Sir Alan Herbert was [illegible] ester and Oxford. Having a [illegible] then joined the Royal Na[illegible] d in France during the Firs[illegible] ar in 1918, and went on to become a Member of Parliament for Oxford University from 1935 to 1950.

Throughout his life A P Herbert was a prolific writer, delighting his many readers with his witty observations and social satires in the columns of *Punch*. He was the creator of a host of colourful characters – notably Topsy, Albert Haddock and Mr Honeybubble – and wrote novels, poems, musicals, essays, sketches and articles. He was also a tireless campaigner for reform, a denouncer of injustice and a dedicated conserver of the Thames.

By the time of his death in 1971, he had gained a considerable following and was highly regarded in literary circles. J M Barrie, Hilaire Belloc, Rudyard Kipling and John Galsworthy all delighted in his work, and H G Wells applauded him saying, 'You are the greatest of great men. You can raise delightful laughter and that is the only sort of writing that has real power over people like me.'

A P HERBERT
PUBLISHED BY HOUSE OF STRATUS

General Cargo
Holy Deadlock
Honeybubble & Co
The House By The River
Light Articles Only
Look Back And Laugh
Made For Man
The Man About Town
Mild And Bitter
More Uncommon Law
Number Nine
The Old Flame
Silver Stream
Sip! Swallow!
Topsy Mp
Topsy Turvy
The Water Gypsies
What A Word

Mild and Bitter

A P HERBERT

HOUSE OF STRATUS

First published in 1936

Stratus Books Ltd., Lisandra House, Fore St., Looe, Cornwall, PL13 1AD, UK.

www.houseofstratus.com

Typeset, printed and bound by House of Stratus.

A catalogue record for this book is available from the British Library and the Library of Congress.

ISBN 1-84232-593-0

ACKNOWLEDGMENT

Most of these bits and pieces first appeared in *Punch,* and I have to thank the proprietors of that paper for their courteous permission to reprint. Two were published in the *Evening Standard* and the *Strand Magazine,* and some were performed in *Streamline,* Mr C B Cochran's revue. My thanks to all concerned, including Messrs Chappell and Co., who published 'Perseverance', with the music by Mr Vivian Ellis.

APH

CONTENTS

I

'I'VE GOT TO BE FUNNY'

I've got to be funny, I've got to be funny,
  But what can a fellow be funny about?
We've too many women and not enough money,
  The present is dingy, the future is doubt;
But I've got to be funny, I've *got* to be funny,
  Not funny tomorrow or funny next week,
  When the world-situation may not be so bleak –
      But funny today,
      This particular day,
With all these absurd 'Accounts Rendered' to pay,
And a man who annoys me is coming to stay.

I study the papers from dawn till dew,
But the comic events are surprisingly few;
And when an event has a comical tone
It is frequently wiser to leave it alone.
      Take Foreign Affairs –
      Well, nobody cares
  For frivolous comment on Foreign Affairs;
      We have to behave
      As if they were grave,
  Although they remind us of Musical Chairs.

Then at home there are so many sensitive toes

That it isn't as simple as many suppose;
It's easy enough
To do comical stuff
In the French or American way,
When you don't give a darn
For the theme of the yarn
Or mind very much what you say;

But I've got to be funny, I've *got* to be funny,
I've got to be funny *in England today*.
Our fathers' pet figures of fun will not do –
The plumber, the painter, the cook and the Jew;
And if you insist
I can give a long list
Of jokes that will never get through.

For the rest, if we look at the news,
How few are the things that amuse!
What with earthquakes in China, disease in Tibet,
Motor-crashes at Kingston and everywhere Debt;
And Folly and Fury and Fudge,
And Budgets unable to budge,
Poor farmers knocked out
By the drought,
Or farmers in pain
From the rain;
Dictators and duds,
And famine and floods,
And shirts a new colour,
More Speeches – but duller –
And the same thing all over again.
I've got to be funny, I've *got* to be funny,
But what is a man to be funny about?

Well, I know what you'll Say: 'Put the papers away

And concentrate only on that which is gay.
There are so many jolly nice things going on –
Take Jane, who is happily married to John;
        They dwell at 'The Rosery', Brawn –
        Four children, a dog and a lawn;
            Their life is a dream –
            What a glorious theme!'
  But, pardon, I've got to be *funny!*
And – this is the kernel and heart of my song –
You cannot be funny when nothing goes wrong.

You cannot make fun of that fortunate two,
And you'll get into trouble with Deans if you do.
        If the couple have many divorces
        Or are ruined by betting on horses,
            They may produce mirth,
            But what is it worth?
        Such topics, again, are taboo.
Oh, it's hard to be funny for money,
  You'll find, if you're that way intentioned,
For most of the world isn't funny,
  And the rest of it mustn't be mentioned.

II

THE SPRING (ARRANGEMENTS) BILL, 1936

Whereas in every lawn and bed the plucky crocus lifts his head, and to and fro sweet song-birds go, the names of which we do not know:

Whereas the woods no more are dumb, the Boat-Race and the Budget come, the Briton swells his manly chest, his mate, as eager, scrubs the nest, and Spring, with light but lavish hand, is spreading madness o'er the land:

It is expedient – but in rhyme – to legislate for such a time:

Be it enacted, therefore, by our King, with Lords and Commons in a fairy ring, assembled joyously at Westminster (or any other place that they prefer):

Provision for Season called spring to

1 (i). It shall be lawful everywhere for citizens to to walk on air, to hang their hats upon the trees and wander hatless, if they please: and notwithstanding any cracked provision in a previous Act give a constable a kiss is not felonious after this.

(ii). All citizens who choose to ride on taxi-tops and not inside: and those who do not use their votes because they're busy painting boats: and any miscreant who hums, instead of doing dismal sums: whoever does a silly thing need only answer ' 'Tis the Spring': and this shall be a good defence in any Court with any sense:

Provided that, in late July, this Act, of course, does not apply.

Financial Provisions *he*

2. *If any person feels he must get out of London* now *or bust, because the Spring is in his bones, but must work for Mr Jones, it shall be lawful for the same to give the Treasury his name, and say 'Upon sufficient grounds I want about a hundred pounds': and there shall not be any fuss concerning sums expended thus.*

Repeal of Redundant Statutes

3. Subsection (i) of Section Four of any Act that seems a bore, and all the Acts concerning beer, and every Act that is not clear (always excepting Schedule A), shall be repealed and thrown away.

House of Commons Reform of Procedure – Music, etc.

4 (i). There shall be banks of maiden-hair arranged about the Speaker's Chair: and roses white and roses red shall hang above the Speaker's head: like some tremendous window-box, the Galleries be gay with phlox: and goldfish, lovely but aloof, shall swim above the glassy roof.

(ii). From now until the First of June all speeches shall be sung (in tune). The Speaker shall determine what hon. Members are in tune, or not.

(iii). When in Committee of Supply the House may hum (but not too high). The Clerk-Assistant-at-the-Table shall choose the key (if he is able).

(iv). A band shall nearly always play (not on the first Allotted Day) behind the Speaker's Chair at three and on the Terrace after tea.

Saving for Committees

5. On any day in May or June Committees shall adjourn quite soon:
Provided, if the cuckoo call, Committees shall not sit at all.

Sittings of the Upper House

6. The House of Lords shall never sit on sunny days till after Whit: and they shall rise, if they have met, when it is foggy, fine or wet.

Termination of Official Report

7 (i). Except as hereinafter hinted, *Hansard* shall not again be printed, and, save as in this Act is learned, all previous *Hansards* shall be burned.

(ii). It is a pity, history teaches, to make reports of people's speeches, and afterwards to be unkind, simply because they change their mind. It is a most disgusting thing to make such comments in the Spring: so, as from when this Act is passed, that day's Report shall be the last.

(iii). And, as respects exceptions, see Subheading (a) of Schedule B.

Powers and Duties of Departments

8 (i). The Secretary of State for Home Affairs shall now proceed to Rome, to Moscow, Washington, Cathay, or anywhere that's far away, and not return to English skies until the Speaker certifies that Spring has ceased to be a fact under the Moss (Collection) Act.

(ii). Meanwhile o'er all his grim domain a lovely golden girl shall reign: and this delicious creature shall give cosmic parties in the Mall (*paying the bills, if she is dunned, from the Consolidated Fund*). The Civil Service, hand in hand, shall dance in masses down the Strand: and all the Cabinet shall wear wild dandelions in their hair.

(iii). It shall be deemed that everyone has come into the world for fun. This shall be printed on the wall of every office in Whitehall.

Penalties for Certain Expressions

9 (i). No kind of crisis shall excuse a man exploring avenues: no lesser doom does he deserve when he is straining every nerve: and special punishment is earned by those who leave no stone unturned.

(ii). The penalty for each offence shall be elastic but immense.

(iii). A pension shall reward the man who modestly does all he can.

Interpretation

10 (i). The greatest care has been employed to make this measure null and void: not one expression in this Act means anything it means in fact.

(ii). Examples we decline to give: the lawyers, after all, must live.

Application

11 This Act applies and shall be good where anybody thinks it should: Provided that, if strong objection should be expressed to any Section, that Section shall not have effect except for those who don't object.[1]

SCHEDULE B

(a)

Any speech, motion, question, amendment or interruption by APH

1. 'The amendment that will be put forward will be designed to secure that coal mines now ancillary to undertakings which are not primarily engaged in the production or treatment of coal, cannot be included in any *compulsory* amalgamation schemes *without the consent* of the owner concerned.' (Mr Runciman, House of Commons, May 18, 1936)

III

PERSEVERANCE

or

HALF A CORONET

An Operetta
In the Gilbertian Manner
(from *Streamline*)

SCENE: *The Terrace of the House of Commons – looking from the windows of the House, i.e. towards the river. The audience sees at the back the parapet of the river-wall, and behind them are the sails of fishing-vessels which, for reasons unknown, are made fast to the wall.*

Discovered, PERSEVERANCE *and* LUCY, *with chorus of fifty* FISHER-GIRLS *in bright-coloured dresses and black woollen stockings. They carry baskets of fish suspended from their shoulders by pink ribbons, and do absurd little movements with admirable uniformity.*

PERSEVERANCE *and* Lucy, *with* CHORUS OF FISHER-GIRLS

Fifty fisher-girls are we
Selling fishes from the sea,
Suiting our ways to our wares:

Fifty fisher-girls or more,
As we think we said before,
Suiting our ways to our wares,
  Though nobody cares:
Each fish in the ocean
We fit with a motion –
With old-fashioned grace
We offer you plaice;
For haddock or cod
We've a coy little nod,
And a virginal pose
For sole or soft roes:
Your fancy exciting
With winkles and whiting,
Although it's not clear
Why we're selling fish here,

Fifty-fish – fifty fish-
Fifty-fish – fifty fish-
Fifty-fish – fifty pretty fisher-girls are we.

[*Enter, arm in arm,* RUDOLF *and* ROBERT, *who, between them, for reasons which will appear, hold the title of Viscount Bunion. They are in court dress.*
RUDOLF *has a very high and fruity tenor voice, and speaks his dialogue as if he has a large potato in his throat and may burst into song at any moment.* ROBERT'S *voice is more normal, and even gruff. He is a baritone or bass. They are twins, but need not be strikingly alike.*
The FISHER-GIRLS, *headed by* PERSEVERANCE, *greet the twins.*]

PERSEVERANCE. Lord Rudolf! Will you purchase a plaice?
LUCY. Lord Robert, may I sell you a sole?

RUDOLF (*brushing them aside*). Pray observe the decencies of etiquette, young ladies. There is no Lord Rudolf –

ROBERT (*gloomily*). Lord Robert does not exist.

RUDOLF. There is only the Viscount Bunion.

PERSEVERANCE. Yes, but which is he?

RUD. and ROB. (*linking arms again and striking an attitude*). *We* are the Viscount Bunion.

LUCY. What, both of you?

CHORUS. Singular coincidence!

PERSEVERANCE. Will you not explain this curious circumstance?

RUDOLF. Certainly, my dear Perseverance. (*comes down stage*) On the death of our father, the Earl, one of us will succeed to the title.

CHORUS. O rapture!

[PERSEVERANCE *clings to* RUDOLF.]

RUDOLF. Yes, but we do not know which!

CHORUS. O disappointment!

[PERSEVERANCE, *with the other hand, clings to* ROBERT *as well.*]

LUCY. But surely, Lord Rudolf, the eldest son must succeed to the title?

ROBERT (*gloomily*). Ah, but we are twins.

CHORUS. O horror!

RUDOLF. And therefore are the same age.

[LUCY *goes up centre.*]

PERSEVERANCE (*to* RUDOLF, *coy*). But though you are the same age it seems to me that one of you must be the elder.

CHORUS. Strange paradox!

RUDOLF. True, my dear Perseverance. Even among twins there is generally, I believe, some trifling element of seniority.

ROBERT. Unfortunately our father has refused to reveal the true facts until his death.

RUDOLF. For he feared that the heir, secure of his future, would spend his youth in profligate enjoyment.

CHORUS. Ingenious precaution!

PERSEVERANCE. But were not both of you present on the occasion you have mentioned? Surely it was a little careless of you not to notice the order of your arrival?

RUDOLF. The reproach is just, Perseverance.

LUCY. Is there *nobody* who can tell you which of you is which?

ROBERT. Our mother – a good Conservative – perished in a one-way street. The hired female who presided over the first weeks of our lives was thoughtfully dismissed. The secret will be revealed, no doubt, in our father's last will and testament, but not before.

RUDOLF. The situation is complicated by the fact that the estate is heavily mortgaged, and the assets will be sufficient to support only one of us. One of us, therefore, will be a peer –

ROBERT. The other, a pauper.

PERSEVERANCE. But unless we know which of you is to be the Earl how are we to know which of you we love the best?

RUDOLF. We appreciate your difficulty, Perseverance. But consider our own embarrassment. I kneel before you, Perseverance. (*does so*)

ROBERT. And I. (*does so*)

RUDOLF. Will you be my bride, Perseverance?

PERSEVERANCE. I love you, Rudolf. But what are your prospects?

ROBERT (*kneeling*). Will you marry me, Perseverance?

PERSEVERANCE. I dote upon you, Robert, but can you support me?

RUDOLF. I may become an earl –

ROBERT. Or an insurance agent.

RUDOLF. I may go to the House of Lords –
ROBERT. Or Carey Street.
CHORUS. Cruel alternatives!
RUDOLF }
ROBERT } How then, can we ask you to love us?
PERSEVERANCE. Or I consent?
RUDOLPH. The only honourable solution that I can see, Perseverance, is that you should do what you can to love both of us, until you are certain which of us is which.
PERSEVERANCE (*very arch – playing to* ROBERT *and* RUDOLPH *alternatively*):

Though I am loath
To plight my troth
With exact particularity,
Yet I might part
With hand and heart
On terms of honest parity:
I will not kiss
The one – like this – (*does so*)
Unless I kiss the other: (*does so*)
Pray hold my hand, (RUDOLPH *takes it*)
But understand
You share it with your brother.
(ROBERT *takes it too*)

CHORUS: Arrangement unromantical!
With equity pedantical
She will not kiss
The one (like this) (*all kiss everybody*)
Unless she hugs the other.
This proposition frantical
Is almost transatlantical
– antical:
Half a loaf is not much fun,

But half a lady's worse than none.

PERSEVERANCE: On Monday night
I'm your delight (*to* RUDOLF)
(But, of course, with due propriety);
On Tuesday (noon)
I change my tune
And bask in *your* society: (*to* ROBERT)
So neither swain
Can well complain
That he is hardly treated,
For if I do
The same for two,
Which is the one that's cheated?

CHORUS: Engagement mathematical!
With equity fanatical
She means to do
The same for two;
So neither one is cheated.
One must not be dogmatical,
But we are still emphatical
– phatical
Half a loaf is *quantum suff.*
But half a lady's not enough.

RUDOLF. Speaking of bankruptcy, unless my eyes deceive me, I behold the Official Receiver.

CHORUS. O terror!

RUDOLF. Not at all. He is the most benevolent institution we have. For it is the only one which makes poverty respectable – and even delightful. Besides, a bankrupt is automatically preserved from the risk of becoming a Member of Parliament.

CHORUS. Merciful exemption!

[*Enter the* OFFICIAL RECEIVER, *with male chorus of* BAILIFFS.]

THE OFFICIAL RECEIVER:

Solo. Of all the fine fellows employed by the King,
Chorus. Tra-la, tra-la, tra-la!
Solo. To make the good citizen carol and sing,
Chorus. Tra-la, tra-la, tra-la!
Solo. I'm one of the latest,
But easily greatest,
For I'm the Official Receiver!
Chorus. 'A popular fellow!'
We readily bellow
For he's the Official Receiver!
Solo. When your furniture swarms with income-tax forms and Notices Final in red,
With magistrates' warrants arriving in torrents and bailiffs asleep in your bed:

If shares go to nought the moment you've bought and soar to the skies when you sell,
If Insurance Collectors and Taxing Inspectors are constantly ringing the bell:
By slaving all day in some odious way you've an income that's worth the returning,
But your daughters and sons, and your dentists and duns, are eating much more than you're earning:
You labour and grind, but are always behind: you might be a mouse or a midge:
You've given up hoping, you fly to the coping of Lambeth or Waterloo Bridge.

You stare at the sinister stream –
Tra-la!
And Death is a dubious dream –

Tra-la!
But the Bankruptcy Act
Is a comforting fact,
And so's the Official Receiver.

As a bird flutters back to its nest –
Tra-la!
As a babe to the sheltering breast –
Tra-la!
How sweet to desist
From the fight to exist
And seek the Official Receiver.

So pack up the wreck of your life –
Tra-la!
Your warrants, your writs, and your wife –
Tra-la!
And hand the whole thing
To the care of the King,
Or rather, Official Receiver!

OFF. REC. You two young gentlemen, I take it, are the Viscount Bunion?

RUD. and ROB. We are, Sir.

OFF. REC. I have news for you. Your father the Earl has passed away. He has in short, ah – kicked the bucket. In point of fact, he is deceased.

CHORUS. O horror!

[PERSEVERANCE, RUDOLF, Lucy *and the* OFFICIAL RECEIVER *at once put their heads together and sing an unaccompanied quartet.* ROBERT, *it seems, cannot sing and stands mute to one side.*]

UNACCOMPANIED QUARTET (*very solemn*):
Death is the terminus of all our travel,
Whether in firsts or thirds our lot is cast:

Some live on clay and some reside on gravel,
But all must hand their tickets in at last:
Death is a riddle man cannot unravel:
Death is the terminus of all our travel.

(*Becoming brighter and brighter*):
Fal-lal-di-diddle-ay,
Fol-lol-di-diddle-o,
Fal-lal-diddle – fol-diddle – fal-diddle-ay!
Death is the terminus to which we go.

ROBERT. Tell us, Sir – for we are naturally interested – what was the cause of this calamitous event?

OFF. REC. Creditors. They were so lacking in respect as to file a petition for the winding-up of the late Earl. The shock was too great for him; and, in short, he wound himself up.

RUDOLF. You have in your possession, perhaps, among his other assets, our father's will?

OFF. REC. I have. It is almost the only asset.

RUDOLF. And in that document does he disclose the name of his elder son?

OFF. REC. That trifling detail is not so much as mentioned.

RUDOLF. Technically, therefore, we are both the Earl of Billingsgate?

OFF. REC. That seems to be the position. (*Bowing* R. *and* L.) I congratulate each half of your lordship.

ROBERT. In that case we shall have to take the same seat in the House of Lords –

RUDOLF. Make the same speeches –

ROBERT. Wear the same coronet –

PERSEVERANCE (*curtsying*). And marry the same Countess.

LUCY. Agreeable dilemma!

RUDOLF. But stay, here comes an elderly female who may be able to disentangle us.

OFF. REC. What should this antiquated ruin know of the matter?

ROBERT. It is our Nurse.
RUDOLF. Nanny!
OFF. REC. On the contrary, it is the Lady Chancellor.
CHORUS. Here comes an old maid!
Ha, ha! What a joke!
She's as plain as a spade,
And as tough as an oak.
The suitors have tarried,
Her plans have miscarried,
She'll never be married.
Ha, ha! What a joke!

Here comes an old maid!
She's extremely decayed,
Her face is mislaid,
She's frowsy and frayed,
She's a sight in the shade.
Ha, ha!
So with chivalrous feelings we bawl
'She'll never be married at all!'
There's one thing ag'inst her,
She's made for a spinster,
But no one's convinced her –
Ha, ha! What a joke!

[*Enter the* LADY CHANCELLOR – *a tremendously tall contralto, in her robes of office, with full-bottomed wig. Either she or an attendant should carry the Great Seal.*]
THE LADY CHANCELLOR (*recitative*):
I am the Lady Chancellor, I am,
But once I was a nurse and drove a pram.
(*Song*)
Two lovely twins they trusted to my care,
Alike in size, in feature, form and hair.
No marks. No moles. But *I* knew which was what,

For one was musical – the other not.
CHORUS. Ah, one was musical – the other not!
The elder babe would crow and croon all day,
And cried for 'Momma' in the key of A:
The other seldom sang, and, if he did,
Was out of tune. Ah, how I loved that kid!
CHORUS. Though out of tune, she dearly loved that kid.

What if my age is rather more than middle?
For his sweet sake I now resolve the riddle.
If one can sing – the rightful Earl is he: (*pointing at twins*)
The other, still more blest, shall marry ME.

OFF. REC. A highly diverting narrative. But, so far as is known, neither of these gentlemen can sing a note.

LADY C. That is easily ascertained. Let them try.

OFF. REC. May I warn your Ladyship that, at the moment, each half of this individual is an undischarged bankrupt.

LADY C. No matter. My miserable honorarium will suffice for two.

OFF. REC. (*looking at* PERSEVERANCE). But not, I take it, for four?

PERSEVERANCE (*taking an oyster from her basket*). It is of no consequence. This oyster has just opened its doors and expelled a pearl of reassuring dimensions. (*holds up an enormous pearl*)

CHORUS. O rapture!

OFF. REC. Intelligent bivalve! Satisfactory pearl! Devoted girl! But still no Earl!

LADY C. (*severely*). Sing, Viscount.

[RUDOLF *sings*. ROBERT *opens his mouth but fails to sing*.
During the following, PERSEVERANCE, *perceiving that* RUDOLF *is the singer, embraces him, and the* LADY CHANCELLOR *claims* ROBERT.]

FINALE

RUDOLF. Take a dainty paradox,
Dress it like a chocolate-box –
Take two babies – mix them well:
Take one spinster – give her H —!
Take some logic – chop it thin;
Take some tunes and rub them in:
One patter-song, and don't forget
Your unaccompanied quartet:
Take a little love, but – hush!
Not enough to raise a blush.
By degrees you'll find you'll get a
Rather popular operetta –

CHORUS. Loved by curate, Kew and Quetta – (*ad lib.*)
And it is a tip-top property –
Yes, there is no properer property
Than a jocular
Never shockular
Proper, popular, popular, operette.

CURTAIN

IV

MULLION

My ball is in a bunch of fern,
   A jolly place to be;
An angry man is close astern –
   He waves his club at me.
Well, let him wave – the sky is blue;
Go on, old ball, we are but two –
   We *may* be down in three,
Or nine – or ten – or twenty-five –
It matters not; to be alive
   Is good enough for me.

How like the happy sheep we pass
   At random through the green,
For ever in the longest grass,
   But never in between!
There is a madness in the air;
There is a damsel over there,
   Her ball is in the brook.
Ah! what a shot – a dream, a dream!
You think it finished in the stream?
   Well, well, we'll go and look.

Mullion

Who is this hot and hasty man
   That shouteth 'Fore!' and 'Fore!'?
We move as quickly as we can –
   Can anyone do more?
Cheer up, sweet sir, enjoy the view;
I'd take a seat if I were you,
   And light your pipe again:
In quiet thought possess your soul,
For John is down a rabbit hole,
   And I am down a drain.

The ocean is a lovely sight,
   A brig is in the bay.
Was that a slice? You may be right –
   But, goodness, what a day!
Young men and maidens dot the down,
And they are beautiful and brown,
   And just as mad as me.
Sing, men and maids, for I have done
The Tenth – the Tenth! – in twenty-one,
   And John was twenty-three.

Now will I take my newest ball,
   And build a mighty tee,
And waggle once, or not at all,
   And bang it out to sea,
And hire a boat and bring it back,
And give it one terrific whack,
   And hole it out in three,
Or nine – or ten – or twenty-five –.
It matters not; to be alive
At Mullion in the summer time,
At Mullion in the silly time,
   Is good enough for me.

V

'THE DOGS'

One can do worse than go to the dogs.

What a long time it seems – it is – since 'the dogs' first came to London! They were frowned upon, as are all new things. Grave moral lectures were delivered, sometimes by racing-men, concerning the distinction between the horse and the dog. Men who betted on horses five days a week were horrified by the thought of other men betting on dogs. For the horse was a noble animal: but the dog – though admittedly the friend of man – was only a dog. Indeed, the greyhound was scarcely a dog.

Moreover, the horse was an asset to the nation, being useful for agriculture and in time of war. But what had the greyhound ever done for his country? Therefore, he who betted on horses was helping to improve the breed of the English thoroughbred and so doing something for the nation, while he who betted on a greyhound was simply betting, in a rather mean and acquisitive manner. Yes, all this was said – though not so nakedly.

For my part, if I must lose money through making unprovoked forecasts about the speed of animals, I care little whether they are horses or dogs. The laugh is on me, anyway. And, at least, I can view the dog without much exertion, whereas nearly all the horses demand a journey and a day off. Moreover, I can see the dogs all round the course, whereas, in my small experience, racehorses are always disappearing into the Dip, or hiding behind coaches, or simply being shut out by bowler-hats.

Yes, one can do worse than go to the dogs. And, in spite of the frowns and the predictions of a short life – 'only a passing craze, old boy; there's no *sport* in it' – they seem to be surviving obstinately. A London evening paper publishes a special Dog Edition, and on Whit-Monday it gave full particulars of thirty meetings in the London area. Four sheets of doggery in tiny type – about thirteen hundred dogs' names in all, I reckoned – with all their form, times, and traps, and recent history, with 'Betting Forecasts' and 'Naps at a Glance', and 'Winning Traps'. What industry! What organization! And what a lot of doggery there must be!

Returning after a long interval to Cream Town, the only course at which I have ever dogged, I noticed a few changes. The hare, I thought, was not looking so well – a little ragged and tired. And soon I saw why. They now let him slip off his electric carriage before it dives into the tunnel at the end, so that the dogs have a brief but enjoyable worry at the skin. The fact that, after having thus found out for certain that the whole thing is a fraud, the intelligent dogs consent to race again is of great scientific interest: it shows either (*a*) that they are not even so intelligent as we thought, or (*b*) that, unlike the rest of us, they are there purely for the sport of the thing and do not really expect to get anything out of it.

And then I missed the bowler-hats – the bowler-hats of the stewards or hound-leaders. There was a grand moment after each race when three white-robed stewards stood before the Grand Stand with the three panting animals to finish first, and in good time together raised their bowler-hats to the company. It was the only occasion, I think, in English public life on which one saw the bowler-hat ceremoniously employed. Now, I suppose because of our symbolic summer, they wear boaters. It is not quite the same thing.

But the rest of the admirable drill and showmanship remains. I like to see the winning three march off down the lighted course with their escorts, while the miserable beasts who were 4, 5, and 6 slink along in the semi-darkness across the fence, and decently to the rear. And I like the six white stewards and attendant hounds marching across the dark ground in quick time with a spotlight on them.

Indeed, for those who can keep their eyes off the odds and their mind off their particular hound, there is, when the daylight goes and the track is lit, a ribbon of brilliant green, with no light in the centre or the stands – there is – hush! – much beauty in the scene; as much, at least, as you will find at most horse-places. And the dogs are beautiful, too, the lean, leggy things, as they speed like arrows over the hurdles or flash past the post in the order which you have predicted. A horse, in motion, is comparatively plain, and hideous if he is also running.

But you do not want to hear about Beauty, pig. You want to know about the dogs from the Investor's Viewpoint.

Well, there are three infallible ways of losing money on the dogs. But I should first explain that to invest in the dogs requires no mean intellectual labour. You have, of course, a mass of 'literature', as any printed paper is called now. You have your Dog Edition, and you have your Race-Card, each of which is a maze of information; and then you probably buy Somebody's card of Tips, which is a mass of Naps. You must learn before you study the Form the meaning of the following technical terms:

awk . . . . awkward
blkd . . . . baulked
bpd. . . . . bumped
bnchd. . . . . bunched
chkd . . . . checked
hpd. . . . . hampered
impd. . . . . impeded
pkd. . . . . pecked

stbld . . . . .stumbled

I cannot myself say what exact difference it makes to a dog whether he is baulked, bumped, bunched, hampered, impeded, or pecked; but it as well to realize to how many dangers dogs are exposed.

You now study the form of the dogs in the first race; and you find yourself in this sort of trouble:

'HADDOCK.
'Tr 2 5th 5 yd (5) By HENRY (T6) 31.47 Bdly blkd 1st bend, 6/1, May 20=30.78
'Tr 1 4th 11yd (5) By MERVYN'S JOY (T5) 31.39 Chkd, Bpd, Faded, 8/1, May 17=31.95
'Tr 2 3rd 13yd (4) By FUCHSIA (T5) 31.93 Blkd, Bpd, Impd, Stbld, 6/1, May 10=31.62
'Tr 4 3rd...'

But the dog Haddock is only one dog, and there are six in the first race; and there are eight races in the evening. And every dog has four different stories (as above) attached to him; so you can see that a conscientious student of form has a busy evening ahead of him. By the time he has properly weighed the bping and impding of the dog Haddock against the blking and chking and pking of the dog Whatisit and allowed for the fact that Haddock was in Trap 1 on the last occasion and is now in Trap 5, whereas Whatisit is now in Trap 2 and – by the time, I say, the student has duly assessed the chances of two or three of the hounds the race is over.

The first infallible way of losing money on the dogs, then, is to study the form – for at the last minute one simply chooses a nice name and loses on that.

But then there are good-hearted and great-minded experts who will do all this loathsome toil for you the day before and present you with the results in short and snappy terms – sometimes in Naps and Doubles.

And the second infallible way of losing money on the dogs is to trust to the experts. Well, that may be harsh; for I have not tested them often. But on this day I know that in eight races my chosen expert named one winner only; that his Nap was fourth or fifth; and, as for his Double, not even the first half of it could do better than third and the second half was worse. But there is more. Referring now to Somebody's card of tips, I find that he did not name a single winner. So that out of sixteen expert prophecies only one was correct. Well, most of us are as wrong about most things as often as that: but we do not give 'Naps'.

The third infallible way of losing money on the dogs is to ignore both form and experts and to trust to your own judgement when the dogs parade. Every Briton is a good judge of a dog: but this is not true of greyhounds. When I back the gay and manifestly vital hound which leaps and walks on air and longs to swallow space, that dog is last: and the only successful hound in which I invested was one of which all men said, upon its appearance, how mean, morbid, sluggish, and unpractical a beast it looked. Never, then, trust to your own judgement.

There are other ways. I believe the best way is the lady's way. One says: 'Blue (or red) is my colour tonight,' and backs blue (or red) in every race. At least there is here no intellectual strain.

Alas! I never tried that way. And it will be clear from what has gone before that I am speaking in no base material fashion when I say again that one can do worse than go to the dogs.

VI

MR MAFFERTY TAKES A LADY OUT

Mr Mafferty, I believe, left his native land at the age of two, but he has read all the Irish plays, and insists on talking like one.

'I know now why men stay at home,' said Mr Mafferty, 'for last night I took a lady out to dinner. I did it to oblige a friend, Mr Haddock, an' he in love with her, so there's no call for your insinuatin' glances. It's a fine young lady she is surely, but hungry itself, though she lives in a rich house, with dogs an' footmen an' the like. I wonder now the like of her would not be takin' a little nourishment at home in the daytime, the way a gintleman could entertain her in the evenin' without sellin' his securities or borrowin' from the bank. An' I wonder there's no two people can meet together in this town without one of them gives food an' drink to the other. Is it unlawful talkin' between meals or what?

'Well, me friend is called away suddenly to the country, an' he asks me to console the lady with me genial society. I drive up punctual to the house in a motor-omnibus, an' in less than half an hour she's dressed an' ready, like a flower of the East in pink satin. An' says I, "What place would you like to take your food? I know a fine small place in Bloomsbury."

' "Bloomsbury's a fine place," says she, "but I know a fine small place behind Piccadilly itself."

'"Well, that's fine," says I; "we can go by the Underground train." For it's not meself was in love with the girl, an' the station two small steps from her house, no more.

'"D'you think I'd travel under the ground in me new pink?" says she.

'"I do so," says I. "It's clean an' dry below. An' you can read the evenin' paper."

'"Jumpin' James!" says she, "it's a quare strange man you are."

'"I am so," says I, an' I hired a motor-cab for the creature.

'Well, Mister Marini's little place was as large as a church, an' full of lords. I never saw so many rich folk before, an' I afeared me black tie would be slidin' up me collar behind, an' me fine gilt studs escapin' in front. Mister Marini an' me young lady is old friends, an' he sends six waiters to us. I picked up the programme of eatin' an' the blood ran cold in me bones, for it's a poor man I am. Bedad, there was nothin' to eat below five shillin's, an' it was three shillin's to sit down only! "I wonder now," says I, "there's no charge made for breathin'. What will you take, young lady? I see they have a nice grilled chop ready."

'"It's a small little cocktail I'll be takin'," she says.

'"Is it so?" says I in wonder, for it's a small slip of a thing she is, maybe nineteen or twenty years grown.

'"It is that," says she. "An *Uncle's Dream* itself."

'"The Saints preserve us!" says I. "Would that be an expensive beverage, Mister Marini?"

'" 'Tis three shillin's only," says the foreign gintleman.

'"Well, let you choose first what food you'll take," says I to the lady, "for it could be I'd not be able to pay for the two."

'"It's little food I'll be eatin' this night," says she, "an' I destroyed with the great fat I have on me."

'"Go fetch the lady a cocktail," says I, relieved in the mind. "An' then will you take some oysters or not?"

'"What's oysters?" says the innocent child.

'"It's a kind of edible bivalve they are," says I; "an' terrible fattenin' in the fall of the year."

'"I'll eat no oysters then," says she.

'"Maybe the lady has a hankerin' for lobsters?" says the head waiter; an' he reels off six or seven lobsters in the French language.

'Well, I cast an eye at the price of lobsters an' I made faces at the waiter the way he'd not be puttin' expensive notions in the lady's head. But the mean feller avoids the glance of me eye, an' she orders a Lobster du Maurier or the like of that.

'"It's a fillin' food, lobster," says I. "You wouldn't want much after your lobster, I'm thinkin'."

'"I would not," says she, "I've a quare small appetite."

'"Would the lady be takin' a pheasant?" says the waiter.

'"I might," says she.

'"You would not," says I, "an' you in dread of the fat. I tell you now what you'd like, surely, an' that's a little chopped ham on a piece of toast. That's a darlin' little dish, now, an' not fattenin', for you'd have the lean of the ham only. There's times I've gone for a week of days eatin' nothin' at all but chopped ham on toast."

'"We've no chopped ham on toast," says the waiter.

'"Then may your bones rattle in your bed this night!" says I. "Haven't you all the birds an' the beasts an' the fishes of the sea in this place? An' is it hard set you'd be to find a small morsel of bread an' a few shavin's from the leg of a pig?"

'"There's no word said about chopped ham on the card," says he.

'"Well, it's the wonder of the world!" says I, speechless.

'An' then the young lady says, "I'll have no more at all, waiter, only a small bowl of soup before the lobster an' maybe the half of a partridge after, with fried potaters an' a few small sprouts; an' after that nothin' at all unless it would be a small piece of an ice-puddin', an' maybe a dainty little savoury to finish, an' coffee an' liqueurs only, an' never a mouthful more, if you please."

' "Have nothin' you don't want, me darlin'," says I tenderly.

'Well, by the end of it, between the two of them, they'd ordered two meals would keep the Brigade of Guards from starvation, with fowls an' fishes an' angels on horseback an' the divil knows what besides. An' I took up the wine-list, an', begob, it opened itself at the champagne page! An' I turned over quickly to the still wines an' burgundies, an' says I, "What wine will you take, young lady? There's a grand Empire Burgundy they have here."

' "It's the strong joy I have to see the bubbles risin' in me glass," says she, "like the stars of heaven climbin' the sky."

' "Is that a fact?" says I. "Well, I wonder now you wouldn't have more joy seein' the red wine of the Empire in your glass, like the red blood of the Australians – an' they shearin' the sheep."

' "I would not," says she.

' "I've seen the great trees of Australia," says I, "as high as the British Museum, an' they bearin' red grapes the size of cannon-balls. An' Number 67 is a nice wine, I'm thinkin'."

' "It's not meself," says she, "would be drinkin' red wine in a pink dress."

' "Is it not?" says I. "Well, if it's white you have your heart fixed on there's a grand little white Chablis would warm the soul of a snake itself. It's Number 30 is in me mind."

' "I've no fancy for the German wines," says she, "since me aunt was drowned in the Great War."

' "It's noble principles you have, surely," says I. "An' there's no nobler wine than a cheap Sauterne, 'tis white as charity an' bottled by the French. Will you take a small sip of Number 17?"

' "It's quare an' heavy I am this night," says she, "after the long day, an' it rainin'. It's no more than a thimbleful I'd be takin', but there's a hunger in me heart for bubbles."

'"God help me!" says I, an' I ordered the champagne, for there's no goin' against a woman at the latter end.

'"The quare extravagant fellow you are!" says the young lady, reproachful. "It's soda-water was in me mind, no more."

'"Soda-water, is it?" says I. "It's a pity now you'd not remember the word before. Maybe it's not lobster you'd be wantin' truly, nor the half of a partridge, but one sardine an' the end of a cold sausage?"

'"It is so," says she. "Why would I be needin' grand food an' drink, an' I a simple girl with the stars in me soul an' a strong love for the wild places? I wonder now you'd bring me to a great place the like of this one, an' I after tellin' you I'd be as happy standin' at the coffee-stall or takin' a poor crust in Bloomsbury."

'"Is it yourself," says I, the blood rushin' to my head – "is it yourself would be as happy eatin' at Bloomsbury as this place?"

'"I would so, surely," says she. "Why would I tell you a lie?"

'"Well," says I, "Mister Marini, is there a public omnibus goes from this place to Bloomsbury?"

'"There is that," says he.

'"Then let you stop it at the door," says I, "an' reserve two places. For it's to Bloomsbury we'll be goin' this livin' instant." An', begob, Mr Haddock, it's to Bloomsbury we went.

'If it wasn't for the passion of love, Mr Haddock, there'd be never a rich restaurant doin' business at all.'

VII

SPEECH DAY
or
CHARACTER COUNTS
(From *Streamline*)

SCENE: *The front part of the platform in the Old School Hall on 'Speech Day'. On the wall at the back the School motto:– 'BIS BAT QUI CITO BAT'.*

The HEAD MASTER, *in cap, gown, and hood, presides. The table before him is piled high with books bound in calf – the prizes.*

At his side sits the Distinguished Visitor, MAJOR-GENERAL SIR RODERICK SWITCHING, *an Old Begonian, who is going to give away the prizes.*

THE HEAD MASTER (*finishing his speech*): …In short, a full and satisfactory year. Lazarus major has gained a scholarship at Bauble, Cambridge – the new wing of the gymnasium is nearing completion – the match with Pewterhouse was drawn – I *think* I may say in our favour (*stamping of feet by the boys*) – and after we have sung 'Carmen' I will ask our newly elected Fellow, General Sir Roderick Switching, to present the prizes.

[*Two very small boys in Etons come forward. Everyone on the platform stands up and joins in the refrain. The* GENERAL *climbs on to his chair, only to find that this good old custom has gone out. He is a little shocked, too, by the* SECOND

BOY, *who, though he warbles in his throat and is difficult to follow, seems to be uttering some queer things.*]

CARMEN CRICKET

BOYS. Carmen Cricket concinamus!
ALL. *O the click of Bat and Ball!*
1ST BOY. Status quota referendum
2ND BOY. Cui bono nisi addendum.
1ST BOY. We salute the sport of heroes
2ND BOY. In the language of the Neroes –
ALL. *Carmen Cricket sing we all!*

BOYS. Carmen Cricket concinamus!
ALL. *O the click of Bat and Ball*
1ST BOY. All our lives may we play cricket
2ND BOY. Win the toss and choose the wicket,
1ST BOY. Get some runs, declare at tea
2ND BOY. And make them bat when they can't see –
ALL. *O the click of Bat and Ball!*

BOYS. Carmen Cricket concinamus!
ALL. *O the click of Bat and Ball!*
1ST BOY. Laugh at Fate, that false cajoler;
2ND BOY. God preserve our one fast bowler!
1ST BOY. Fairly may the foe be mastered;
2ND BOY. Anyhow we'll beat the bastard –
ALL. *O the click of Bat and Ball!*

BOYS. Carmen Cricket concinamus!
ALL. *O the click of Bat and Ball!*
1ST BOY. Angels kind attend our matches
2ND BOY. And make Eton miss their catches.
1ST BOY. And when we have made a million
2ND BOY. Lead us to the Last Pavilion –

ALL. *O the click of Bat and Ball!*
Carmen Cricket sing we all!

[*Cheers. The* GENERAL *rises. More cheers.*]

[*The* GENERAL *is pompous but not impressive in appearance. The more he talks about 'Character' the more one wonders why.*]

SIR RODERICK (*after many clearings of throat*):
I'm very glad to give away the prizes:
I congratulate the boys who've won the prizes,
But I think I ought to say, if you'll allow,
To encourage those who haven't won the prizes,
That in after-life the ones who win the prizes
Are not always those who win the prizes now:

(*with great satisfaction and pride*)

I was always at the bottom of my class
When I was a boy at school:
Examinations I could never pass
When I was a boy at school:
(*beaming*) And now I'm a General
– a General
– a General
And now I'm a General
And earn large amounts.
But where are all the clever boys who used to do my sums?
They're hidden in the Church, the Civil Service or the slums.
Arithmetic's a bore
And not the slightest use in war –
Brains don't matter – it's character that counts.

Patter – spoken through music

Yes, brains aren't everything. I know when I was at Dudley I was always bottom of my class. (*laughter – great delight on all faces except perhaps the head master's*) The bottom class too. (more laughter) In fact, I was bottom of the school for four years: and they were the happiest years of my life. (*loud cheers*) You'll find, my boys, that the men who make good in the world are generally those who begin at the bottom and work up. (*cheers*) As for Latin and Greek – (*sings*)

I was always last in Latin and in Greek
When I was a boy at school:
I was whacked for Latin once or twice a week
When I was a boy at school:
(*very gay*) And now I'm a General
– a General
– a General
Now I'm a General
And earn large amounts.
The language of Shakespeare's good enough for me and you –
Well, what did Mr Aristotle do at Waterloo?
In the face of savage foes
What's the use of Latin prose?
Brains don't matter – it's character that counts.

All the same, I hope you boys will not neglect your Latin and Greek. It's a fine discipline; and discipline is what we need. There's too much laxness and slackness about. I'm afraid I was a sad scamp at school. (*delighted laughter*) I well remember eating gooseberries in the arithmetic class. (*laughter*) But, after all, arithmetic isn't everything. Truth – Straightness – Discipline – if you learn these lessons you can let the clever ones carry off the prizes. I've always said I'd rather my boy got a Blue than wrote a Blue-Book! Ha!

I always say I learned to handle men

When I was a boy at school:
We took a bat and gave the scholars ten
When I was a boy at school:
And now I'm a Governor
– a Governor
– a Governor
Now I govern Gundrabad
And earn large amounts.
But what's become of all the dirty brainy little swots?
They're doing all the dirty work in all the dirty spots.
And they're sorry, I dare say,
They did Algebra today –
Brains don't matter – it's character that counts.

Ha! I wish my old friend Johnny Gore was here today. Ha! Poor old Johnny. He was a thorn in the flesh of the masters. (*cheers*) Always at the bottom of his class, too. (*laughter*) And now he's Bishop of Rangoon. I'm sorry to see they've pulled down the lavatory behind the Fives Court – because that's where Johnny Gore and I used to sit and smoke during the Science Lessons. (*loud cheers*) Ah, well, you should be proud of men like Johnny Gore. It only shows that brains ain't everything.

I was always using cribs – ha, ha! – in form
When I was a boy at school:
And smoking blotting-paper in the dorm –
When I was a boy at school:
But now I'm a Baronet
– a Baronet
– a Baronet
Now I'm a Baronet
And earn large amounts.
After all, it's not the goody-goods do credit to their schools:

The boy who breaks the records is the boy who breaks the rules.

I broke every rule I could
And I think it did me good – Haw!
Brains aren't everything – it's character that counts.

[*The first* BOYS *come up for their prizes, receive them, bow and pass across the stage, where they halt, holding the books guiltily and with signs of shame. When seven or eight have passed, the* LEADING BOY, *who wears spectacles and looks a typical scholar, turns and approaches the table again, the others backing him up*.]

LEADING SCHOLAR (*politely – all hold out their books*):

Sir, would you mind
If we declined
These valuable tomes,
Though they would cause
Prolonged applause
In our respective homes?
We wrongly thought that we came here
To study and to swot:
God may forgive us, but we fear
The football team will not.
And if some brainless bully jumps
Upon our beds tonight
And beats us up with cricket stumps
You'll say it serves us right:

ALL (*suddenly fierce*):

So keep your dirty prizes
And we timidly suggest
That you put your dirty prizes
In the place that you think best.

[*They all throw their prizes at the* GENERAL. *Uproar. The Boys link arms and sing mutinously*:]

Let's all be bottom of the class –
As long as we're boys at school.
Examinations we decline to pass –
As long as we're boys at school.
And then we'll be Generals
– and Admirals
– and Governors
Then we'll be Generals
And earn large amounts.
Let's use cribs and learn to handle men,
Let's get a bat and give the scholars ten;
In the face of savage foes
What's the use of Latin Prose?
Brains don't matter – it's character that counts.

[*The prize-winners are taken out by the* FIRST XI *and thrown into a pond.*]

VIII

'I WANT YOU'

A Little Grouse

Will people who are rich and busy enough to have private secretaries and telephone-operators kindly remember that there are other people who may also be busy but are not rich enough to have these conveniences?

Mr Cube (shall we say?) wishes to speak to me, though it is on the cards that I have no wish to speak to Mr Cube. Mr Cube is in a large office, well-manned, or rather well-womanned; and it is nice and easy for Mr Cube to say to his secretary, Miss Potts, 'Ring up Mr Haddock'. Having said that, he goes into the next room and wanders about the building. Miss Potts rings through to the private operator, the private operator calls the Exchange, and the vile bell rings at Mr Haddock's house.

It is a hot day and I am working in the garden. I rise mutinously, put down my papers (which the wind blows into the pond) and run into the house.

I remove the receiver and pant into the transmitter mouthpiece. The girl at the Exchange says, 'Are you Riverside 18943?' I say, 'Yes', and she says, 'I want you'. I say, 'Who are you?' but she has gone away.

After a minute another girl says, 'Is that Riverside 18943?'

'Yes.'

'Is that Mr Haddock's house?'

'Yes.'

'Is Mr Haddock at home?'

'Speaking.'

'Is that Mr Haddock?'

'Yes!!'

'I *want* you,' she says brightly; very brightly and happily she says it, as if I were just going to hear that I had been left a fortune.

I say, 'Who are you?' But she has gone away.

I wait for a minute or two, drawing pictures on the wall.

Then a third girl says, 'Hullo?'

'Hullo.'

'Is that Mr Haddock's house?'

'Yes.'

'Is that Mr Haddock?'

'Yes.'

'Mr A P Haddock?'

'*Yes!!!*'

'I *want* you,' she carols, bird-like.

'Who are you?' I say; but she has gone away.

I have no idea who any of these young women are. They pay no attention to anything I say. They all want me – few men can have been wanted so much – but the moment they have got me they go away. The incalculable mystery of Woman!

I wait. I wait a full minute. Tired of drawing on the wall I kick holes in the sideboard.

At last the third young woman who wants me says, 'Are you there?'

'I am. Who are you and why do you want me, please?'

'I am sorry to keep you waiting,' she says very sweetly. 'Mr Cube has gone out of the room.'

'Who is Mr Cube?'

'Would you mind holding the line? Mr Cube wants to speak to you.'

'Then why did he go out of the room?'

No answer. She has gone away. Fanatically devoted to Mr Cube's interests, she takes no more notice of what I say than if I were a sheep bleating at the entrance to the slaughter-house.

Against my better judgement I hold the line. For all I know Mr Cube may be an editor or the Prime Minister's secretary; he may have to tell me that all the time I held a winning ticket in the Calcutta Sweep. Besides, the third girl has a sweet voice.

I hold the line till my ear swells.

Then the sweet voice says, 'I am very sorry, Mr Cube cannot be found at the moment, but he is somewhere in the building'.

'What is the building?'

'I will call you again.'

'Who is Mr Cube?'

But she has gone away.

The episode has lasted about five minutes. I return to my work, fuming.

Five minutes later the foul bell rings again. Again we go through the protracted ritual by which Mr Cube is put in touch with the outside world. Again the three girls pass me along, as men throw bricks from one to another, unloading a barge. They do not care how long I wait or what questions I ask – I am mere telephone-fodder for Mr Cube.

At last a loud and masterful male voice says, 'Hullo!'

'Hullo.'

'Look here, old chap, about tonight. You know there's no doubt in my mind that we've got to be firm with Footle and his lot or he'll stampede the whole Committee. Well, I'll tell you what I've done – '

'I beg your pardon?'

'Hullo? Hullo? Is that you, Mortimer?'

'No. It's Mr Haddock. I was told somebody – '

'Mr Haddock? Oh, I beg your pardon. I thought my secretary said – Hullo? Is Mr Haddock there then?'

'Yes. Speaking.'

'Is that you, Mr Haddock?'

'Yes.'

'Mr A P Haddock?'

'Y E S!'

'Oh! Well, Mr Haddock, I hope you don't mind my ringing you up. It's like this – '

But let us not prolong the painful story. Mr Cube has no intention of giving me money. On the contrary, he wants me to do something for him; he wants me to make a speech at some ghastly dinner, he wants me to lecture at a school, he wants me to write an article about a deserving charity, he wants me to insure my life… And he has taken up ten whole minutes of my priceless time besides poisoning my mind with irritation. Curse you, Mr Cube! Let me tell you that my time is as valuable to me as yours to you, and, having no cloud of young women to assist me, I have even less time to spare. I do *not* mind your ringing me up, but I hotly object to your ringing me up on the instalment system.

Curse you, Mr Cube!

IX

NINTH WICKET

The bowling looks exceptionally sound,
   The wicket seems unusually worn,
The balls fly up or run along the ground;
   I rather wish that I had not been born.
I have been sitting here since two o'clock;
   My pads are both inelegant and hot;
I do not want what people call my 'knock',
   And this pavilion is a sultry spot.
I shall not win one clap or word of praise,
   I know that I shall bat like a baboon;
And I can think of many better ways
   In which to spend a summer afternoon.
I might be swimming in a crystal pool;
   I might be wooing some delicious dame;
I might be drinking something long and cool –
   I can't imagine why I play this game.

Why is the wicket seven miles away,
   And why have I to walk to it alone?
I hope that Bottle's bat will drive today –
   I ought to buy a weapon of my own.
I wonder if this walk will ever cease;
   They should provide a motor-car or crane
To drop the batsman on the popping-crease

And, when he's out, convey him back again.
Is it a dream? Can this be truly me,
Alone and friendless in a waste of grass?
The fielding side are sniggering, I see,
And long-leg sort of shudders as I pass.
How very small and funny I must look!
I only hope that no one knows my name.
I might be in a hammock with a book –
I can't imagine why I play this game.

Well, here we are. We feel a little ill.
What is this pedant of an umpire at?
Middle and off, or centre – what you will;
It cannot matter where I park the bat.
I look around me in a knowing way
To show that I am not to be cajoled;
I shall play forward gracefully and pray…
I have played forward and I am not bowled.
I do not like the wicket-keeper's face,
And why are all the fielders crowding round?
The bowler makes an imbecile grimace,
And mid-off makes a silly whistling sound.
These innuendoes I could do without;
They mean to say the ball defied the bat,
They indicate that I was nearly out;
Well, darn their impudence! I know all that.
Why am I standing in this comic pose,
Hemmed in by men that I should like to maim?
I might be lying in a punt with Rose –
I can't imagine why I play this game.

And there are people sitting over there
Who fondly hope that I shall make a run;
They cannot guess how blinding is the glare;
They do not know the ball is like a bun.

But, courage, heart! We have survived a ball;
   I pat the pitch to show that it is bad;
We are not such a rabbit, after all;
   Now we shall show them what is what, my lad!
The second ball is very, very swift;
   It breaks and stands up steeply in the air;
It looks at me, and I could swear it sniffed;
   I gesture at it, but it is not there.
Ah, what a ball! Mind you, I do not say
   That Bradman, Hobbs, and Ranji in his prime,
Rolled into one, and that one on his day,
   Might not have got a bat to it in time...
But long-stop's looking for my middle-stump,
   And I am walking in a world of shame;
My captain has addressed me as a chump –
   I can't imagine why I play this game.

X

SCENE SEVENTEEN

SEQUENCE 49, Scene 17, did not, on paper, present many difficulties. Just a simple piece of dialogue:

MURIEL. Give me that letter!
GEORGE (*crunching the letter in his hand*). Never!
MURIEL (*she hears a twig snap in the jungle and whispers*). What is that?
GEORGE. Elephants.

That was all. But when I arrived on the 'location' they had been working at this scene for four hours.

The scene of the incident was a clearing in the jungle of Ceylon, near which it was known that a dangerous 'rogue' elephant was roaming, seeking somebody to trample on.

But the scene of the 'shooting' was a desolate area of stubble-fields and barbed-wire fences in Herts. Two hundred yards away from the tropical grove was a British railway-station, which appeared to be the centre of the shunting operations of Great Britain. Through this station express trains ran frequently and noisily, careless of the trouble they gave to the producers of a sound-film operating in the open air. The studio unfortunately was built before the talkies were thought of.

It was a typical spring day in August – 'showers and bright periods', as the forecast describes it. A fitful breeze blew across the fields and made noises in the microphones; the sun appeared now and then between racing clouds, and rain fell every fifteen minutes.

The difficulties of reproducing the hot stillness of a tropical jungle in these conditions can scarcely be exaggerated. Nor was the tropical atmosphere heightened by the numerous arc-lamps, cameras, hanging microphones, bits of scaffolding, and labyrinthine wires that surrounded the tropical palms and banyan-tree, not to mention three or four directors, five or six sound experts, twenty-five cameramen, and a miscellaneous army of electricians, carpenters, and tropical sceneshifters.

There are three main troubles in the production of a talkie out of doors – the actors, the sound, and the light. The first thing is to decide what the actors are to say and to get them to say it correctly and audibly. When I arrived the actors were still being rehearsed; they seemed patient but mad. *George* had hissed 'Never!' for the forty-first time, and *Muriel* was about to hear the broken twig and whisper, '*What is that?*' when an express train rushed roaring through the station.

A man was sitting about a hundred yards away beside a telephone connected with the sound-cabinet far away in the studio; and this man shouted, 'Can't be heard!' Muriel with pardonable irritation shouted back, 'I'M *WHISPERING!* WHAT IS *THAT*?' And George yelled, 'ELEPHANTS! MY SACRED AUNT!'

But these were the only signs of strain I detected: the patience of everyone was quite amazing. In Scene 17, Sequence 49, there are, as you will have noted, three separate sound-effects, all rather fine – the crunching of the letter, the snapping of the twig, and the whispering of *Muriel*. After long labours, rehearsals, and tests, the correct volume for all the sounds and speeches was ascertained and fixed. *Muriel's* whisper was no longer likely to break the ear-drums of the film-fan, and the snapping of the twig no longer sounded to the unseen fellows in the sound-cabinet like a twelve-inch log falling from a great height. All that remained was to turn on the four expensive lamps which were to bring the English sunshine up to tropical standard, start the sound-machines, set the cameras going and *shoot* the scene.

The sun was shining brightly. A red light shone. The tropical lamps shone. 'All quiet, please!' Perfect silence. A green light shone. A cold breeze blew across the fields. *Muriel,* wilting in the heat of Ceylon, said, '*Give me that letter!*' The cameras madly photographed her. And then from nowhere a big black cloud rolled up and buried the sun; and the darkness of Britain descended on Ceylon.

For fifteen minutes the whole crowd patiently watched the cloud. Then it rained for ten minutes. Then the sun emerged. A red light shone. 'Quiet, everybody!' Deathly hush. Lamps, cameras, green light. Scene 17 was off again. *Muriel* wound up her weary emotions for the fifty-seventh time and said, 'Give me that letter'. *George* said –

But at that moment round the corner came the 'Flying Scotsman' or some such train. *Muriel* made a rather pathetic little whimper and I went off to tea.

When I returned it seemed that Scene 17, Sequence 49, was really about to be recorded.

The tropical sun was visible, and though it was now low the arc-lamps supported it powerfully. The breeze had fallen with the sun, and there was a strange quiet, broken only by some desultory shunting. The red light shone. The green light shone. The cameras whirred. Away in the sound-cabinet the sound-gentleman listened tensely. And then an awful thing happened. *Muriel* forgot her words.

Thrilled, no doubt, by the prospect of finishing with Scene 17 at last, *Muriel* stared blankly at *George* and said nothing at all for a full half-minute. And at last she murmured diffidently, '*Where is the letter?*'

George stared at her and shook like a jelly, realizing that to this question it was impossible to reply 'Never!' and he said, '*I don't know*'. But the quick-witted fellow then remembered that he had the letter in his grasp, so he added, '*Here it is*', and handed it to *Muriel*. They then turned off the expensive lamps and began again. No cross word passed. Everyone seemed to realize that this sort of thing was only to be expected. I was proud to be a Briton.

The sky was now clear, but the sun had nearly set. At the next attempt it was *George* who lost his nerve, and when *Muriel* said, '*Give me that letter*', *George* replied, '*All right*', and tore it up.

Perfect patience continued to reign. I thought as the night fell that *Muriel* perhaps had a suicidal impulse or two, but neither she nor the directors expressed their secret thoughts.

The biggest blow, perhaps, came about sunset. More lamps had been brought out, there was neither rain nor train, both *Muriel* and *George* remembered their words, said them perfectly and even acted a little (this was the hundred-and-first time), and the whole scene was played through without interruption or fault of any kind. Smiles and sighs of relief all round. And then the cameraman revealed that the film had run out half-way through the scene.

Not a word was said. I went home and left them at it. But I believe that Scene 17 was successfully recorded about nine.

I know that, later, when the film was finished, the film was too long, and Scene 17 was cut out altogether.

And now you know:

(*a*) Why the 'pictures' have sometimes a certain spasmodic effect.

(*b*) Why the radiant heroine of one scene looks as if she had slept under a steam-roller in the next.

(*c*) Why film-actors are highly paid.

(*d*) Why the invention of the 'talkies', though a marvel of modern science, has not so far perhaps made many staggering contributions to Art.

And (*e*) one or two other things.

XI

CRICKET IN THE CAUCASUS
or
THE VOLGA BATMEN
(Translated from the Russian)

I

'I Tell you what it is, Andrey Andreyevitch,' said Stepan Pepushkin impatiently, 'if the cricket competition does not soon begin it will be dark before it is finished. And then, you know, we shall be hampered by the wolves.'

'What is the hurry?' replied the old man, chewing grass. 'I am too drunk to umpire yet. Natalya Popova cannot find the bats. And, besides, the young men have not yet settled the dispute about the teams.'

'Sometimes,' replied the other passionately, 'I think I see the stars in your old eyes, Andrey Andreyevitch; and sometimes I do not understand you.'

Stepan Pepushkin was a poet. He wore a peaked cap and black knickerbockers. He was eager for the new game, which would bring back poetry to the village, the Commissar had said. 'How can there be a dispute among brothers?' he cried.

'Well, you see, it is perfectly simple,' said the old umpire. 'I think I can stand now. I will get up. What a disgusting creature I am to be drunk on Wednesday! And Olga Merinin says the harvest will be late. What was I saying, Stepan Stepanovitch?'

'You were raving quietly,' replied the young man. 'There is Natalya, carrying the two bats like torches over her shoulders. How beautiful she is!'

'The young men are quarrelling. Boris Borisovitch has emptied the whitewash pail over Lopakhin; and now we shall have no crease. But all this is highly intelligible when you come to think of it.'

'If I were to kill Maria Andreyevna,' said the poet dreamily, 'would you marry again?'

'Excuse me, the trouble is that our village has been collectivized under the Decree. Everything is in common. We are all in common. We are all brothers. Naturally, therefore, say the young men, we cannot have two teams of brothers playing against each other, for there can be nothing brotherly in trying to get the better of one another. But the Commissar has a paper from Moscow. He says there must be two teams of eleven, each with a captain; but the young men will not have captains. It is all rather unpleasant. I think I shall lie down again.'

'Eleven is a beautiful number,' said the poet. 'Two ones. Two ones – two captains – two bats of forest wood. Some day, Andrey Andreyevitch, I shall go to London where this beautiful game was thought of.'

But the old man was asleep.

Stepan Pepushkin walked over to the debate of the young men. He went straight up to Natalya Popova and kissed her. 'Will you marry me?' he said loudly, because of the noise of the speakers, many of whom were talking in common. She had very brown eyes, like a small cow in springtime. She wore a Tartar skirt and knee-pads for the wicket.

'I think I am engaged to some of the others,' she said. 'Besides, you are a poet, Stepan, and there is no place for poetry now. We should have no food.'

'If I were to write in prose,' said the young man, 'would you love me?'

'Prose is more respectable, to be sure,' said Natalya Popova, 'but, excuse me, everyone is active and vigorous now, ploughing and making grain for the State or combating the counter-revolutionaries. You are only a dreamer; Olga Merinin told me she found you feeding nightingales in the wood. What is the use of that when Russia is starving, Stepan Pepushkin? To-day, to take an example, the Committee will not let you take part in the batting. They have appointed you to count the runs. I tell you what is in my mind, Stepan; I am sorry I let you kiss me.'

Stepan smiled dumbly and listened to the speakers.

'Comrades,' shouted Serge Obolensky, the humane slaughterer, 'the solution is evident. We cannot have two hostile teams competing against each other, for this would be to play into the hands of the Capitalist Governments, which seek to divide the workers. But we can all play on the same side.'

'*Pravda!*' 'Well spoken, Serge!' '*Yashmak!*' cried the cricketers.

Big Lubov, the bearded schoolmaster, came to the rostrum carrying a stump. 'I have a proposition.'

'*Nitchevo!*' '*Chuchuk!*' 'A proposition!'

'My proposition is that all runs should be shared in common.'

'*Pravda! 'Yashmak!*' 'All runs to be shared in common!'

But Bortsov, the Commissar, stepped forward. 'I have a paper from Moscow. At Moscow they say that you are idle; the grain lies unreaped, the bins are empty.'

'*Tchai!*' '*Merovestia!*' cried the angry villagers.

'Moscow says that the will to compete and act energetically must be born again in you. Therefore they have given you this cricket which the English workers play. Therefore you must have two teams striving for victory, and therefore each worker shall keep his own runs, striving to gain more than his comrade.'

'Kill the Commissar!' cried every one. 'Capitalism!' 'The counter-revolution!'

'I will kill the Commissar!' yelled Big Lubov the schoolmaster. 'Give me a bat, Natalya Popova,' he said in a softer voice; for Big Lubov loved Natalya.

'There are only two bats,' said the girl, 'and they must be restored to the Government after the game. It would be a pity to break them.'

'*Pravda!*' said Lubov; and he drove the sharp stump which he carried through the Commissar's heart.

'And now let us begin the game,' said the schoolmaster.

II

'Now that we have killed the Commissar,' Serge Obolensky was saying, 'we have no one who can explain the rules of cricket. But Russia is like that.'

'Who wants rules?' said young Nicolai Nicolaievitch. 'Rules were made for the bourgeois.'

'*Pravda*. True. But, excuse me, it would be convenient if we could come to some agreement about the method of our proceedings. To take an example, Nicolai Nicolaievitch, we know that there are two sets of stumps, for the Commissar told us so much; but where in the world are we to put them?'

'It is simple enough, Serge Obolensky. We will put one set here and the other over there.'

'Yes, Nicolai,' replied the older man patiently; 'but where?'

'There.'

'I recognize the energy of your mind, Nicolai – but how far away?'

'Give me the Commissar's paper. Twenty-two yards – that is versts. *Cuculin!*' said the young revolutionary in triumph.

'No one in the village can throw a leather ball so far. I tell you what, we will let each man bowl according to his capacity. The strong man shall throw from a great way off and the weak from a little distance. Thus we shall establish equality. Big Lubov, to take an example, must throw at the batsmen from the next field, and I shall throw from here.'

'But,' said the young cynical clerk of the bank, 'suppose that the strong man pretends to be weak, then he will have an advantage.'

'Then,' said Serge Obolensky simply, 'we shall kill him.'

III

Big Lubov and Natalya Popova were still batting. All the village had bowled the round ball at them, some from this place and some from that. None of the peasants had hit them. Big Lubov defended his body nimbly with his great bat. But the young men did not like to throw the ball at pretty Natalya. They threw it away from her, so that she could not strike it with her bat. So it came about that Lubov had gained seven runs, but pretty Natalya had made none.

Old Volodja's best cow lay in the shade watching the game. Dreamily, sitting on the cow, Stepan Pepushkin wrote the runs in his book. He thought that Natalya was like a tulip.

'Ho, Stepan!' Big Lubov cries, 'how goes the count?'

'Lubov – 9 runs,' answers the poet; 'Natalya Popova – 7 runs.'

'*Nitchevo!* How is this? Not once has Natalya struck the ball.'

'From time to time I give her a run,' said the poet, 'because she is so beautiful.'

'*Yashmak!*' At first Big Lubov was angry. But he loved Natalya and he shrugged with good temper. When Big Lubov shrugged it was like a storm on the hills. Trees fell down.

'Besides,' said Serge Obolensky cunningly, 'since all the runs are to be shared in common, Lubov Lubovinsky, the question has no significance. Strictly speaking, the count is Lubov – 8; Natalya – 8.'

'*Botsch!*' shouted the schoolmaster angrily. 'No man or woman shall take *my* runs!' For Lubov had begun to enjoy the cricket, and the will to win was in his great heart, which was shaped like a pear.

'You are a *molak*, Lubov!' cried Nicolai Nicolaievitch. 'Run-hog! *Menshevik!*'

'Bowl, thou,' replied the big man with a threatening motion, 'or I will bat thee.'

Presently Lubov had made 13. Stepan gave Natalya two more runs because of the pretty curve of her waist, which was like the prow of a small ship. Natalya Popova was 9.

Then Alexis the blacksmith took the ball.

Lubov cries out: 'Ho! blacksmith, you come too close! Stand yonder by Obolensky in the farther field!'

But Alexis throws the ball strong and low and strikes the schoolmaster in the stomach.

'*Yashmak!*' 'Hit!' 'Lubov is out!' cry the peasants.

'The blow was irregular,' cries the batsman angrily. 'He came too near. What is the verdict, Andrey Andreyevitch?'

All eyes turned to the aged umpire. But the umpire was still asleep.

'He is drunk,' said Serge Obolensky.

'I tell you what,' said Lubov, 'is it not a very extraordinary thing that all the time, while we have been playing this game, the umpire was lying drunk at the place called square-leg, and none of us perceived it?'

'Russia is like that,' said Serge Obolensky. 'My father's sister kept beetles in her bedroom and fed them on sunflower seeds. Nobody knew.'

'Practically speaking,' the schoolmaster remarked logically, 'the game, so far, has not been happening, for the official, in a manner of speaking, was not present. It follows therefore that I am still batting.'

'In that case,' said the cunning Nicolai, 'you have not made 13 runs, but no runs.'

'*Pravda!*'

Lubov weakened. He thought that none of the peasants would make so many as 13 runs.

'Besides, as you will be the first to appreciate, Lubov Lubovinsky, this umpire is only a mouthpiece for the voice of the people. Indubitably he is incapable; but what of that? The voice of the people has said that you are out.'

'Out!' 'Out!' '*Slava!*'

Lubov with a bad grace gave up the bat, saying, 'As for you, Andrey Andreyevitch, tonight I will give you to the wolves'.

The old man woke. 'The queer thing is, brother,' he said, 'that I have forgotten your name.'

'Russia is like that,' said Serge Obolensky.

'I have just remembered,' said Big Lubov unpleasantly, 'that I have a pistol in my breeches pocket. If any brother or comrade makes more than 13 I will shoot him through the head.'

IV

All the peasants batted in turn and were thrown out. Boris Polunin was stunned. Michael Andrid ran away. Only Natalya Popova remained always at the stumps. Natalya had 11 runs; but Stepan would not give her any more now for fear of Big Lubov's pistol. Alexis the blacksmith had made 7. The others had made nothing. Meanwhile Big Lubov had become exceedingly dogmatic and unpopular. When the last man was out he said, 'Well, it must be evident to all of you that Lubov Lubovinski has gained the victory.

The angry shouts of the villagers drowned his speech; and Alexis the blacksmith said, 'Excuse me, the affair is not concluded. Stepan Pepushkin has not yet tried his skill.'

'*Pravda!*' 'Stepan!' 'Pepushkin the poet will put the schoolmaster down.'

They summoned Stepan to the stumps, and gave the ball to Nicolai Nicolaievitch. The young poet was overjoyed to be batting with Natalya. On his way to the stumps he took her in his arms and kissed her.

'Your hair is like the wild jasmine which grows in the Caucasus,' he said. 'Now, Natalya, if I am not mistaken, you are going to see that I am not a dreamer only.'

Nicolai prepared to throw, but the poet stepped forward, lifting his hand. 'Excuse me, Nicolai Nicolaievitch,' he said, 'but, do you know, this is a highly significant moment? Here am I, a young man who never in his whole life has played with bat and ball before. I have never been clever with my hands. At carpentry and needlework I was the duffer of my school. I never could knit or tie up parcels. Truly, I don't know anyone so clumsy with his fingers. I am always dropping my tea-cup, upsetting things, pushing things over. As you see, Nicolai, I am quite unable to tie my cravat in a presentable bow. The only tool I was ever able to use was a lead pencil. And yet – '

'Pardon my abruptness, Stepan Pepushkin,' said Nicolai, 'but if you are going to relate to us the history of your life it seems to me that the fieldsmen had better sit down.'

'That is as you please, Nicolai Nicolaievitch.' And all the peasants sat down on the grass.

'As I was saying,' the batsman continued, 'the extraordinary thing is that here I am with this really most unfamiliar instrument in my hands, and, do you know, I am superbly confident? I am absolutely convinced that I am going to succeed in the game, and gain more runs than this blustering schoolmaster. Is it not remarkable?'

'*Pravda,*' said the bowler, yawning slightly.

'The reason for all this is, I think, perfectly evident. It is Natalya – Natalya Popova, standing there with her Government bat like a torch of a new truth. Now that the Union of Soviet Republics has inscribed cricket upon its advancing banners I think you will agree that we shall conquer the world. Cricket was the one thing that Holy Russia lacked. Cricket will save Russia. Cricket – '

'Excuse me,' said Serge Obolensky, rising to his feet at mid-off; 'night is falling, Stepan Pepushkin; the grass is wet with dew, and I perceive that wolves are gathering at the borders of the field. It would be convenient to most of us if we could continue the game.'

'By all means,' answered the poet. 'But do you know, in spite of my confidence it has now occurred to me that men are but mortal and the future is uncertain? It is just possible that Nicolai Nicolaievitch will kill me with the ball. Permit me therefore to embrace Natalya Popova before we begin.'

'Naturally, Stepan Pepushkin.'

This ceremony concluded, the poet prepared to defend himself. Nicolaievitch threw the ball very hard at his head. Stepan put his bat before his face, and the ball, touching it, flew into the forest, scattering the wolves.

'Run, Natalya Popova!' cried the poet, and they ran. Old Volodja, the long-stop, was fat and slow. They ran nine runs.

The ball was carried back at length, and Stepan, panting, faced Nicolaievitch again.

Big Lubov stepped forward. 'I tell you what,' he bellowed, 'I have just realized that all this business is simply a waste of time. When you come to think of it, there are crops to be garnered, cattle to be tended, cows to be milked. The moon is rising, and here we all are throwing a leather ball at Stepan Pepushkin. Is it not preposterous? What in the world does it matter, I ask myself, whether Stepan gains more runs than Lubov or not? Naturally it is most unlikely that he will overcome me; but will the State be any the better for it if he does? Andrey Andreyevitch is asleep again. Let us all go to the village and drink *tchai*.'

'What you say is extremely reasonable,' said Serge Obolensky, 'but, excuse me, you should have said it before. It is evident that Stepan Pepushkin has a talent for the game, and it would not surprise me if he were to overcome you.'

'*Pravda!*' '*Yashmak!*' cried the peasants, who hated the schoolmaster.

Nicolaievitch threw the ball at Pepushkin's face a second time. The poet struck the ball towards the wood.

'Run, Natalya!'

'I run, Stepan. Do thou run also!'

A big wolf runs out of the wood and takes the ball in its mouth.

'Run, Volodja! The wolf has the ball. Follow and help him, Boris Borisovitch!'

The wolf runs into the wood. Volodja runs after the wolf. Boris Borisovitch runs after Volodja. Serge Obolensky runs after Borisovitch. Alexis the blacksmith runs after Obolensky. Olga Merinin runs after Alexis. Nicolai Nicolaievitch runs after Olga Merinin. The other peasants follow; and last of all, Andrey Andreyevitch, waking up, totters into the wood, where the wolves devour him with the others.

Only Big Lubov remains in the field, watching with a sour smile while Stepan and Natalya run up and down, hand-in-hand, between the stumps. Stepan has made two-hundred-and-ninety-four. Out of breath, he pauses; Natalya folds her strong arms about him.

'You are a true man, Stepan Pepushkin,' she whispers. 'We will go to Moscow together and make fly-papers for the Government.'

But Big Lubov has picked up the Commissar's paper.

'It is all very well,' he says spitefully, 'but, do you know, Pepushkin, we were playing without the bails? Moscow says that without the bails the game does not exist.'

Natalya wept.

'After all, then, Stepan, I find that I do not love you.'

'Russia is like that,' said Stepan Pepushkin.

XII

MR MAFFERTY HAS A HAIR-CUT

'The hair's a little thin, is it?' said Mr Mafferty, taking his head out of the basin. 'Well, maybe it is thin, Mr Barber. An' what way would it not be thin, an' you diggin' in the roots of it with your sharp fingers, an' tearin' it out with your fierce machines, an' frettin' it with your rough towels, an' washin' it away with your cascades of water, like a Chinaman tormentin' the sands of the river for a few grains of gold? It's the wonder of the world, I'm thinkin', if there's one hair clingin' to the poor crown of me head, an' it swollen and sore with the great buffetin' it's had this day. It's not thin the hair is at all, Mr Barber, but sensitive itself. It isn't a doormat you have in front of you, or a frayed rug, or a piece of a carpet is hung in the backyard on a Saturday mornin' to be beaten by an old woman, an' she chokin' with the dust. It's a human head, an' tender as a little child's. But maybe it's in the stable you worked as a boy, Mr Barber, an' you mistakin' the top of me skull for the back of a horse, the way you'd be scrapin' an' scrubbin' it with your steel brushes to make a shinin' surface a girl could see her face in, an' she lost in the wood on a dark night. There'll be a grand shine on me head, surely, after this mornin's work, but it'll be the shine of nakedness and the glory of a bald crown. Will you wait now while I chase the soap out of me eyes, for there's a longin' in me heart to be lookin' in the glass an' takin' a peep at what you've left of me.

'That's better now. I can see with one eye. Let's be viewin' the remains.

'So that's it, is it? The Holy Popes! did you ever see the like of that? Let you cast your mind back now, Mr Barber, to a piece of a talk an' conversation we had a great while ago, an' I throwin' out a small kind of a hint I'd have a little off the top an' divil a hair off the sides. You mind that, is it? Then it could be that you might have a note made in your capacious memory of the great oaths you let that time to be watchin' me wishes as careful as a young bride, an' she not wedded a week of days. An' if it's the truth I'm sayin', will you throw your tired eyes in the glass, Mr Barber, an' see the wreck an' havoc you've made of me noble head, an' it clipped an' shaven from ear to ear like a parson's lawn or a bagatelle-board itself? *Thin,* is it? If it's thin that it is, what word would you use for a man had no hair at all? There'll be no welcome anny place for me from this out, I'm thinkin', unless it would be Portland prison or the county jail. An' it's a hard thing, Mr Barber, to take an honest man an' turn him into a burglar with a pair of scissors an' an electric brush between the sittin' down of him an' the risin' up.

'But it's me own blame, surely, for it's meself was engrossed in the flow of your conversation, the way I'd not be noticin' what you were at, an' you charmin' the ear with the fine tales of your family, an' your prognostications of rain, an' your brother that keeps the chickens, an' your wife's sister has the asthma an' went to America itself. It's lost I was in the story, Mr Barber, an' half in love with your wife's sister already, an' she rangin' the ocean an' the countries of the West to be makin' her fortune in the movin' pictures. Halfway to Hollywood I was meself, an' it's a fierce thing for a man to be brought back from America in the flick of an eye to find his own head is like a football made out of the skin of a wet seal, an' it piebald. But it's not I would be blamin' you, Mr Barber, for we've great trouble in this world, ivery one of us; an' when a man has his wife's sister in his mind, an' she coughin' on the high seas, he'd have a right not to be frettin' himself will he be cuttin' a hair here or a hair there or maybe an ear itself. But it's not meself will be takin' a shave of the face this day, an' you distracted thinkin' of your brother's hens an' the fall of the rain.

'Is it a small bottle of lotion I'll be buyin' now, Mr Barber? It is not. It's a quare, fine, gratifyin' liquid, that one, I'm not denyin'. There's some kind of a magical oil in it isn't oily at all, the way the hair will never be greasy. An' there's some kind of a powerful astringent in it isn't astringent at all, the way the hair will never be dry. An' there's some kind of a supernatural glue in it, the way the hair will never fall out. An' there's some kind of an exceptional fertilizer in it, the way ten hairs will be growin' where one grew before. An' there's some kind of a miraculous polish in it, the way the hair will glow like the skin of a tiger, an' he preenin' an' prowlin' at the time of matin'. An' there's some kind of a juice of the hyacinth in it, the way the hair will curl like the fingers of a flower, an' it rollin' across the brow like the billows of the sea. It's a tonic it is, an' a stimulant, an' a brain-food, an' if you gave half a drop to a man with one leg it's two he'd have at the dawn of day. It's like the wine of Juppiter himself, it's what they drink in the Moon, it has the rose beat for scent, there's never a flower could stand up to it at all, an' if you take one smell of it you'll not be lookin' at a lily again on this side of the grave. There's all the perfumes of Arabia an' India an' the United States in one small teaspoonful.

'But no, Mr Barber, it's not meself will be buying a bottle. And I'll tell you for why. I had a bottle the last time, an' by a quare sort of an accident I spilled a little drop of the liquid on me old Persian prayer-mat lies before the fire. Believe me or believe me not, Mr Barber – for it's all one at the end of Time – but in the half of a day, Mr Barber, that same small prayer-mat had grown so large it was fillin' the whole room, the creature, the way I'd not be openin' the drawin'-room door at all for fear it would be spreadin' over the hallplace an' maybe creepin' up the stairway itself. An' after that, for the sake of Science, I let fall a drop or two on the bit of a croquet-lawn I have, an' it as bare as the south face of a billiard-ball. Well, if it's a lie I'm tellin' you Mr Barber, let you poke me with a razor between the stomach an' the midriff, but that same lawn grew up so thick with weeds an' the like it broke down me neighbour's wall, crash, in the midnight, the way a man would swear it was an explosion did it, and he comin' fresh an' ignorant from the Isles of Bute or a far place entirely. So it's in dread I was to be puttin' it on me head, Mr Barber, an' I thinkin' I'd be flowerin' cabbages or burstin' out with a great mop of black hair like the natives of Australia, to be trippin' the feet of me an' I walkin' the wood. It's not meself, Mr Barber, would take much pleasure goin' about the city with a long trail of hair behind me hangin' from the head, an' maybe furred like a rabbit from me top to me toes. Let you keep silence, then, Mr Barber, for it's never a word I'm sayin' against the agricultural properties of your rare lotion, but the contrary altogether.

'An' now, Mr Barber, if you'll find me bowler-hat it's away I am out of this place for ever. What's that? Is it a bill itself? Is it money you have in your gross mind? Away now, Mr Barber, I'd be ashamed breathin' the same air with you! Is it *payin'* I'd be to have me grand head destroyed, an' I the mock of the city from this out? I wouldn't pay a tailor to cut great holes in me trousers, an' I wouldn't pay a doctor to cut off me right hand, an' I askin' for a soothin' medicine. An' why would I pay you for an Eton crop, when all I looked for was a little kindness an' to be tidied round the ears? It's yourself will be payin' at the latter end, I'm thinkin'. I'll not ask you for a contribution an' damages this moment, Mr Barber, but it's me own solicitor will be rampagin' at your doors before the moon rises on the city this night, an' he makin' the heart of you a jelly with writs and the like. Good mornin', Mr Barber, an' misfortune follow you from this day to your life's end!'

XIII

'STRUBE'

(With apologies and compliments)

A rose by any other name
Would smell as rosy; all the same
It is important – yes, it is,
To know how STRUBE pronounces his.
For instance, does he rhyme with 'tube'?
I cannot tell you. (Nor can STRUBE.)
Full many a wife informs her hubby
'The only man I love is STRUBE';
While there are those who rudely dub
This brilliant little fellow STRUBE.
By others he is rhymed with 'booby',
But somehow that does not suit STRUBE;
And I have heard the artist blubber
When men accosted him as STRUBE.
It is a fearful thing to think,
Wherever Britons sit and drink,
In Madagascar and Ceylon,
And Africa and Kensington,
Where'er they speak the British tongue,
However far the Empire's flung,
All day our countrymen exclaim,
'How *does* this man pronounce his name?'

Canadians wake their wives at night
And mutter, 'No, that can't be right.'
Australians cooee through the scrub
'STROOB? STROOBY? STRUBBY? STROOBER?
STRUB?'
We know the secrets of the sky
And how the stars behave, and why;
We know so much it makes us ill,
But this conundrum beats us still.
No doubt you think the simplest plan
Would be to *ask* the little man.
Well, you are wrong, for when I pounced
And said, 'Hi! How are you pronounced?'
He took his horsewhip from the shelf
And said, 'I do not know myself'.
So we must leave it, I suppose –
The only thing that *no one* knows.

XIV

GIVING UP SMOKING

Thank heaven, I have given up smoking again!

This is the morning of the second day and the thing is now fixed. You can scarcely imagine the relief of it. How well I feel! What vitality and vigour!

I could bite through the leg of that chair, kick a hole through that table or run about knocking everybody's heads together. In fact, I have felt like doing these things since just after luncheon yesterday.

Gad! I feel fit. Homicidal, but fit. A different man. Irritable, moody, depressed, rude, nervy, perhaps; but the lungs are fine. And if I do bash somebody over the head it will at least be said in my defence that I had the strength of mind to give up smoking.

And then, the *mental* difference! The mind more active, the imagination less sluggish. True, at the moment I can think of nothing but pipes and cigars; but the mind is busy. True, I am now travelling through the Red Sea and the pipe is never so alluring in the tropics. True, also, I have a cruel sore throat. But these little accidents have really nothing to do with it. I have always meant to give up smoking for good, and now it just happens that I have.

What a filthy foolish habit it was. Have you ever examined the interior of a pipe just after a smoke – a good old long-service, 'favourite', disgusting pipe? Incredible! One might as well put a straw in the gutter and have a suck at that. Better, indeed, for the gutter as a rule contains no nicotine.

And what sentimental twaddle we used to talk about it! All this Baldwin-and-his-pipe stuff, for example. Mr Baldwin ought to be ashamed of himself. Obviously he oversmokes; and that explains why – I mean, I know myself exactly the effect it has on the brain. People say it's so 'English', and even women will say that they like to see their husbands smoking a pipe. Silly fools! They cannot know what they mean. The writers too, with their 'Odes to Tobacco', 'My Lady Nicotine', and so forth. 'My Lady Nicotine,' forsooth! Might as well rhapsodize about 'My Lady Tannin' or 'My Lady Lipstick'.

'English', indeed! Bah! Is it really characteristic of our race to burn a vegetable substance in a small bowl just in front of the eyes and nose and then suck the residuary juices (which are toxic) into the mouth? Is this really a distinguishing mark of the pioneers of civilization? Again 'Bah!'

Gosh, I feel fit! And gosh, what a temper I'm in! Gosh, what an appetite! I could bite that lifebuoy through!

It pleases me to think of the time, trouble, and transport (to say nothing of cash) which I shall save – am saving already. The *stuff* one carried about! Every time one dressed, every time one went out, every time one changed one's clothes there was the same trouble: Have I got everything? One pipe (generally two), one tobacco-pouch (and is it full? and, if not, where's the tin?), the matches, the pipe-cleaners, the knife or Smoker's Companion for poking or cleaning. And some poor slaves, of course, carry cigarettes as well. What a lot of trash! Bulging out the pockets, spoiling the figure! Here I sit in my tropical suit, with empty pockets at last, a flat surface, and the right shape.

And free of that endless match-trouble. He does not notice it, maybe; but life for the pipe-smoker is really coloured by the number of matches in his box. He acquires a full box – elation; someone removes it – agony; it dwindles towards emptiness – growing anxiety; the last match flickers out – despair; no matches to be had anywhere – madness, murder, anything.

And then, the *labour* of pipe-smoking! In the bad old days when I smoked, that is to say, the day before yesterday, I used to sit in this same corner at the after end of B deck and write – and *smoke*. Naturally, in the Red Sea, one sits in a breeze if possible; and when the mind is being used the pipe goes out, I find, or used to find, about once in every two minutes; and one then ceased thinking and lit a match; and it was instantly extinguished by the breeze; and one lit two more and tried again; and then one got up, went round the corner and lit the pipe in the lee of the smoking-room; and then one returned, collected the thoughts and began work again.

Well, you will understand that on a morning when the breeze was fresh and the concentration-of-mind strong the pipe-lighting intervals amounted to a considerable period. You may say, of course, 'Well, if the mind is concentrating to that extent, why smoke at all?' But it is quite useless to ask silly questions of that kind. The answer is, 'One does'. Or rather, 'One did'.

All that, however, is now dead and done with. Today, a non-smoker, I sit here working away steadily without interruption, unless it might be to look at a passing flying-fish or porpoise or, once in a while, to pop into the smoking-room to read the wireless news or stand some poor devil the first drink of the day. No pipe-trouble, no breeze-trouble, no match-trouble.

No dead-match-trouble, for instance. What a problem – what to do with dead matches when sitting on deck! Being a tidy person and attached to the Chief Officer, I have never cared to drop them on deck, for this maddens him. Sometimes I thrust them tidily back into my match-box; and then ladies came along, borrowed my matches, extracted four dead men in succession, and reviled me. Nor was it any use to remind them that the match-box was mine, and that people who could not keep matches of their own deserved what they got. So I invented a third plan. I allowed the deads to accumulate in a little pile till they numbered six or seven, and I would then make a special expedition to the side of the ship and throw them overboard. But these little walks took time, you know; and what with walks to the rail and walks round the corner, lighting matches and lending matches, filling the pipe, cleaning the pipe, prodding the pipe, and knocking out the pipe, slipping down to the cabin for more tobacco, slipping into the smoking-room for more matches, I really shudder to think how much of the working-morning was occupied with smoking or trying to smoke.

'Was' – mark you. For all that is a thing of the past. Never again. Still, it would be interesting, in a morbid sort of way, to know exactly what was the loss of efficiency, reckoned in man-hours or output units, of those bad old days. Some things one can measure quite accurately – the time taken, for example, in filling and lighting a pipe. Let us see. (I will just slip down to the cabin and get the things.)

Filling the pipe, I find, done leisurely and meditatively, takes forty-five seconds at least. But the tobacco-pouch was then to hand: allow fifteen seconds for routing about under tables and chairs and papers (it is generally more) and it works out at a minute, or about three or four full minutes every morning. Then there was finding the matches and lighting the four or five abortive matches – say ten seconds each or a minute altogether. Two minutes gone, you see, before we reached the actual business of lighting the pipe at all. First there is the little walk round the corner, then comes the lighting of the pipe. Now how long did that take? Let us see.

A-a-a-h!...

About a minute.

And how long did it take to smoke a whole pipe through?

Let us see...

XV

'PR': OR, STANDING FOR OXFORD

(Educational – for Adults only: and few of them will understand it)

And, by the way, many thanks to the Electors. This is probably a breach with precedent; it may, for all we know, be a Corrupt Practice. But we will risk it. So many thanks to the Electors, without whose assistance, after all, the Candidate would never become a MEMBER.

Thanks, too, to all the – as it were – stage-hands. These, it seems to us, seldom receive due recognition at a General Upheaval. Votes of thanks to Returning Officers are made, inaudibly, to yelling crowds from the balconies of Town Halls, but I never heard of a vote of thanks to all the willing citizens who sit in draughty schoolrooms and check the voting-lists, who cart the ballot-boxes about and count the electorate by fifties in caves.

Especial thanks are earned by those who mind the machinery of a constituency where everything is done by post and according to the rites of Proportional Representation. For they have the labour (*a*) of sending out many thousands of voting-papers to the wrong addresses; (*b*) of opening the envelopes of the quite numerous electors who, by some miraculous chance, receive their voting-papers and record their votes; (*c*) of sorting the papers not simply into Blacks and Whites but into sub-divisions of preference, such as 'Black (1) White (2)' – 'Green (1) Black (2)'; and (*d*), after all this, of having to do some really disgusting arithmetic. All this being remembered, the fact that our Result was declared two hours after the closing of the poll may justly be the cause of pride among the workers, and now receives our public acknowledgment. Also, by the way, it says something for the system of postal voting.

The Counting – what an ordeal! We have suffered the agonies of numerous 'first-nights', but this beat all. At a 'first-night' the author can always lurk at the back of the dress-circle, and, if the show looks like a 'flop', withdraw for consolation into the bar. But, by an unaccountable oversight, there is no bar at the Old Clarendon Buildings, Oxford.

The long table is cleared for action. The Vice-Chancellor of the University, courteous and lucid, explains the course and meaning of the mysteries which are to be performed. About him sit the Registrar and his assistants, and the representatives of the four Candidates. All are gowned except the infamous Haddock, who never took his degree and has not even a hat.

Of the Candidates, whom we will call Blue, White, Red, and Haddock, only Red and Haddock are present. From secret cupboards they take the bundles of papers and dump them on the table. They begin alarmingly with four heaps, castles, mountains of Blue-Whites, that is, of papers on which the less intelligent Bachelors of Arts types have marked | BLUE | 1 | first preference) and | WHITE | 2 |. It seems that all the graduates in the world have voted in this extraordinary way. We murmur to our Agent, 'What a hope!' He whispers, 'Never mind. I think you may save your deposit. But now they are taking out our little 1's. There is one goodly pile, but against the great masses of 'Blue-Whites' it looks anaemic. White's personal pile, though, is even less impressive. By fifties, the acolytes count the Blue-Whites –

'five hundred, five-fifty...one thousand, one thousand and fifty...three thousand...four thousand seven hundred and fifty...' On he goes, relentless. '...fivethousand...six thousand... seven thousand...' Our presence is ridiculous. We must have lost our deposit, our dear little, or rather our large £150. We heard the other day that one of the dons had started a 'book' about our losing our deposit. Well, well, good luck to him!

For though, no doubt, innumerable gallant Bachelors and Masters of Arts have given us their *second* preference that will not save our deposit. Indeed, by the bizarre provisions of the Representation of the People Act, if all the 22,000 electors did that it would not save our deposit. For to do that one must receive not (as in the ordinary Election) one-eighth of the votes polled, or even one-eighth of the votes reckoned in the final count, but one-eighth of the *first preferences.*

This must be the most absurd provision in any Franchise Act. For the whole point of the Single Transferable Vote is that, though you have only one vote, you have two or three choices, and your second (or third) preference may in the end be the effective expression of your vote; in other words, in the final reckoning your '2' or '3' may become a '1'; and thousands of the votes recorded in the 'result' began as humble '2's' and '3's'. It is ridiculous, therefore, to assess the acceptability of a Candidate by the number of '1's' he received.

If we had known that this was the law ten thousand wild horses tethered in a line would not have been able to urge us towards the Returning Officer on nomination day. But the thing is done; and here we are. One consolation is that our £150 will be forfeited to the University and not, as usual, to the Crown. And that naughty betting don will be happy.

But now they have counted the '1's'.

Blue	7,365
Haddock	3,390
Red	2,683
White	1,803

Good gracious! we are second. And the total of the votes cast is 15,241; and eight times 3 is 24, so that the little old deposit is *safe*! But, goodness, what about poor White? How much is eight 8's?… 57. No, no, that can't be right. It isn't. We calculate that White should have 1,905 first preferences. But he has only 1,803. So *he* will lose his deposit. Which seems unfair and ridiculous; and when he is in Parliament he must do something about it. For elected, surely, he will be.[1] Look at those mountains of second preferences – those Blue-White mountains.

They are now attempting some truly revolting arithmetic; and everyone in the room is doing sums – except the infamous Haddock, who is incapable of them.

We are not even sure that we can explain what they are trying to do.

The votes cast number 15,241. There are two seats to be filled; and they will go to the first two Candidates who score one-third *plus* 1 of the total votes – that is, 5,081; for it is obvious that *three* Candidates cannot do this. This figure is called the 'quota'.

Now, Blue has his quota already, and he is declared elected. But he has a surplus of – what is it? Well, do it yourself:

Blue	7,365
Quota	5,081
	2,284

I make it 2,284. And, according to the principles of 'PR', it is unfair that those 2,284 votes should not be effective, and so

1. We had been told, erroneously, that it was possible, under this sytem, for a candidate to lose his deposit and yet be elected.

large a body of opinion be represented solely by the election of Blue.

So they take the *second* preferences indicated on Blue's papers and distribute a *fraction* of them among White, Red, and Haddock. Not *all* of them, mark you, because, if that was done, some of the chaps would be getting two votes. Each chap has only one *vote*, but it is transferable. So they calculate first what number of votes ought to be transferred to White, having regard to

(*a*) the number of papers on which he was second choice and

(*b*) the size of Blue's surplus. (Is that clear?) And how they do that we have no more notion than the Man-in-the-Moon.

Indeed, at this point, we tell you frankly, we had ceased to take any serious interest in the proceedings. For, whatever the answer to the sum might be, it must, we thought (with an eye on those mountains), be a figure sufficient to give White his quota and take him in. We had saved our honour and our deposit; and meanwhile it was pleasant to sit and watch the dons doing sums.

A soothing silence filled the room. From time to time someone would say, 'I make it 1,416'. Another would murmur, '1,417'. And from another corner came, '1,418. But what's your fraction?' It was all like a pleasant family party busy at a word-game or puzzle. We felt a little like the guest who has come in late and is not in the game; and from time to time we whispered, we confess, to our Agent, 'What *exactly* is going on?' Indeed, we remember the following passage of dialogue:

The Independent National Candidate (*whispering*). What do you make it?

The INC's Agent (*ditto*). Two thousand and three.

The INC. Is that right?

The Agent. Probably not.

The Registrar (*with justifiable severity*). S-sh! How can we *multiply* if people *whisper*?

(*Collapse of Independent National Candidate – and quite right too.*)

Hours seemed to pass. Everybody in the room was still doing horrible sums – distributing some of the 2's on the voting-papers which were marked 'Blue 1' between White and Red and Haddock – distributing them, that is, in proportion to Blue's surplus, that is, his total votes, 7,365, *less* the quota (5,081), which comes to 2,284. Is that clear? No.

Well, supposing that White was marked '2' on twenty of Blue's 1-papers, the Sum, we think, would be: As 20 is to 2,284, x is to 20 – x being the votes to be transferred to White. Or it may be something quite different. We cannot tell.

But if it were possible to build a play or film round Proportional Representation (which we doubt), *this*, we know, would be the 'dramatic' point, the 'high-spot'. For if, after this calculation, some Candidate reaches his quota, he is elected, and there is no more to be done. But if *not*, then some Candidate is bottom and the second and third choices on *his* papers are distributed. And, between ourselves, we had observed that there was a very goodly heap of papers marked

RED	1		HADDOCK	2

We did not, however, expect the business to go on so far that we should enjoy the benefit of those inspired papers. White's transfer-fee was fixed at last at 717, which took him up to 3,520 (Haddock being 3,390).

But then, after another period of anxious arithmetic, we received, with sharp surprise, a dividend of 474, taking us up to 3,864.

Red made a nice little break of 93 and became 2,776.

We began to take a serious interest in the match.

The score-board (second innings) now stood as follows:

Blue	7,365	elected
Haddock	3,864	
White	3,520	
Red	2,776	
	17,525	

The third innings began.

Poor Red is now at the bottom; and the game is to bag all the 2's and 3's on his papers and distribute them between Haddock and White.

And this time they distribute not a proportion but the *whole lot*. This, we suppose, is because, Red being knocked out, none of the votes on his paper has counted at all yet, and every vote must count somewhere.

At this point the page on which we were making notes began to look like a Lower Fourth Arithmetic Book or the casual jottings of a lunatic: it is covered with addition and subtraction sums, and vague isolated figures merely wandering about, like the Floating Vote; there are also a good many triangles and unfinished faces.

But those who played the game properly tell us that from the benevolent Red (bless him!) we received a delicious parcel of 1,315 2's and twenty-seven 3's, making us 5,206. White received only 154 2's and twenty-three 3's, and went up to 3,697.

The quota being 5,081, Haddock was declared elected. The final score was:

Blue	7,365
Haddock	5,206
White	3,697
Red	2,776
	19,044

What would have happened next if we had not reached the quota we are quite unable to tell you. But I believe they would have shuffled all the papers and started again.

It will be observed that we began with 15,241 votes (total); that after the second innings there were 17,525; and after the third, 19,044. Yet they still assure us that everybody votes only once. The first jump is easily explained away, we agree; but the second baffles us.

It will be observed also that on the final count White had one-fifth of the total vote recorded, and may justly complain about his deposit.

We believe that on the whole, in proper circumstances, PR is a good thing. But in no form is it offensively easy to understand; and, where any form is used, it ought, we feel, to be explained (by somebody, we mean, who understands it better than we do). The young Bachelor of Arts who has just gained a vote is (unless a political student) unlikely to have any knowledge of these mysteries, and should, we feel, receive with his voting-papers a little 'non-party' instruction.

At all events, some sad misconception prevails. Many intelligent and kindly persons suppose, for example, that they are doing the best thing for their favourite Candidate by 'plumping' for him – that is, by putting '1' against his name and ignoring the other Candidates. The experts assure us that this is quite erroneous, that you cannot damage your favourite by giving his rival a '2' as well, though you may damage their common cause by not doing so.

Then there is the 'Split Vote' delusion, from which we suffered much. Some patriotic undergraduates at Oxford announced that our nomination was 'unpatriotic and disloyal' on the ground that we 'might split the National Vote', and about the town we met many anxious elders who had the same fear.

But (as we were assured before we deposited our name and money) it is mathematically impossible to 'split the vote' under this system. That is one of its great merits. It is sensible to use such expressions only where the voter has a single choice, and therefore, if there are two Candidates having the same cause, he must plump for one or the other. Suppose that Mr Baldwin and Sir Stafford Cripps are opposed to each other in an ordinary degraded non-University constituency, and that Mr Ramsay MacDonald pops up suddenly on nomination day, the National cause is embarrassed and may be lost.

But suppose that, under PR (as practised by the University), Mr Baldwin and Mr MacDonald are opposing Sir Stafford, and that Sir John Simon turns up at the last moment as a National Candidate. Those who passionately desire to see Mr MacDonald in Parliament may then have a grievance against Sir John; but apart from that he cannot be accused of endangering the National cause or 'letting Cripps in'.

The National voter's right course is to mark his paper thus:

BALDWIN	1
MACDONALD	2
SIMON	3
CRIPPS	

There is no room here to explain the whole doings; but roughly, we gather, it works this way:

(1) Baldwin (we assume) is elected first.

(2) Then, if either MacDonald or Simon is elected second, the National Cause has not suffered.

(3) If Cripps goes to the bottom he cannot be elected and the National cause has not suffered.

(4) But if Simon, the interloper (or, for that matter, MacDonald), goes to the bottom, then all the second preferences marked on his paper will be transferred to MacDonald (or Simon),

becoming 1's, and the National cause has not suffered by Simon's intervention.

If, *in spite of this,* Cripps is elected, it means that he would have been elected in any case, without Simon's intervention.

And, if that is not right, we give the whole thing up.

We met on polling-day a most distinguished lawyer and statesman, who, notwithstanding our efforts to dissipate error, was still muttering gloomy forebodings about 'splitting the vote'. We tried to explain that this was impossible; but he replied that he had no use for Proportional Representation anyway, and we parted. And we thought, 'If such is the attitude and such the knowledge of that great man, how can we expect the newly degreed BA, the busy stockbroker or far-off Rector to understand how the darn thing works?'

However, all's well, *etc*... But next time – if there is a next time – we shall enclose with our Address an explanation of the Single Transferable Vote – in verse.

It would be more seemly (and less expensive) if the University did the job – in prose.

XVI

'BUMPING'

That is what the very old Parliamentary hands call it – 'bumping'. A good expression. It means the process of bobbing up and trying to catch the Speaker's eye and bobbing down again when the eye is not caught.

I suppose that to make a true case of bumping the vain attempts upon the Eye should be numerous. Tell a very old hand that the world has just missed a nation-saving oration because you could not catch the eye and he will answer: 'That's nothing. In the old days I remember bumping twenty or thirty times and then not "getting in".'

One statesman tells a sad tale of his youth, how he prepared a speech for some special occasion months ahead, amassed with industry all the statistics and relevant quotations, mastered his theme and laboriously rehearsed his address, how the great day came at last, how he bumped from 4.0 p.m. till 11.0 p.m., and then went home unheard.

Anyone who has done only a modest course of bumping will admire such tenacity, and all must wonder at so great an itch for self-expression. For bumping is a wearisome exercise; and ought to be counted among the records of Parliamentary achievement. Ghoulish persons, at the end of a Session, count how many times this or that legislator has voted and spoken, and these figures, I believe, are sometimes quoted at elections as evidence of industry, or vile neglect of duty. The picture can never be complete unless it includes the statistics of bumping.

The undelivered speeches should be recorded, as the stillborn babies are. In the American Congress, I have been told, this is done. A man may hand in a written speech, to be printed and distributed to his delighted constituents, without even opening his mouth. Excellent system! For though few men are satisfied with the speech they have just made, remorse for what has been said is never so keen as regret for what could not be said. If only all the undelivered speeches had been released, what a different place the world would be!

Those, then, who with some inconsistence complain that Parliament is 'only a talking-shop', and that some Members do not talk; and those who write so genially to the papers, thus:

> 'What are all these MPs for? Most of them do nothing. And they all get £400 a year'

should try, at least, to imagine the agonies of bumping, and, if their Member has no more than a good bumping record, be as kind to the poor fellow as they can.

The debate begins. He is fresh and alert – though probably fearful, for he is in the most frightening corner of the world. He is armed and burdened with documents, with the Order Paper, and the White Paper, and the Report of the Departmental Committee, and the Bill in question, and little clusters of figures, and two cuttings from *The Times*, and a passage copied from an old statute, and *Hansard* for the day before yesterday, and some nasty quotations from old speeches of the Minister, or somebody's Election Manifesto. And, by the way, let the ungrateful constituents remember this – that he has not reached even this, the pre-bumping stage, without much anxiety and noble toil. When the constituent reads:

> 'Mr Blissbone (*East Buggins – Con.*) continued the debate…'

it looks easy. But Mr Blissbone may have been labouring for days to produce that small result, only his preparatory exercises, unlike those of the Boat-Race boys and Big Fighters, are not made public.

But let us return to bumping. We left Mr Blissbone fresh and alert. Since then the Minister has finished moving the Second Reading of the Tannin Traffic (Regulation) Bill, and Mr Smith, an ex-Minister on the other side, has replied. At that point, if only Mr Blissbone could have intervened, the course of history might have been changed. For Mr Smith closed with a provocative passage to which Mr Blissbone had a spontaneous and devastating reply. But, alas! another large Liberal gun, Mr Jones, took the floor. To him also Mr Blissbone has a great many wise and unanswerable things to say; and one particularly witty 'sally'. So when the Liberal sinks back into his seat, Mr Blissbone leaps to his feet and fixes his compelling gaze upon the Deputy-Speaker (for the Speaker is now having his tea-interval). So do about twelve other legislators. There is a ghastly pause and hush while the Eye passes from figure to figure. For an exciting second Mr Blissbone thinks that the Eye has chosen him, but the Eye has found a Privy Councillor, and such great men have precedence. The Privy Councillor puts forward Mr Blissbone's own main argument but (in Mr Blissbone's opinion) imperfectly, so that Mr Williams, next on the Opposition side, is able to tear it to pieces. However, Mr Blissbone will now be able to decimate Mr Williams, and up (with ten others) he hopefully bumps. But Mr Williams has made an unprovoked attack upon Mr Fish, who had had no intention of speaking at all, but is now admitted, indignant, into the fray. And after him those Liberals start chipping in again.

So pass the sad hours. The Speaker has returned: but nearly everybody else has gone out. A small but determined – and, yes, an increasing – body of bumpers remains; more wish to speak, though fewer wish to listen.

Meanwhile, neither Mr Blissbone nor his oration are quite what they were. The speech, that majestic structure of logic and human feeling, designed and spaced and decorated with such care, is already a thing of the past; for the main parts of it have been harshly demolished and set up again so often that everyone is sick of them. It can be but a snappy little speech now at the best. Even those telling retorts to Mr Williams and the Liberal are now out of date and useless, grand though they would have been at the right and magical moment.

The Speaker has gone out for his dinner-interval. Mr Blissbone bumps on. He would like to go out too. His mouth is parched; he has had no tea. He does not want tea now. But if he slips out he may miss his opportunity – and surely when this incredibly erroneous fellow on the other side has ceased, he, Mr Blissbone, will get his chance. The sad thing is that he no longer cares so much as he did in what particular form the Tannin Traffic (Regulation) Bill passes on to the Statute Book. The flame of his conviction has not dwindled, but it no longer seems to matter much, and his head is beginning to ache. But Mrs Blissbone is waiting faithfully in the Gallery and his constituents will expect something. Outside in the Smoking-Rooms and Dining-Rooms and Libraries his happy fellows chatter and dine, conspire, or study Blue Books, indifferent to his sufferings. The indicators announce to them that Mr Wallop is now addressing the House: but no machine informs them that Mr Blissbone is still bumping.

So far he has accepted stoically the cruelty of Fate. But soon, maybe, he begins to scent injustice. That fellow who has just been called has not, surely, been bumping half so long and has things much less important to say. Perhaps the Whips are leagued against Mr Blissbone. Perhaps the Cabinet are determined that he shall not be heard. There – another bump; and another of those interlopers is up. It seems to Mr Blissbone that all this has happened to him before; and if ever he was a member of a University Union or a school debating society it has. But sufferings which are good for a mere boy are far from fitting, he reflects, for a ripened legislator.

But let us leave poor Mr Blissbone, still bumping. In the end, no doubt, he will catch the Eye, but it will not now, we fear, be a very good speech. And then, it is just possible that, however benevolent the intentions of Mr Speaker may be, Mr Blissbone may never 'get in' at all. For time is passing; it is nine now, and presently, refreshed with dinner, the big guns will begin to boom again. Then Mr Blissbone will have to put away those notes and quotations, retrieve the disappointed Mrs Blissbone and deliver the masterpiece to her. And tomorrow, far away in East Buggins, the ungrateful constituents will say that they wonder their Mr Blissbone didn't have something to say about that there Tannin Bill. Or perhaps they will not even notice. What a world!

XVII

ODD SPOTS

It is proposed, we hear, 'on an early day' to put down the following Question:

'To ask the Chancellor of the Exchequer whether he has observed the use of unnecessary full-stops in titles and headings on the Order Paper, of which examples are

AT THE COMMENCEMENT OF
PUBLIC BUSINESS.

NOTICE OF MOTION.

And whether, for the sake of economy and good printing, he will request His Majesty's Stationery Office to give attention to the diminution of redundancies.'

There can be no ill-feeling about this, for His Majesty's Printer and Mr Punch's Printer follow the same practice. But the latter is relenting. At the top of a *Punch* page you will read –

PUNCH *or the London Charivari*
July 29 1936

It used to be –

PUNCH, OR THE LONDON CHARIVARI.

April 24, 1869.

But you will still read –

CHARIVARIA.

The *Observer's* printer is on the same side:

ITALY'S SWEEP.

Transformation of the War.

An Astonishing Campaign.

End of the Ethiopian Empire.

Sanctions and Ruin.

(BY J L Garvin.)

I do not know of any other paper which has the same habit. *The Times* headings and titles are austerely stopless –

THE TIMES MONDAY APRIL 20 1936

even where the title of a leading article is a complete sentence –

THE COUNCIL MEETS

and even *Punch* and the *Observer* permit PRICE SIXPENCE and TWOPENCE to stand alone: but *Punch* is

PRINTED ON WEDNESDAY.

and the *Observer* is enjoying its

145TH YEAR.

What these two great organs do is not my business. But the King's Printer is spending my money; and every day in his voluminous and excellent labours he must be spending much of it on redundant full-stops. I can count nineteen which appear to me at least to be redundant on a single page of the Order Paper before me; and in the first Session of Parliament there were three thousand pages.

I have too great an admiration for the King's Printer to suppose that he does anything without a plan and purpose: and I should like to ask him, with respect, what is the plan and purpose behind all this full-stoppery. Full-stops and colons and commas are not ornaments but instruments. (At least, I never knew any one who obtained aesthetic pleasure from the contemplation of a full-stop or semi-colon; and not even the most modern poet has offered to the public a lyric consisting of nothing but commas, though that may come.) They are intended, surely, to assist the understanding of written words by indicating what words should be connected or divided; and where a word cannot possibly be connected with any other word, as

TWOPENCE

or

NOTICE OF MOTION

there is surely no need for a punctuation-mark.

The full-stops therefore in

ORDERS OF THE DAY.

and

MIDWIVES BILL; – SECOND READING.

are mere superfluous adornment (and I am not hotly in favour of the semi-colon). But if we are to have superfluous ornaments on the great Order Paper of the House of Commons cannot we do better than the rather drab and unexciting full-stop? Why not

AT THE COMMENCEMENT OF
PUBLIC BUSINESS!!!

Notice of Motion?.,

ORDERS OF THE DAY a/c

MIDWIVES BILL;:@ – A SECOND READING£

This might at least stimulate interest in a dull programme of business.

And His Majesty's Printer is strangely inconsistent. When he is printing the Order Paper he is all spotty, like the *Observer* –

21ST APRIL, 1936.

But when he is printing *Hansard* he is, at the top of the page, as austere as *The Times* –

8 APRIL 1936

– though on the cover he slips back to

WEDNESDAY, 8TH APRIL, 1936.

The volume is numbered thus –

VOL. 310, NO. 67.

But the pages of the Order Paper are simply numbered thus –

1471

Why not –

1471.

Why not –

OFFICIAL REPORT.
PARLIAMENTARY DEBATES.
HOUSE OF COMMONS.

What does it all mean?

And you, reader, do you put a full-stop at the end of your signature? You will find that you do if you write a letter to most of the daily papers, though in the same papers there is no full-stop after the names of the contributors – a queer distinction. I find that about a third of my correspondents do this thing. I wonder why. I often do it myself, but that is because I have a special signature to show the bank that my cheques are genuine, and a full-stop is part of this cunning device. But have you the same excuse? Look into your heart, reader. And look about the world. You will find that once you have given your mind to this affair the world is much more exciting; for though, as so often happens, 'there is nothing in the paper', the hunt for odd spots will still furnish interest. And do not say that this is an unimportant matter. A spot on the Order Paper of the House of Commons is, as it were, a spot on the sun.

XVIII

TEA

In spite of all the warnings of experience, women, and even men, continue to drink tea. It may therefore not be out of place to explain how tea is grown.

Tea is grown in the high hills of Ceylon, the island of delight. There is a tale of a young planter's bride who carried to Ceylon a parcel of a kind of weed called China Tea and offered it to her lord; but you may take if from me that tea is grown in Ceylon.

The tea industry is full of surprises. Tea is cultivated by Public School men who dislike tea intensely; and it cannot be grown by anyone who has not been educated at a Public School. The tea-country presents an extraordinary spectacle – thousands of square miles of steep hills covered with the obnoxious little tea-bush and by Public School men, who have to live on gin because of the climate. Every few miles there is a charming bungalow, inhabited by a charming planter, with a charming wife; and at longer intervals there is a charming country club, where in the evenings the planters and their wives endeavour to forget the miseries of exile, the name of tea, the state of the market, and the hardships of their lives. Four thousand feet up, their gardens are ablaze with the garden flowers of England; the constant sight of these familiar blooms cannot fail to remind them painfully of the Homeland far away; and most of the flowers grow obstinately all the year round. I have seen planters weep as they showed me their honeysuckle, carnations, and violets; many of them root up their rose-trees rather than be reminded of home. They look out over deep valleys, gorges, rivers, waterfalls, at the high peaks crowned with virgin jungle; but the grand prospect is ruined for them by the loathsome seas of tea which surround them. So in the afternoon they repair to the club, and try to forget tea with rugger or cricket-matches, tennis or bridge, and even gin. And they drive home rather late at night so that in the darkness they may not see the tea.

But in the morning the tea has to be faced. The planter emerges from his bungalow and surveys with disgust about seven mountains covered with tea. And he says, 'Why the — did I plant so much tea? Why not, for example, gin?' He then looks at his morning paper and, observing (a) the price of tea and (b) the price of gin, he repeats his query with increased emphasis. And indeed there is no answer to it, except that Ceylon has no luck, and, if Ceylon planted gin, gin at once would go the downward way of rubber.

Tea is planted by sprinkling tea-leaves in straight lines on a hillside. It will be seen therefore that before anything can be done someone has to have a pot of tea. This is what the planter's wife is for. But the thing is not quite so simple as that. The fact is – and no one yet has been able to explain it – that tea will *not grow except for a Public School man*. Experiments have been made in what is called Board School planting, but the bush is always anaemic and frail. The moment, however, that an old Cheltonian or Wykehamist puts on his tie and drives round the estate the bushes shoot up vigorously and bear quantities of fresh green tea-leaves. There it is, one of the inexplicable devices of Nature, and you can't get away from it. Nor is it any use for a Board School boy or one Educated at Home to wear an Old Etonian tie. The thing has been tried, but Nature is not deceived, and the bush perishes of a malignant blight.

One or two things have to be done before the tea can be exported; though, given the Public School man, the process is delightfully simple. The bushes must be pruned every year or two and the leaves are plucked constantly. The actual pruning and plucking are done by native labour (not by the natives of Ceylon, who have never understood the dignity of labour, but by Tamil coolies from Southern India). But the labour, to be effective, has, of course, to be watched by an Old Carthusian or Marlburian. Given one Old Carthusian to ten thousand acres, or two Old Marlburians to six hundred coolies, the system has been proved to be highly satisfactory.

When the leaf has been plucked by Tamil maidens it is carried to the factory by oxen and coolies. There the leaf is placed on a hot tray and *withered*. The *withering* is a fairly simple process and can be watched by an Old Harrovian. After withering, the leaf is placed in a large mangle and *rolled*. *Rolling* is a highly scientific process and must be supervised in the proportions of one Old Wykehamist to two Old Westminsters (or four Old Salopians). What with all this withering and rolling the process of

FERMENTATION

now begins.

I am sorry to have to use that ominous word in connexion with this well-advertised 'Temperance' drink. But it is the scientific and the accurate word: and you may as well face the fact that *tea is a fermented liquor*, like all the others. It is to this quality in tea that we may attribute all that deplorable back-biting, tittle-tattle, and fish-faced malice which are associated with tea-parties. Having been thoroughly fermented the leaf is placed in an oven and baked. Everybody puts on the old tie for this and a telegram is sent to the Headmasters' Association.

The leaf, when placed in the oven, resembles chopped seaweed and smells like a bad orange; and there is no doubt that the first man who made tea was under the impression that he was making a new kind of manure. At this stage certainly he cannot have imagined that it might be fit for human consumption. When it was taken out of the oven, however, the planter discovered that he had been making *tea* all the time. Even now, I believe, there are days when the planter wonders gravely whether there can really be women who will pour water on such a mess and drink it. Probably, if it was now rerolled or put in a freezer or trampled by mules, it would ferment again and turn into something quite different – gum or leaf-mould, a new explosive or a dangerous alcoholic drink. It may be that a fortune awaits the planter who will take the treatment of the tea-leaf a stage or two farther.

But by now it is time to go to the Darrawella Club, and the present state of the tea is such an improvement on the former that most planters decide not to risk any more. It is therefore disinfected, graded, and packed. The long bits of manure are put on one side and called Broken Orange Pekoe (on account of the smell already referred to). The short bits are called Orange Pekoe, and both are sent to England in wooden boxes, there to interrupt the labours of the kitchen and inspire the envy, hatred, and all uncharitableness of the drawing-room. After that the planter goes to the club for a healthy gin. And I wish I were there to drink his noble health.

Tea, by the way, is 'not recommended' by the celebrated Dr W H Hay.

II

What is tea, the tax on which is causing so much oratory and indignation? The tea-tree, I learn for the first time today, is 'closely related to the well-known ornamental shrub the Camellia', and its Latin name is *Camellia Thea, Linn*. This attempt of the lowly tea to climb into high society is touching, and it is surprising that tea's publicity-men have not made more use of its aristocratic connexion. 'Camellia Wine' might bring in many who scorn the simple tea.

But many things are surprising about tea. The hold it has upon the Island Race, for example. Look in your *Encyclopaedia Britannica* at the figures of 'Importation and Consumption'.

'Great Britain and Northern Ireland,' it is there asserted, '*consume more tea than all the other countries combined.*' In 1927 we imported for home consumption

416,152,552 lbs.

The United States, generally supposed to be fair tea-tipplers, were second on the roll, but imported only

88,518,696 lbs.

And the total figure for all countries was

792,348,500 lbs.

So that GB and NI swilled more than half the world's supply.

And this habit follows the flag. Australia and Canada, with their tiny populations, were third and fourth in the list.

The figures for 'Tea consumption per head' are rather thrilling too:

	lbs.
Great Britain and Northern Ireland	9.4
New Zealand	9
Australia	8.3
Irish Free State	7.6
Canada	4
Holland	3.2
South Africa	1.7
United States	.84
European Russia	.27
Germany	.18
France	.07

Staggering figures! Is it not strange that the Island Race, scorning the horrid habits of foreign lands, should make such surrender to a heathen product and extract its principal beverage from a shrub which cannot even be grown within its own borders?

The tax, now raised to 4d. (Imperial) and 6d. (foreign) has been even higher. In the bad days of William and Mary it was five shillings a pound. In 1852 it was 2s. 2½d. In 1900 it was 6d., in 1904 8d. and in 1914 (how did we endure it?) a shilling.

One important mathematical problem which arises in the present discussion is: *How many cups of tea go to a pound?*

Experiments I have made gave me the answer: 'About 200.' But I allowed one for the pot, and my spoonfuls may have been too generous. For another encyclopaedia I possess, published many years ago, says: 'Ts. costing up to 1/8d. per lb., should make about 220 cups to the lb., while more expensive Ts. make about 280 cups. A gargle of T. is strongly recommended for sore throat.'

It is a sum to which every citizen should try to find an answer. Miss Ellen Wilkinson, MP, in an eloquent assault upon the increased gargle-tax, spoke of a factory canteen which proposed now to raise the price of a cup of tea from a penny to a penny-farthing, because a farthing is the smallest amount that can be put on to the cost. 'That,' as she rightly said, 'represents an increase of 25 per cent.' But 2d. is very far from 25 per cent of two shillings; and the answer is surely that the canteen are profiteering, though it may be that they are being compelled to profiteer by our queer coinage. For, supposing that there are 200 cups to a lb., 200 farthings make 4/2d. (do they not?); so that the canteen is making a profit of 4s. on a tax of 2d.! The proper person to abuse, therefore, is not the Chancellor but the canteen. It will then be said, 'But how are they to get the tax back?' Well, it remains to be proved that they are not getting too much for their cup of T. already. For they are charging 200 pennies, or 16/8d., for serving a pound of tea which cost, perhaps, 2s.; and 200 cubes of sugar can be bought for 6d. I do not know about 200 dollops of milk, or the 'overheads', but I suspect that there should be a margin there.

Nevertheless I sympathize with the poor tea-drinkers, provided that they do not paint too brightly either their own virtues or the merits of their delightful beverage. I agree that *all* 'the little comforts of the poor' (Mr Attlee's moving description of T.) are taxed too highly. But T. will still be the most-favoured comfort. A pound of tea, they say, lasts our dear friend the Average Man nearly six weeks, since he consumes only nine pounds a year; and on a pound of Empire tea at, say, 2s., he will now pay a tax of 16 per cent. But if he buys a sixpenny packet of ten cigarettes he pays a tax of 50–60 per cent; and if he buys a glass of the best bitter he pays a tax of 45 per cent; and these comforts will not last so long. He cannot, if he is poor, buy whisky at all (though beer may be bad for his rheumatics) since the tax on that is 200 per cent!

And the staggering fact remains that the Naughty Comforts (Tobacco, Beer, Wine, etc.) are to contribute to the revenue this year the sum of £185,000,000 (enough to pay for all the Defence Forces and, I think, Education as well) and the Good Comforts (Tea, Coffee, Cocoa, Sugar, etc.) only £20,000,000.

The Average Teetotaller and Non-Smoker, therefore, pays at least *nine times* less in indirect taxation than the Average Low Fellow like you and me. But he has the same voting power and the same claims on the Defence Forces. So vast a discrepancy could only be justified in a democratic State by some outstanding virtue in the favoured citizen. But where is this? Those who avoid tobacco and beer do not do so as a rule because they are good, but because they do not like tobacco and beer. They choose their own diet and 'comforts', as others do; and, though they may be congratulated on choosing those least heavily taxed, they have no obvious claim to be regarded as specially good citizens. Indeed, if it could be shown that they shunned tobacco and beer in order to avoid taxation, we all know what should be said against them. Moreover, in my experience it is the ferocious T.-drinker who is most eager to take on all the dictators in Europe and increase those noble international commitments for which we are now beginning to pay.

And where is the particular virtue in T. (apart from its undoubted fitness for use as a gargle)? It is a mild stimulant, like coffee; but my medical dictionary asserts that coffee is more wholesome. It is a comforting habit, like the cigarette or pipe, and like those it may be used to excess. It is a convenient way of making milk and hot water palatable. It is delightful. If there were no more T. we should all suffer inconvenience and regret; and I should be specially sorry for that excellent breed, the planters. But the health of nobody, I think, would suffer. It cannot, strictly, therefore, be described as a 'food' or even a 'necessity'. Indeed, there is a good deal of evidence that, as used today in many quarters, it comes near to being a vice and a clog on the wheels of the nation's work.

The world may well connect this huge national habit with that increase of softness which most of the world perceives or suspects in our nation today. But everybody likes T.; and so do I. And if the T.-fans would leave it at that I should sympathize more warmly still. But they will put on this insufferable air of virtue. And so, with some reluctance, I record the hard truth about T.

T., by the way, is *not* recommended by the celebrated Dr W H Hay.

XIX

HAMLET, PC

(From *Streamline*)
(A Modern Tragedy. With apologies to
WS and LH-B.)

SCENE: *A street.* L. *and* R. *are two Belisha Beacons. The stage represents a Belisha pedestrians' crossing, controlled by* POLICE-CONSTABLE HAMLET, who is discovered L.

A FRIEND (*crossing R. to L.*).
Hail, noble Hamlet. I am for 'The Grapes'.
HAMLET. Would I were so! Good-day!
FRIEND. Good-day, good Hamlet.

[*Exit*]

HAMLET (*looking at first Beacon, soliloquizes*).
O most unnatural of the orbs of night,
Art thou the droppings of the harvest moon?
Sometimes I take thee for a Minister:
Sometimes I fear these moons have made me mad:
And then methinks they have an aim and purpose
Not yet revealéd –

[*Enter* MRS HAMLET *R., distracted, and holding a newspaper and a small piece of paper in her hand.*]

MRS H. Hamlet!
HAMLET. How now, wife?

What, not enough? Did not I kiss thee twice,
And swoon among the perfume of thy lips?
What, will you bring our bed upon the street
To affront the godly and stop up the traffic?
Pass over, Kate.
MRS H. O husband, speak not so:
For my intelligence must not delay.
Hamlet, be resolute, for we have need –
(*trembling*)
I have a ticket in the Irish sweepstake!
HAMLET (*shocked*).
Oh! Oh! most damnable! Most óbscene wrong!
Out, usuress! Foul avarice, avaunt!
And, by the way, it is against the law.
MRS H.
I know my fault, and would have hid the fact,
But Hamlet – Hamlet – we have drawn a *horse!*
HAMLET.
A horse! A horse! O mounting infamy!
This is to say 'I have a ticket for Hell
But be of courage, for it is First Class!'
I could endure it if you named a dog
Or some august adventure in the Stocks:
But horse – O that corrupting quadruped,
Whose vile contagion doth infect the land,
Breathing the stench of stables o'er the town
And in one pit embroiling lord and lackey…
What is its name?
MRS H. She is called Chorus Girl,
By Merry Marquis out of Governess:
And they do say the filly has a chance:
The going will be soft –
HAMLET. O worse and worse!
MRS H.

Hamlet, the prize is thirty thousand pounds
And I could do with it –
HAMLET (*frenzied*). Hence, plausible jade!
Give me the ticket. Let me tear it up.
Would I could tear the poison from thy mind,
And call down thunderbolts upon my conscience
To blast it clean of guilt – (*is going to tear it up*)
MRS H. Stay, Hamlet, stay!
For here comes one that will relieve thee on't.
[*Enter a stout horsy-looking* MAN.]
MR POTBELLY. This is the fellow?
(MRS H. *nods secretly*)
Sir, without preamble,
I come the herald of a syndicate,
Which, for one half of this unlawful paper,
Will straight deliver thee one thousand pounds.
Here is my cheque.
HAMLET (*taking cheque*). O thou most damned villain!
What, split in twain the opportunity
And leave intact the stain upon me soul?
[Seeing a pedestrian approach, he stands centre of stage, facing audience, and holding up hands to guard the crossing, the ticket in one hand and the cheque in the other.]
One for fifteen! Thou knave!
[*Enter* GIRL.]
GIRL. Good officer,
What is the way to Kew?
HAMLET (*wildly*).
The way to Kew?
March north, march east, march west, then north again.
There are a thousand gardens under Heaven,
Nor doth it signify i' the account of Death
In which dull hemisphere you rest tonight.
All homes, all harbours, human destinations,

Are broken twigs upon the tree of Time,
And men but sparrows –
[*The* GIRL, *supposing she has to do with a lunatic, scuttles off across the road and exit.*]
(*To* POTBELLY) Did you say a thousand?
POTBELLY. If I say two – ?
HAMLET. Then the offence is doubled.
MRS H. (*intervenes*).
Hamlet, if some distemper in the mind
Disqualify thee to retain the half,
Wilt thou not name a figure for the whole?
POTBELLY. Sir, for the whole – five thousand pounds –
HAMLET (*dignified*). Go to!
Such money stinks.
POTBELLY. But Time's a disinfectant:
What stinks today tomorrow hath perfume.
Come, Sir, be prompt, the race is run this hour.
Methinks already the lunátic mob
Heave at the barriers and cry 'She wins!'
HAMLET. Who wins?
POTBELLY. Why, Chorus Girl – for Gordon's up!
MRS H.In that case, sir, we will not sell the creature!
POTBELLY.
Nay, ma'am, be warned: for Chance is mischievous:
Methinks I see a dog run through her legs.
(MR *and* MRS H. *in a dither*)
Better a little than the hope of more –
Better a remnant than the chance of nothing.
MRS H. (*distracted*).
O me! O me! O Hamlet, be resolved!
Our son is seven and his lungs are weak,
The twins are suffering: and –
HAMLET. Peace, Kate! Peace!
[*Now quite mad, he goes up to Second Beacon, clasps the staff and peers into the face of the globe.*]
O my sweet oracle, advise me now!

POTBELLY (*aside*).
Mark how the madness marches! He will sell.
(MRS H. *watches in horror*)
HAMLET (*to the Beacon*).
Thou art my friend, I know thou art my friend:
Thou art the noblest of the Cabinet:
Thou art the Mayor of Little Burbleton.
To beacon or not to beacon: that is the – Nay!
To sell or not to sell –
MRS H. Dear lord, perpend!
Remember Mabel, who is bronchial.
HAMLET (*raving*).
A lottery. By Section 26
It is unlawful for a man to sell
A ticket in a lottery. But what?
A constable is not a man. *Argal* –
He is a Beacon. Ha! Here's laughter! Ho!
(*pleased with himself*)
A man's in his humour, and there's the humour on't!
(*fiercely*) Cry knave!
[*Enter* OLD LADY]
OLD LADY.
Kind constable, I pray you will direct me –
Where is St Pancras?
HAMLET. Madam, who can tell?
[*Exit* OLD LADY. HAMLET *continues, gently, to* MRS H.]
I think, my chuck, I will be scrupulous,
I will be delicate. Shall we not bestow
This tainted pledge on yonder greedy fellow,
Free of all charge, fee, payment or commission –
MRS H. Nay, Hamlet, nay! –
HAMLET. And thus at once be free
Of gold and guilt – of thirty thousand pounds –
MRS H. O husband!
HAMLET. Aye, and thirty thousand shames!

(*holding out ticket and cheque to* POT.)

MRS H. (*intervening*). Sir, heed him not. He is distempered quite. (*to* H.) O think of Antony, whose lungs are weak!

POTBELLY. And quickly think, good sir, for they are off.

HAMLET. Lungs! Lungs! Aye, marry, lungs are lungs, i'faith.

(*withdraws ticket:* POT. *takes cheque – addressing the Beacon again, cunningly*)

What dost thou think, Sir? Is it very sin
To sell my soul for our sweet Antony?

(*swaying, he causes Beacon to shake its head*)

Look how he shakes his orange-pate at me!
Here's argument, here's proof and circumstance.

(*turns to* POT., *his mind made up*)

I'll sacrifice me conscience to me son!
Take thou the ticket, Sir – give me the cheque.

[*A newsboy is heard shouting.*]

MRS H. What tumult's here?

POTBELLY (*clinging to the cheque*). I think the race is run.

[*Enter* NEWSBOY, *still calling 'Eenee Poimeer – Big Race – Winner!'*]

HAMLET. Speak, child, and the event make manifest.

NEWSBOY (*instead of handing over a paper, bursts into blank verse*).

Twice seven horses, Sir, confront the gate,
Rosemary, Counting House, and Who Goes There,
And Love Lies Bleeding and the Manton Colt,
The French horse, Mélanie, Bluebottle, Mustard,
Peer's Frolic, Yellow Jack –

POTBELLY. Enough! Enough!

It doth not signify what horse began
But which concluded –

HAMLET. Speak! Did Chorus Girl

With valiant neighing o'ercome the envious field?

(*takes out note-book*)

NEWSBOY (*looks at Stop Press*).

O gentlemen, three horses' names are here –
First, second, third, respectively the gainers –
But in this brief invéntory of honour
I cannot find the name of Chorus Girl.
She was not placed. I think she did not start.

MRS H. O heavy day!

HAMLET. O doubly dreadful day!
The guilt lies thick on us, but not the gold.

POTBELLY. I am very glad, Sir, that you would not sell.

HAMLET (*plucks Beacon from the ground and brandishes it terribly, like a battle-axe, over* POT.).
Thou damned, dastard, double-dealing drain,
Which doth draw off the filth of all the world
To fill thy soul with wickedness, and feed –
Die, sewer-rat – die, gutter-bug!
(*strikes him with Beacon*)

POTBELLY. O Sir! (*dies*)

MRS H. O Hamlet, you have slain the gentleman.

HAMLET (*takes out truncheon: makes some notes*).
This odd event will have to be reported;
With signal obsequies dispose the slain.
Then let the trumpet sound. Now, Hamlet, die.
(*strikes himself on the head with truncheon and dies:* MRS H. *falls on his body and dies*)
Trumpets *Black-out*

XX

BIG SWIM

On a warm sunny afternoon in September 1934 a clean-shaven man might have been observed swimming methodically towards Westminster. Indeed, he *was* observed, by a small boy on Hungerford Bridge, who spat upon him. I did not for my own sake wish for any wider recognition. When I am swimming the fewer people who recognize me the better I like it. But what began as a 'pleasure'-swim finished up as an athletic record, and it is our duty to posterity and truth to record all such 'records', for otherwise some upstart swimmer may appear in years to come and claim that which is not his. So let the tale be told.

I had dived – or, more accurately, I had passed head-first – into the River Thames from a coal-lighter situated forty yards west of Waterloo Bridge. I was swimming, slowly but gracefully, towards Hungerford, or Charing Cross, Bridge, assisted by the flood-tide. My little 'pram' dinghy floated ahead of me, the plan being that when I was tired I should climb into the dinghy and row back over the tide to the parent ship, which was tied up to the coal-lighter. I thought that I should be tired very soon. I am always tired of swimming very soon, especially in the muddy waters of London river; and if anybody makes me laugh I sink.

However, I swam on, reflecting how odd a thing it was that a rational man, at ease in comfortable clothes, should go to the trouble of removing them in order to travel a short distance at the expense of great exertion in a liquid composed of such miscellaneous elements as the Thames at Waterloo. I wondered how many Channel-swimmers would have swum the Channel if they had had to swim it in Waterloo water, which has no buoyancy at all and, so far from supporting the swimmer, seems all the time to be dragging him down to the extremely muddy floor of the river. Moreover, it tastes very strongly of I know not what.

On the other hand, the swimmer has a delightful view of the heart of London. Turning on the back, I surveyed the remnants of Waterloo Bridge, and, through one of the arches, the noble curve of the bank to Blackfriars and St Paul's Cathedral beyond. I wished once again that they would adopt my proposal for a Waterloo Tunnel – have no bridge at all and throw open that tremendous view. The tunnel-building and the bridge-breaking could proceed simultaneously. Or perhaps not. The engineers, I dare say, would have some fussy objection to the whole scheme. Nevertheless, I thought, it is good, and, turning on to the left side, I swam on feebly past the Shell-Mex building.

Perhaps it was the sight of the great Clock (which someone has wittily called Big Benzine), provoking thoughts of Time, Measurement, and so forth, that first put into my head the idea of making a record. At any rate it suddenly occurred to me that *no literary man had ever swum from Waterloo Bridge to Westminster Bridge.*

Or had one? I swam backwards for a little, reflecting and gazing at the pale blue sky. Lord Byron? No. He was careful and chose salt water for his feats. Mr Bernard Shaw? John Drinkwater? No. Not even 'Beachcomber', swinging his great staff, had done this thing. I was first in the field.

At that moment a shadow swept over me and I perceived that the body was approaching Hungerford Bridge. A small boy perceived this too and spat upon the body. What satisfaction this gesture gave him I cannot tell, but I hope it was great. 'My boy,' I said politely, 'it was not thus that in olden days the youth of Britain greeted a pioneer at grips with the elements. Besides,

I am paying for your education, and your ethical standards disappoint me.'

We then drifted into the protected waters under the bridge. This bridge, as I have said before, has been unfairly maligned. From the mariner's, swimmer's, or fish's point of view those round red columns, with the sun slanting between them and the tide swishing round them, have a certain simple grandeur. There is light and shade under the bridge such as is not found under a common stone arch; and if a train rumbles over the bridge as one swims through the experience is awesome. Indeed, I am surprised that the London Society and the Fine Arts Commission do not arrange a joint swim under Charing Cross Bridge.

However, we swam on into the Westminster Reach, weary but determined. This is a very fine reach to swim along. A fish's-eye view reveals all kinds of beauties unsuspected by you who merely walk upon the Embankment or clank along in trams. Under my right arm I beheld the stately pile of Whitehall Court dominating the skyline, residence, I believe, of Mr Bernard Shaw, a strong swimmer; and I wondered if he slipped out before breakfast on fine mornings for a dip. But just then we met one of the pleasure-boats which ply in summer from Westminster Pier. The crews of some of these vessels have a genial but embarrassing habit of pointing me out to their passengers as their ship passes mine and making complimentary remarks through megaphones. Not long ago, being tied up to the Tower Pier (it was the day we saw the dead porpoise drifting by), I heard these words booming across the water: 'RIGHT AHEAD IS THE TOWER BRIDGE ON YOUR LEFT IS MR A P HADDOCK IN HIS BOAT.' Flattering, but hardly fair to the Tower Bridge. And here and now I beg these good fellows to desist from the practice.

This day, being almost entirely submerged and having wet hair over the eyes, I did hope to preserve a decent anonymity. But the rather literary nose, I suppose, still bravely held above the waves, gave me away, and I heard, far too loud: 'ON YOUR

LEFT YOU WILL DISCERN THE SHELL-MEX BUILDING AND SAVOY HOTEL THE GENTLEMAN SWIMMING IS MR A P HADDOCK THE WRITER.' I waved a feeble hand in deprecation and sank.

Coming up, spluttering, I had a mind to abandon all thought of the record; but the great clock of Westminster beckoned me forward, no more than three hundred yards away, and I splashed on behind my little boat. Alone. No man fed me with Bovril or played tunes on the gramophone to cheer my spirit. Was there ever such a feat?

As I passed the Air Force Memorial a small blue canoe approached me containing two young men. And one of the young men said, 'Are you Mr Haddock?' I sank again.

A literary man engaged in a record swim ought not to be addressed without a formal introduction, and never in so brusque a manner as to cause his submersion. I came to the surface determined to teach the young men a lesson in water-etiquette. But I was short of breath; they were very pleasant young men; they had come down from Oxford in their canoe and merely wished to be directed to Charing Cross, where they proposed to land. So I put them on their way and swam on.

Did I say 'swam?' Now comes the really heroic part of the adventure. The goal was near – but, oh, so far! The body was now an enormous weight, the arms could scarcely thrust themselves from the water, the legs kicked anaemically below; the whole frame seemed subject to some magnetic force relentlessly pulling it towards the bed of the river. Huge dirty waves rose up and slapped the face; the lungs worked like pistons inadequately supplied with oil; the eyes could see but dimly the crowds upon the bridge, the great clock of Westminster far up in some quite different world. But the flood-tide was running at about three knots, and in fact we did reach Westminster Bridge. Crowds leaned over the parapet with mocking or indifferent eyes, but blind to the inner drama of what they saw, perceiving with due surprise and curiosity a man swimming under Westminster Bridge, but wholly unaware that he had started from Waterloo. Now – *now* we should not have complained if some friendly citizen had recognized us and raised a cheer and saluted a record. But history repeated itself and a small boy spat, not knowing, poor little pagan, that he was spitting on a record.

We turned on our back, faint but satisfied, floated through the bridge, and off the Terrace of the House of Commons climbed slowly into our little boat – *the first man of letters to swim from Waterloo to Westminster!*

Then we rowed back and had a good gargle.

XXI

'WITHOUT DUE CARE'

Old Mrs Alice Bird is dead –
    'Crossing the road without due care';
The driver said she lost her head –
    'Crossing the road without due care';
        She disobeyed the simple rule,
        'Be very careful, quick and cool
            When motor-cars are there';
        So she is dead, the silly fool –
    'Crossing the road without due care'.

Old Mrs Bird was much to blame,
    'Crossing the road without due care',
For Mrs Bird was rather lame
    And should have taken SPECIAL care;
        She had, it seems, deficient sight,
        Her intellect perhaps was slight,
            Her nerve required repair,
        So she is dead, and serve her right –
    'Crossing the road without due care'.

Old Mrs Bird came up to Town
    From Chipping-under-Bone,
Where limousines are seldom seen
    And one-way streets unknown;

The notices of every kind
She studied with a frown:
'LOOK LEFT, LOOK RIGHT, BEFORE,BEHIND,
LOOK SIDEWAYS, UP *AND* DOWN!'
And since her eyes were only two
(And both were placed ahead)
She did not quite know what to do,
And so the woman's dead.

She meekly stood upon the kerb,
Wishing that she could fly
And hoping she would not disturb
The motors rushing by;
But after waiting quite a space
She tired (I know not why)
Of standing in the selfsame place
And watching cars go by.

Like swallows homing to their mates,
Like sinners followed by the Fates,
Like elephants with urgent dates
The endless motors flew;
And Mrs Bird at length was heard
To whisper this disgraceful word,
'Although no doubt it seems absurd,
I'm in a hurry too.'

She took a step into the road
And cars for miles around,
As if she were a slug or toad,
Made an offensive sound –
A cross between a siren's hoot
And a rhinoceros' roar,
A sound which said, 'You bug! You brute!

You imbecile! You bore!'
And Mrs Bird withdrew, deterred,
To where she was before.

The day went on, and Mrs B.
Still to the kerb was tied,
While those whom she desired to see
Were on the other side.
But as the sun began to sink
There came a little lull.
A tiny little lull there came,
And Mrs Bird said, 'Now I *think*
That I can cross, but all the same
I wish I were a gull.'

I have remarked that she was lame,
She knew no acrobatics,
She could not sprint for half the Mint,
And what is more, the darned old fool,
She quite neglected when at school
The Higher Mathematics;
And so she could not calculate
By algebra or cards
Bow long it takes a Snitzler '8'
To travel fifty yards
(When doing fifty miles an hour
And hooting fit to frighten,
Containing sixty horses' power,
And on the way to Brighton).
Nor could she tell that such a car,
If it is stopped, will skid
(You know what country-people are),
But that is what it did.
And almost everybody passed
This verdict on the blow –

'Twas not the car that went too fast,
   But she who went too slow.
And I agree – but then, to me,
   There is no god but Speed;
When England's one great asphalt floor,
Where motors, more and more and more,
Move ever faster than before,
And whizz and wheeze and hoot and roar,
Though walking may become a bore
   Life will be good indeed.

Old Mrs Alice Bird is dead –
   'Crossing the road without due care';
The driver said she lost her head –
   'Crossing the road without due care';
      She should have burrowed underground,
         Or crossed the road by crane,
      Or taken one terrific bound,
         Or hired an aeroplane;
      For such as she are sure to fall
         If they proceed on foot;
      'Twere wiser not to cross at all,
         But stay where they are put.

She will not very much be missed,
But it upset the motorist;
And we must add her to the list –
   'Crossing the road without due care'.

XXII

GIVING AWAY

As the day of his daughter's wedding approaches a father gradually rises to a position of comparative importance in the home. The process is very gradual. At first he is taught to do elementary duties in connexion with the affair – to sit at home while the ladies go shopping, answer the telephone and take simple messages about the colour of curtains, the number of choirboys, size of shoes, voltage, linoleum, choice of hymns, dimensions of bridesmaids, and would the young lady prefer coral ear-rings, a bicycle, or fish-knives?

Next he is allowed to sign a few documents and go through easy interviews with relatives and lawyers, provided that he gives no trouble. All this is done in the home, and there is not much danger of the man doing serious damage.

But later it is realized with a sudden shock that eventually he will have to be allowed out in public, and even, owing to an old-fashioned liturgy, play a small part in the ceremony. In other words, *he too will have to have some clothes*. The two old suits have served well enough for seven years, but now his appearance has begun to matter. It is discovered, for example, that the man does not possess a top-hat; and it is even regretted that many years ago the top-hat was taken out and used in charades for the Battle of Trafalgar scene. And he will have to have some new shoes.

Further, he will have to do things; and being, like most fathers, weak in the head, he is almost certain to do the wrong ones. Bridesmaids, being female, may be trusted to carry out their duties with intelligence and aplomb. But the haggard sire is a worry.

No honest father, we think, will wish to quarrel with these assumptions. We would only protest, mildly, that things ought to be made a little easier for the poor fellow. The more backward and obtuse the pupil the greater care should be taken, surely, to see that instruction is definite and plain. There should, in short, be a *Wedding Handbook for Fathers or Those About to Give Daughters Away*. But there is not. All is nebulous and difficult.

If you glance at the Marriage Service you will see at once the sort of thing we mean. A number of searching questions are put to the bride and bridegroom, but in each case they are provided with precise and easy answers. They have only to mutter 'I will' from time to time, and all is well. Moreover they have the parson handy if they should put a foot wrong.

But when they have said their 'I wills' the parson says sternly to the world in general: 'Who giveth this Woman to this Man?'

The Father (if he be 'giving away') is then expected to make some accurate and sensible reply.

But no words are given to him. There is just a blank. Alone of all that varied company of actors the father has not only to perform but to write his own part. For even the parson (unless he chooses to throw in a homily) has not got to make anything up. Only the father, *ex hypothesi* the feeblest intelligence present, has to do this thing. And, mind you, he is standing all alone, conspicuous in an open space, with no one to prompt him.

Well, being involved recently in an affair of this kind, we gave our minds to the matter. We inquired what one did of all the expert females we knew. And none of them knew. At least – and here is the point – nobody knew *for certain*.

Some said that we should answer '*I* do'.

That looks easy; but you try it. Evidently there must be an accent on the 'I', for that is the important word. But if you over-accentuate the 'I' the assertion tends to have an arrogant note which repels one. (You try it, as we did, in the bath and Tube.) On the other hand, the response is sadly inadequate and bare. It suggests, evidently, the retort: 'Who are you?' For the parson, who has taken great pains to find out who the bride and bridegroom are, has, in theory, not the slightest idea who *we* are. So at one stage we proposed to say:

'I, her Father, do,'

or,

'*I* do,' adding in brackets ('her Father').

And then we thought, 'Well, after all, why the Father only? What about Mamma?' It *is* a defect, we think, in the Marriage Service that the Mother, who does all the work and has all the worry, has no official place in the proceedings at all (though she is generally allowed into the vestry at the end, and may kiss the groom's father).

So we told the ladies: 'Apparently we have a free hand. We shall say:

"I, her Father, give this Woman (as you call the bride) to this Man. But in this transaction I *should* like, if I may, to be associated with this Woman's Mother (my Wife), who is, after all, the One who Matters. And I have her authority to say that, reluctantly, because she likes her, she is giving this Woman too. And while I am about it – " '

'Stop! Stop!' they all cried. 'You can't make a *speech!*'

Well, we don't know why not. It may even be that that was the original idea of this queer hiatus in the ritual; it was a gap in which the Parents were intended to utter any thoughts or announcements they had in their minds. Announcements especially; for there are all sorts of things the Mother wants to say and has no chance to say, as, for instance –

'And while I am about it, if anyone cares to pop in at home and see the presents on the way to the reception, do. Drive round by Standish Road because Gale's Gardens is a one-way street…' And so on.

But they wouldn't have that.

We offered to strike a nobler note, to compose and deliver a poem in rhymed couplets, celebrating the glorious institution of Marriage and expressing in a moving fashion the sensations of parents as they give their young away. If ever a father did seize this opportunity to deliver himself at length we don't see how anyone could stop him. He might, for example, give a poetical account of his family tree, which would be strictly relevant to the question put to him:

> Your Reverence, I am the latest Haddock.
> Full twice three hundred years have swung
> through space
> Since Padraic, that first Haddock…

But they wouldn't have that either.

Very well, then. Now, the next thing was the march up the nave. As you know, all the mothers, aunts, sisters, bridesmaids, and other expert females, having worked for weeks to get the bride into a fit state to present herself at the altar, go off to the church first and leave the bride alone in the house, sick with nerves, on the verge of hysterics. Well, when I say 'alone', they leave the poor creature with the only half-wit of the party, the father; and they trust to him to cope with any hysterics that may crop up and bring her safely to the church at a given hour. But everybody knows that that is just the moment when the bride feels like calling the whole thing off. In other words, the experts withdraw their services at the critical moment. A most extraordinary arrangement.

Well, we had inquired about stations, and the experts said that we marched on the bride's *port* hand; and we rehearsed it thus. But at the last moment the bride and another female insisted firmly that our place was on her *starboard* hand. 'Well,' we said, 'you women ought to know,' and we rehearsed it thus.

Arrived at the church, we dutifully placed ourselves on the starboard hand. We were just approaching the nave when a strange but kind lady ran up and hissed, 'The *other* side! The *other* side! I ought to know – I've done this four times.'

Without having time to ponder this odd information, we slipped round and took station on the port hand. The lady, of course, was right, and we passed up the nave in good order, without, as we were expected to do, walking too fast, casting the twin bridesmaids to the ground and dragging them through the dust.

We handed over the Woman to the Man, tore her bouquet from her, and thought that we were nearly through. All we had to do now was to say, 'I do'.

But the verger whispered: '*When your time comes take her right hand and hand it over.*'

We trembled. Not one expert had mentioned this. It had never been rehearsed.

And, surveying the country, we wondered how it was to be done. The Priest, the Woman, and the Man, stood in a little archway with a dense jungle of flowers and vegetation on either side. We were on her left hand, in *échelon*; how were we to get at her right? We decided not to try.

But the verger whispered again: 'Take her *right* hand and pass it over.'

The man seemed to attach importance to the thing. He ought to know what was right; and we do not like to disappoint those who are trying to get things done in the best way; so, when the time came, we said, 'I do', and thrust ourselves between the jungle and the Woman; and we whispered, 'Your *right* hand'.

But the Woman's right hand was already firmly clasped in the Man's. Wondering, no doubt (if she noticed the Father), what the Father was butting in for, she paid not the smallest attention to the Father's last request; and we backed away as gracefully as possible, not quite trampling on the twins.

If the Woman is not lawfully married it is not our fault. But we give this warning to all fathers whom it may concern: 'Make them write down plainly *exactly* what you have to do, before you sign on'.

XXIII

THE PREAMBLE

Closing-time[1] in the following districts is now as follows:

Westminster (including Knightsbridge)	11.00 p.m.
Kensington (including Hammersmith)	10.00 p.m.
Chiswick	10.30 p.m.

And these districts are adjacent, the one to the other, respectively.

So, having been solemnly and loudly shepherded out of the '— Arms' in Kensington at 10.0, the citizen can walk a few yards and continue his conversation for another hour at the '— Arms' in Knightsbridge. Or, by strolling over the Western frontier of Hammersmith at 10.0, he can have another half-hour in Chiswick. Or, again, by crossing Hammersmith Bridge, another half-hour in Barnes.

The like of this, I think, is not to be found in Paris. In either case this hypothetical gentleman will hear two 'Last orders, please!' and probably have two lots of 'final rounds'. The Kensington Licensing Justices may not know it, for they are never at the '— Arms'; but it is the Last Ten Minutes that most often does any mischief that is done. It follows mathematically

1. Or rather, strictly, 'the end of permitted hours': for, technically, there is now no 'closing-time'.

that where there are two sets of Last Ten Minutes twice as much mischief is done.

The Kensington Licensing Justices, therefore, have a heavy load of responsibility: and it is a hard thing indeed that virile and impecunious Hammersmith should be under the regime of the royal and rich but namby-pamby Borough, whose citizens and justices, having fine houses and clubs and hotels in which to spend their leisure hours, do not wish to congregate in pubs.

In the old days, when we were writing plays at the Lyric Theatre, Hammersmith, much damage was done to British Drama by the said Justices; for, since the bar was closed by their order at 10.0, it was important to finish the Second Act by 9.55 at latest in order that some at least of the dejected audience might be able to console themselves and be persuaded to remain in the theatre. If the curtain came down at 10.1 the Interval must be dry; and it is a very hard thing for a dramatist to have to cut his Second Act about in order to fit the edicts of the old ladies and gentlemen of the Kensington Licensing Bench.

Now, I do not think that you will find the like of these things in Paris or any other French city. And that, we are authorized to say, is one answer to the question we have recently heard: What exactly is the point of the Public Refreshment Bill, 1936?

The answer does not satisfy us.

A

BILL

TO

Amend the laws concerning public refreshment.

Whereas it appears that the laws concerning public refreshment are vexatious and unreasonable, and are not well fitted to the good sense of Englishmen and the conditions of the present time:

And whereas the said laws, as at present administered, are a hindrance to improvement in the resorts of the people, a cause of intemperance, a burden upon trade, a danger to the King's revenue, and a discouragement to foreign travellers proposing to visit this realm:

And whereas it is commonly accepted that England is now to be considered as a part of the continent of Europe, and should so conduct herself in all proper and peaceful affairs: and in this affair it is expedient that she should follow the good and civilized customs of France, which, by reason of the said laws, is now not possible:

Be it therefore enacted, by the King's Most Excellent Majesty, by and with the advice and consent of the Lords Spiritual and Temporal, and Commons, in this present Parliament assembled and by the authority of the same, as follows:

ADOPTION OF THE LAWS OF FRANCE

1. The laws of England concerning the provision of public refreshment, including the sale or supply of wine, beer, spirits, and the like, shall be made, *mutatis mutandis*, the same as the laws of France.

HOME
are
SECRETARY'S
this
POWERS

2. The Secretary of State shall ascertain what the laws of France at the date of the passing of Act, and shall, from time to time, make all such orders and regulations as are necessary to give effect to Section One of this Act. Such orders and regulations shall be laid in draft before both Houses of Parliament, and when both Houses by resolution have approved the draft, either without modifications or with modifications and additions to which both Houses agree, they shall have the force of law:

Provided that the Secretary of State shall within six months of the passing of this Act make regulations for the protection of persons employed in the refreshment trades and for the restriction of their hours of labour.

REPEAL OF LICENSING ACTS, &C.

3. On the coming into operation of any orders or regulations made under Section Two of this Act, any statutory or other provisions of the English law which are inconsistent therewith shall cease to have effect.

SHORT TITLE AND APPLICATION

4. (*i*) This Act may be cited as the Public Refreshment Act, 1936.

(*ii*) This Act shall not apply to Scotland, Northern Ireland or Wales.

At least His Majesty's Government cannot say, as they have said about all other attempts at Licensing reform, that it is a 'piecemeal' measure. It is the most comprehensive Licensing Bill ever presented to Parliament. It covers everything, with a sheet-and-a-half of paper.

But its promoters, we feel, must be very young and inexperienced. What vagueness! Surely they know that in modern legislation every 'i' and every 't' must be dotted or crossed respectively, as the case may be, by, with or from? Here all is nebulous. What is this extraordinary suggestion that the Home Secretary should 'ascertain what are the laws of France' and imitate them? It is true that if the Home Secretary should happen to visit France he would observe that in this department of life all is civilized and sane, that the citizen can get what he wants when he wants it, but does not cause Parliamentary debates and Bills by taking too much. It is true that Mr Baldwin has said that 'our frontier is now the Rhine'. It is true that at the time of Jubilee, when for a brief space the laws of London were almost like the laws of Paris, the people of England did *not* disgrace themselves. It is true that at that time many statesmen delightedly described the behaviour and gaiety of the people as 'almost Continental'. But is it seriously supposed that *England* is going to take lessons from the said Continent? A million times No!

The one feature of this deplorable document which we can commend is the revival of the Preamble. In most modern measures the preamble, if there is one, is a feeble and anaemic thing. But the legislators of the past knew how to use it. It rolled; it thundered; it said things. Consider, for example, the preamble of the Treasonable and Seditious Practices Act, 1795:

> We, Your Majesty's most dutiful and loyal subjects, the lords spiritual and temporal, and Commons of Great Britain, in this present Parliament assembled, duly considering the daring outrages offered to Your Majesty's most sacred person, in your passage to and from your Parliament at the opening of the present Session, and also the continued attempts of wicked and evil disposed

> persons to disturb the tranquillity of this Your Majesty's kingdom, particularly by the multitude of seditious pamphlets and speeches daily printed, published and dispersed, with unremitting industry and with a transcendent boldness…

Or the cheery overture to the Suspension of the Habeas Corpus Act, 1803:

> Whereas a treasonable and rebellious spirit of insurrection now unfortunately exists in Ireland…

We like too the vigorous preamble to the English in the Law Courts Act, 1731:

> Whereas many and great mischiefs do frequently happen to the subjects of this kingdom from the proceedings in courts of justice being in an unknown language, those who are summoned and impleaded having no knowledge or understanding of what is alleged for or against them in the pleadings of their lawyers and attornies, who use a character not legible to any but persons practising the law: to remedy these great mischiefs, and to protect the lives and fortunes of the subjects of that part of Great Britain called England, more effectually than heretofore from the peril of being ensnared or brought in danger by forms and proceedings, in courts of justice, in an unknown language, be it enacted…

One knows at once what Pitt's Militia Act is about, and is at once excited:

> Whereas a well-ordered and well-disciplined militia is essentially necessary to the safety, peace and prosperity of

> this kingdom: and whereas the laws in being for the regulation of the militia are defective and ineffectual...

But the purpose of most modern measures has to be explained by a long and extremely dull Memorandum: and even then the purpose is not always plain, even to His Majesty's Judges. And, by the way, the explanatory Memorandum must not be 'argumentative' and may be censored by the officers of Parliament. In a preamble the legislator can say what he thinks. But then, it is not the thing to say what one thinks. Members, according to the *Spectator*, were 'shocked by the terms of the Public Refreshment Bill'. Dear, dear!

XXIV

MR MAFFERTY GOES TO THE DENTIST

'Good mornin', Mr Dentist,' said Mr Mafferty, entering the fatal chamber, 'it's a bright day, surely, an' at this rate, as you say, I wouldn't wonder at all if we had a warm August, or maybe September. No, there was no rain fell in me fine suburb this mornin', only a little hail at breakfast-time an' a small shower of snow as I left the house. Yes, it's quare an' cold for the time of year, as you say, an' the crowd an' traffic in the streets is excessive, as you say, an' the Government slides slowly down from blunder to blunder, as you say, the way you'll see an old pig rollin' down the rocky hillsides of Killibeg, an' it dyin' of the Pigs' Mischief, an' maybe we'll have summer again in a year or two, as you say, an' in the meantime there's worse lives than suicide, as you say, an' it's a strange thing a man would be puttin' himself to the trouble of killin' an' murderin' the poor old tobacco-woman at Putney, as you say, the one that's dead in the evenin' papers this mornin'.

'But in the name of torment, Mr Dentist, for what cause do you think I'd be troublin' me dejected mind with speculations of that like on this morn of mornin's? It's well enough for your own self to be standin' there by your instruments of torture with a glad welcome in your eyes an' a great smile upon your face, an' the merry talk on your lips concernin' the rain, an' the income-tax, and the latest murder, an' the like. But it's meself came knockin' at your door this noon with never a laugh in me heart. Isn't it destroyed I am, and tremblin' a week of days since we fixed this meetin', and I not able to be takin' pleasure in the light of the sun, or the shine of the stars, or the sound of music or the kiss of a young girl, for the black thoughts do be crowdin' in me mind of fillin's an' excavations an' extraction itself? If I've given me mind to anny person but yourself since the time of breakfast the day before yesterday, it's the lord of liars I am. You've blackened the week for me, I'm tellin' you. An' now let you cast off the mask of kindliness an' goodwill an' keep silence about the Government, for I've not the heart to be discussin' trivialities in this place. Take out your knives an' pokers an' I'll show you me teeth.

'Yes, you may look round the mouth if you're wishful, Mr Dentist, but let you keep your hands from pickin' an' proddin', an' makin' holes where there was no holes before. It's the fine salubrious set of teeth I had before the dentists took to cuttin' them up, like a row of white stones you'd see borderin' a flower-bed an' they polished with the rain. There's maybe one or two at the back has been excavated an' filled with metal by your great profession, but there's no flaw in the rest of them at all, only it's a delicate kind of tooth they are, an' sensitive, by reason of the rare breed they come from. So I'd not be insinuatin' an' scrapin' at them with your sharp points, Mr Dentist, for fear they'd crumble like the petals of a rose an' it blown by the wind. Nor I'd not be grindin' at them with your terrible wheel, Mr Dentist, for fine as they are it's the quare slender foundations they have, an' I wouldn't wonder but with one revolution of that machine you'd see them fallin' from me head like hailstones in the time of Spring, by reason of the vibration. So let you have done with that idea from this out, Mr Dentist. But if you'd like a quiet peep with your little glass an' no more, you're welcome, surely.

'No, there's no pain at all. No, there was never any pain. Well, I won't deceive you, maybe there was a little pain on Saturday last, an' maybe there was a small little pain on Sunday. But since

Monday mornin', when we fixed this meetin' on the telephone, the pain's been smaller and smaller, an' now there's no pain at all. It could be that I imagined the pain, Mr Dentist, for it's the quare fanciful fellow I am, seein' things everywhere that no man saw before or since, an' apt to be dreamin' at night, the way I'd be hard put to it sometimes to look back into the past an' say did this or that happen at all, or was it a dream entirely? I'm thinkin' it's a bad dream vexed me on Saturday an' Sunday, an' I tossin' in the night-time.

'Or maybe there's a kind of a magic in you, Mr Dentist, an' it needs no more than the sound of your soft voice on the public telephone to heal an abscess or take away pain. Annyway, here I am sittin' cosy in your great chair, an' not a twinge or unpleasantness in me mouth at all. I'm thinkin' me teeth was never better, so it's good you've done me already, an' you've no call, you understand, to be plannin' anny drastic action with picks an' shovels an' wheels an' the like, for I'll not require it.

'But I see it in your mind, Mr Dentist, to be askin' me what for I'd be comin' to see you at all with me teeth in the grand condition they are. Well, I've told you for why. It's the healin' spirit an' presence of you I'm after seekin', and if I sit here a small while longer, I'm thinkin', talkin' easily the way we are, it's not me teeth only will be the better for it, it's such a way you have with you. I suffer from indigestion, Mr Dentist, an' it's a martyr I am to rheumatism, but there'll be no more of them troubles from this day to the world's end after one dose of your medicinal society.

'But I wouldn't like you to think I'd be wastin' your precious time: an' now you speak of it there's a small matter besides is in your own line of business. I've a sore tongue, Mr Dentist, continually, an' that's a great fret in the life of a man, an' he talkin' an' eatin' from one day's end to another. No, it wouldn't be the tobacco at all, for it's the quare moderate smoker I am. There's no smoker, Mr Dentist, smokes so moderately as meself, without the word of a lie. I don't believe it's more than twenty pipes I'd be smokin' in one day, or maybe thirty in the rainy times. For you know well there's no man in this sad country takes the liquor or the baccy because they like them at all, but to keep their sanity only, an' they wanderin' in their minds with misery by reason of the rain an' the hail an' the taxes an' that like. I've had a great spate of misfortune lately, Mr Dentist, an' there's a quantity of rain fallen, but it's the quare small smoker I am nevertheless, so it can't be that is frettin' me tongue. I'm thinkin' there might be a sharp corner of a tooth in me mouth that's tearin' me tongue with every syllable I'm speakin'. How would it be now if you were to set down that murderous instrument you have an' take a wary search for jagged edges with your finger only? You can't find annythin'? Well, that's a wonder now, an' a pity besides; but I thank you kindly for your kind intentions.

'An' now, Mr Dentist, I wouldn't say I'd be givin' you anny more of me time, for it's a pressin' appointment I have for luncheon, an' there's a great grief bitin' the heart of me to think I'll not be takin' you with me, an' you not known to the lady. It's a fine talk, surely, we've had this day; an' you've done me good, Mr Dentist, you've done me good – an' what more can one man say to another than that? Good-day to you, Mr Dentist; an' maybe I'll be payin' you a visit another day if I have the pain again.'

XXV

THE PURSER

(as too many passengers seem to see him)

Yes, that is the Purser – with lots of gold lace
   And nothing whatever to do;
Not an officer really, but quite a nice face,
   And matters immensely to you;
For he is the one who is really to blame
   For whatever annoys you at sea,
But the joy of his life is to remedy same,
   And he will for a moderate fee.

   So go to the Purser and slip him a tip;
   His temper is terser with every trip,
         But bang on his door,
         For that's what he's for,
   And say what you think of his horrible ship.
And if there is nothing to make you profane
Invent an excuse, if it's only the rain:
The man isn't happy unless you complain –
         So go to the Purser.

The moment the steamer is clear of the wharf
   Proceed to the office and say,
'My cabin would be a small size for a dwarf;

You cannot expect me to *pay!*
I would not confine a white rabbit of mine
To a prison so meagre in plan;
I am told that they snore in the cabin next-door,
And something is wrong with the fan.'

Go to the Purser and be impolite;
Call at the office from morning till night;
Tackle the chap
While he's having his nap –
The Purser is wrong and the passenger's right.
Make it quite clear that you are not a mole
And cannot exist without air in a hole;
Add, by the way, that the ship mustn't roll –
That's the fault of the Purser.

As the voyage proceeds you may find that your needs
Take even more time to explain;
The food as a rule is the work of a fool;
It is foggy again and again;
The sailors will trek overhead on the deck
Just as sleep is approaching your eyes;
Your boy is too fond of that staggering blonde –
And what does the Purser advise?

Go to the Purser and give him some lip –
After all, you have paid for this odious trip,
And you never allowed
For a positive crowd
Of Parisian vamps in this part of the ship.
A man at your table's unpleasant to see,
So either you go to another, or he;
And why is fresh milk not provided at sea?
Inquire of the Purser.

And don't hesitate to pop in and relate
   Any personal matters you can;
Describe all the rows you have had with your spouse
   And ask him to speak to the man;
If your daughters insist upon staying up late,
   If your husband will love you no more,
If you cannot digest or are putting on weight –
   Well, that's what the Purser is for.

   Go to the Purser and sing him this song –
   The passenger's right and the Purser is wrong,
         And, alone of the crew,
         He has nothing to do
   But listen to nice little speeches from you.
The Captain has only the ocean to fear;
A furnace is fun to the Chief Engineer;
But the Purser has people to manage, poor dear –
         And God help the Purser!

XXVI

NEW ROADS

So the New Road is coming at last, and we among whom it is coming should, I suppose, be glad and gay and speak happily of Progress. For roads are the mark of Civilization, the triumph of Man. But, in fact, I can discover nobody in the neighbourhood who is keen about the New Road, except a few citizens who have property to sell (and even they are not enthusiastic).

Mr Bernard Shaw recently informed the world that as a potential visitor to Ethiopia he was on the side of the Italians, who were making roads, and against the Ethiopians, who were shortsightedly obstructing the benevolent road-builders.

I suppose, therefore, that Mr Shaw would be on the side of the London County Council and the Middlesex County Council, which, whatever I say, are going to drive this new road past our comparatively quiet homes. But in this controversy I am for the Ethiopians, who say, 'We do not *want* your excellent road'.

People kept bringing Ballots to the door and asking us what view we took about the Italians' road-making in Ethiopia. But nobody asks us what we think about this road-making in Hammersmith.

Yet, one would have thought, we deserve to have our say – if it is only a despairing squeak. For we who live just here are the only people in the country who can *never* benefit from the new road (excepting always the few citizens who have property to sell). Those of us who are going to be turned out of our homes to make way for the Road are quite content where we are; and those of us who are going to be allowed to remain are quite content with our communications. Seven minutes' walk to the Underground, five or six to a tram or bus in the High Road: this is swift enough for us. Indeed, so far as the communications are imperfect we like them, because imperfect communications keep the place quiet, not only for us but for all the citizens who like going for walks on Sundays.

But – we are told – we must not be selfish, like the Ethiopians.

Well, I don't know why not.

However, let us be noble and think of the Interests of the Community. What are they?

The Interests of the Community, it seems, demand that more motor-cars should be able to pass more swiftly through this part of London. At present, it seems, they can only go comparatively slowly along the High Road, and there are 'traffic jams'.

But how splendid! For many years, in the Interests of the Community, I have been saying that motor-cars went too fast along the High Road and ought to go slower. At last, it seems, my dream is coming true. And now they are going to spoil it all.

My heart leaps up when I behold a lovely traffic jam, as the poet remarked. Sometimes, gliding under Cannon Street Bridge in my little ship, I see a monstrous traffic jam on London Bridge – a beautiful, endless, two-way traffic jam – two great battalions of stationary vehicles. I put my engine into neutral and, letting the vessel drift, regard the great jam with pleasure. For this, I think, is a wholesome thing for the Community, which has bowed down to the false god Speed and thought by multiplying motors to add a cubit to its stature. I am sorry for the poor bus-drivers; though even for them a jam may bring more ease than pain. But up there, I think, as the tide carries me under London Bridge (which, by the way, has a slight but disturbing suggestion of being about to fall – in an easterly direction) – up there, I think, the big souls, the philosophers, sit calm and meditative, not raging vainly against the passage of time; while the small, the restless, the unpunctual ones, who always start too late and cannot sit still, being incapable of thought, are fuming and fussing and suffering, as they should. The little pedestrians, like pigeons, trip in and out among the great wheels, dreaming, and all, for a short space, has good order and proportion in the world of Speed. I put the engine ahead with a deep sigh; and sometimes, as, at six knots, we glide through Tower Bridge, I look astern and see that the Jam is still in being.

How foolish, then, to suppose that you can warm my heart towards the New Road by telling me of traffic jams in the old one! As well expect an Ethiopian to shed hot tears over the involuntary descent of an Italian aeroplane.

But let us return to the Community. What is this Community which the Councils and the Ministry (and Parliament) are going to serve by enabling it to pass at high speed through this now quiet corner of the town? The Community, I am sure, is a very good fellow; and if we met we should be friends. But we do not know it; and it does not, I fear, care half a hoot about us. For, *ex hypothesi*, it has never driven through our little corner and will never suspect how quiet we were before the New Road came,

It has, for the most part, I think, a nice house, or cottage, in the country. It would complain bitterly if we proposed to drive a new road through its quiet garden or suggested that it should travel by train; so it is not, at bottom, I think, much less selfish than we are. Indeed, on the ethical ladder it stands pretty low. Since it acquired a car it has become slothful; it has almost lost the use of its legs and cannot bear to walk to a common station and catch a degrading train. So it bustles in and out of London on its frequently redundant car, and because the poor little corner where we reside is in its way a great motor-track has to be blasted through our midst. Well, good luck to it! *Sauve qui peut!* But don't let us have any nonsense about the Interest of the Community; for this means the Interest of the Internal Combustion Community and nothing else. The fruit and vegetables and milk and everything arrive in London quite fast enough by the High Road; or, if not, there are two courses open – send more of the stuff by train or widen the High Road, whose unfortunate inhabitants cannot be worse off than they are already. And, by the way, remove the 'bottle-neck' which is the cause of the congestion. This was proposed by the London County Council some years ago; but a few shopkeepers objected. They matter. We don't. Nor does Quiet.

There are not so many quiet untidy corners left in London, where one may saunter along old passages at the backs of churchyards and boat-yards and clusters of old cottages without a sound of London's traffic; and it is, I think, in the Interests of the Community that these should be preserved. Those, however, who plan new roads are not impressed by that kind of argument; so we will argue no more. Indeed, it is too late; for already they have begun to knock the place about. We used to say, 'But surely they will never go through all these Recreation Grounds – our Open Spaces, our Lungs!' But they are. We used to cry, 'But they couldn't go through the churchyard!' They are taking a great chunk off the churchyard, just missing the altar. Progress marches on, and we will argue no more.

But when the correspondents tell us with amusement that the Ethiopian feebly brandishes his sword at the Italian aeroplanes I do not laugh. I know exactly how the Ethiopian feels.

XXVII

EAT LESS LIPSTICK

I know now. For years I have been wondering why young women will make up their mouths to look like letter-boxes or bits of wet sealing-wax. I long ago gave up the idea that it was intended to please the men; for women have long ago abandoned the pretence that they do anything to please the men. Also I know by inquiry that every man of courage and sense continually tells his favourite lady that he prefers her mouth to look like a mouth and not like a sea-anemone or a piece of raw meat. So I know that women know that nearly all men think that what nearly all young women do is disgusting. They stop short, of course, of telling the ladies that they will get no supper until they wash their faces (which is what we ought to do). And so it goes on. Goes on? The thing is increasing. Within the last few months the lips of London's ladies have gone up seven shades of scarlet. The merest shop-girl now has a mouth like a bad inflammation. Walking down Piccadilly is like walking through the wings of a theatre. The aristocracy used to scorn the actress because she painted her face, but very soon the actress will have to put on more make-up, not less, when she joins the aristocracy after the play.

And meanwhile the chemists and the cunning cosmetic-mongers are madly battening on Woman's weakness. New shades of stickiness are issued daily. I have a Beauty paper before me, with some new lines illustrated in colour. 'Lipsalve medium scarlet, bright scarlet lipsalve, bright rose lipsalve, deep rose lipsalve.' (The colour in the illustration is in every case the same; but what of that?) There are kiss-proof lipstuffs and indelible lipstuffs and permanent lipstuffs and stormproof lipstuffs. And too many young women look more and more revolting. In the old days, when a man kissed a woman for the first time, his first thought was, 'Will she marry me?' Now his first thought is, 'Where can I wash?'

Well, I know that women have always done many things in the way of decoration not to attract the gentlemen but to annoy the other women. And I have thought that that perhaps was the reason of the Flaming Lip Competition. But now I know. The last young woman I lectured upon this insanitary subject let the cat out of the vanity-bag. She said, 'Yes, I know you dislike it – but I like the taste of it'. The thing is a food, a sort of sweet, a common indulgence, a new vice. Our womenfolk, if my young friend is right, spend the whole day licking their lips. They eat in the theatre, they eat in the streets. The red lips of your lady-love are not a Cupid's bow but an emergency ration.

Odious conception! This thing must stop. Or at least we must have fewer lectures from women about the horrid habits of men. Our pipes are dirty, we freely admit; but how dare they talk to us about our dirty pipes! At least, we do not pretend that they are aids to beauty.

And where is all this 'Beauty' business to stop? This paper before me has three well-illustrated pages on what every young girl ought to do to her eyebrows. The great thing about our eyebrows, it seems, is that most of them ought not to be there at all, and the others are in the wrong place. The Creator, when creating Woman, had not read *Woman and Beauty*, and so was not aware that 'long narrow eyebrows add delicacy to the round face, whereas thick wide brows will exaggerate the round appearance of an already wide face,' and 'for the *petite* type of face a short delicate eyebrow is desirable. The Oriental type of face demands long narrow eyebrows dipping slightly towards the nose and slanting upwards at the ends... So, before starting to pluck out the hairs, decide upon the line you intend to achieve.'

Life is busy for the ladies nowadays:

'Eyelashes that are thin and colourless can be made to look thicker, longer, and silkier by moistening them with brilliantine, brushed on with the finger in an upward direction.

'When making up the eyes, first shade the upper lids with shadow-powder, as in the centre picture – grey-blue for those with fair and mid-brown colourings, and hazel-brown for the real brunette.

'You can darken your eyelashes with water cosmetique – brown or black, according to your colouring. Darken only the edges of the lashes, brushing very lightly away from the eyes.

'If you want to make your eyes look large take your eyebrow pencil and draw a short line from each outer corner out towards the temple. This line must not be too clearly defined but should be gently spread with the tip of the finger to take away the hard line.

'A surprisingly youthful and soft expression can be imparted to the eyes by moistening the tip of the little finger with cold cream or brilliantine (the merest suspicion, of course) and rubbing it along the edge of the upper lids.

'For the beauty of your eyes you will need:

An eyebath,
A good skin-food,
Boracic and rose-water lotion,
Brilliantine,
A soft baby's brush,
An eyebrow pencil,
Eyelash darkener.'

That is for the eyes only. What, I wonder, must be the

equipment required to keep the rest of a normal woman beautiful?

Realize, sir, these are not instructions to a young actress making-up for the first time, they are things your lady-love is invited to do in civil life, as it were. Perhaps she is on the way to the rendezvous now, the lovely natural thing: presently she will be in your arms and you will be gazing deep, deep into her peerless eyes, whose lids are shaded with grey-blue shadow powder: but modestly she casts down those long dark lashes which you love, darkened with brown-water cosmetique, surprisingly soft and youthful with the merest suspicion of brilliantine. 'Kiss me,' you whisper and, raising the long dark lashes, she reveals those large eyes, made to look large with the eyebrow pencil which drew that delicious short line from each outer corner out towards the temple. Her little nose, her shell-like ears – but I do not know what she has done to them; probably they too are mere compositions of skin-food and hair-oil. But hark! a sound. Cautiously (or incautiously) she puts a finger to her lips. 'Lend me your hanky, darling,' she murmurs. 'Angel, what's that upon your finger? Blood?' 'No, Cecil, it is medium rose lipsalve. Don't kiss me, darling, for the stuff is expensive. Besides, I'm hungry.'

And you, sir, what do you say? I leave it to you.

XXVII

BATTER SWEET: OR 'NOT CRICKET'

AN OPERETTA

Music by Vivian Ellis

(*With respectful compliments to Mr Noel Coward, who has surprisingly neglected the National Game.*)

PROLOGUE

Front-cloth, a nursery. An elderly lady, strikingly beautiful in spite of her advanced years and white hair, is wheeled on L. in a bath-chair.

A small boy bounds on R. carrying a small cricket-bat.

MAX. Oh, Granny, may I play with this bat?

LADY BANE (*gently*). Mais, mon petit, c'est le '*bat*' de Grand'-mère. Where did you find it?

MAX. In your secret cupboard, Granny. (*smelling the bat*) It smells of lavender.

LADY BANE. You know you mustn't play with Granny's toys.

MAX (*stoutly*). But, Granny, when I grow up I'm going to be a soldier and kill the Australians.

[*He makes a violent gesture with the bat, as if bringing it down upon the head of an enemy.*

LADY BANE *is much moved and sobs quietly.*]

MAX. Oh, Granny, what is it?
LADY BANE (*sings*). La vie est dure
Un peu d'amour –
Et puis bonjour.
(*Music*)
MAX (*clinging to knee, L.*):
Granny, tell me, Granny, have you
anything upon your mind?
I'll give you a penny.
Let me tenderly partake
Of your evident heartache –
Will you tell me the tale?

Can it be some poignant recollection
has revived an old affection?
Can it be that this little toy
Has awakened the brittle joy
Of a dream that is stale?
LADY BANE. Ah – ah!
MAX. Does it bring back again
The ecstasy and subtle pain
Of yesterday?
LADY BANE. C'est vrai.
(*frantic with reminiscence*)
Fling away – all fettering things,
Find a way – of bettering things;
Shatter whatever
Spoils our endeavour
To keep our love gallant and gay.
Let us dream – romantical things,
Though they seem – impractical things;
Let romance lead you
On, for I need you.
If things impede you
Fling them far away.

SCENE I

SCENE: *Lord's Cricket Ground on the occasion of the Oxton and Camrow Match. A sunny day.*
Time: The present – and the end of the luncheon interval.

THE PARADE

(*Music*)

FIRST SPECTATOR. The wicket's wearing.
SECOND SPECTATOR. And how is Madge?
THIRD SPECTATOR. The bowling's putrid.
FOURTH SPECTATOR. What batting!
FIFTH SPECTATOR. Have a good lunch?
SIXTH SPECTATOR. They can't play forward nowadays.

[*Enter three* YOUNG CRICKETERS, *arm-in-arm. Flannels, blue blazers, caps, and scarves and long cigarette-holders. Each carries, or rather dangles, a bat.*

A bell rings and a policeman begins to clear the ground.

The crowd melt away gradually.]

Sprigs of nobility we,
Twigs on the Family Tree.
Like everyone else in the plays of dear
Howard
We're flowers that wonder just why we
have flowered –
Delicate cuttings of class,
Why are we kept under glass?
Life's such a bore –
What are we for?
Sprigs of nobility we – we – we, sprigs of
nobility we!

At our most expensive schools the
masters taught the rules
Of cricket, football, squash – in fact,
of all games,
And sent us up to college with the
satisfying knowledge
That life is just another of the
ball-games.
If a boy can keep his bat
Perpendicular (like that),
He is sure to be successful as a
banker;
If he's handy in the slips
He is certain to eclipse
The businessman whose game is
Crown and Anchor.
In every trade and calling take the
richest and the greatest –
Their brains may be appalling, but
their bats, you'll find, were
straightest;
While huddle in the jails
Or on the gallows dangle
The miserable males
Whose bats were at an angle,
And those who dropped a sitter
Or played forward to half-volleys
In squalor long and bitter
Must expiate their follies.

Sprigs of nobility we,
Twigs on the Family Tree,
We've wielded this curious weapon
correctly
And so we may count on an income

directly;
Possibly, probably shove
Into His Majesty's Gov.;
Still, we implore:
What are we for?
Sprigs of nobility we – we – we, sprigs of
nobility we!

[*Exeunt R. the* YOUNG MEN. *Enter R. (higher up) two* UMPIRES *in white coats, carrying enormous books labelled 'The Laws of Cricket'. One should be tall, one short and round; both, if possible, basses. They enter pompously to Handelian music.*]

BOTH. We are the British Umpire,
Of Equity the model,
And the hearts of our race beat twice
the pace
As to the pitch we waddle.
FIRST U. These are the Laws,
SECOND U. . . . . .do . . . . .
FIRST U. . . . . .do . . . . .
SECOND U. . . . . .do . . . . .
FIRST U. These are the Rules,
The cause of fear
SECOND U. To knaves or fools
Who flout 'em.
FIRST U. But we have heard
They're not quite clear,
SECOND U. And so a word
BOTH. About 'em.
FIRST U. Few men can say –
SECOND U. Not I, for one –
FIRST U. What is or is not cricket;
SECOND U. But, briefly, anything may be done,

FIRST U. So long as the other side stick it.
The bowlers may strike batsmen down
With hideous blows on trunk or crown;
SECOND U. A captain may compel the foe
To bat in darkness, fog or snow;
FIRST U. And if the foe does not protest
SECOND U. We take it all is for the best.
FIRST U. All dirty tricks shall we allow,
SECOND U. Provided no one makes a row
Or dies upon the wicket.
FIRST U. But if a player starts a jaw,
SECOND U. That player has infringed the law,
In short, it is not cricket –
FIRST U. Not cricket –
SECOND U. Not cricket –
BOTH. Not cri-i-i-ck –
Not cri-i-i-ck – (*ad lib.*)
In short, it is not cricket.

[*Both turn and march up-stage to their posts, one going off R.*

The Camrow team come out on to the field to take their places.]

BALLET

[*Loud applause as* HOWARD *and* SECOND BATSMAN *emerge from the Pavilion (R.) and proceed towards the wicket.* HOWARD *touches his dark-blue cap and hitches up his trousers. His bat is a veteran bound with many strappings, and is a tawny brown. He is a tenor – dark and sinister.*

SADIE *runs forward and confronts him. She carries under her arm a small, new, very white-looking bat.* SECOND BATSMAN *goes on and off – up-left.*

BASIL, *the Camrow captain, 'clean-limbed' and athletic, stands down left, ready to field, and listens grimly to this scene.*]

HOWARD (*halting*). You!

SADIE. Howard, I hear you are captain of Oxton now.

HOWARD. Yes. Isn't it foul?

SADIE. Isn't it rather big to be at the top of the tree?

HOWARD (*with a bitter little laugh*). It's a lonely place, Sadie, the top of the tree. There's nothing up there but last year's birds'-nests.

SADIE. You're so unserious.

[*With sudden passion he kisses her.* BASIL *observes the gesture with dissatisfaction.]*

HOWARD (*breaking away*). How beastly! Sadie, we shall have to marry. Do you mind?

SADIE. I should hate it. (*intense*) Howard, let's get away from our horrible set – away to the South, to the sunshine.

HOWARD. To escape from our horrible set you'll have to go North. The South is crawling with it.

SADIE. Nobody but you could make cricket decadent. And yet – I hate it too. Will you make a hundred today?

HOWARD (*shaking his head*). Running wearies me. Besides, a century's so snobbish.

SADIE (*a sudden decision*). Howard, if you make a hundred I'll marry you.

HOWARD. And if I make nought you'll live with me. Is that it?

SADIE. I want to see if you can do something *big*. (*holding out her bat*) I have bought you a bat.

HOWARD. I have a bat.

SADIE (*looks at his bat with disgust*). But it's strapped up like a duchess. Use my little clean bat, Howard.

HOWARD (*looking at her*). My dear, a virgin bat is no more use than a virgin cow.

SADIE. Oh, Howard! (*pressing him*) To please me!

HOWARD. Angel, I can't carry two bats.

SADIE. Why not? The tennis-champions carry six.

HOWARD. But they play with six balls. (*yielding, puts her bat under his arm*) Very well, fish-face.

[*He is going to embrace her but she stops him.*]

SADIE (*looking down at his pads and fingering his gloves*). Darling, I don't think you ought to kiss me in those things. It's *too* inelegant.

HOWARD. Darling, how right you are! Off with them!

[*She kneels and unbuckles his pads while he takes off his gloves.*]

SADIE *and* HOWARD:

Fling away – all fettering things!
Find a way – of bettering things.
Shatter whatever
Spoils our endeavour
To keep our love gallant and gay!
Let us dream – romantical things,
Though they seem – impractical things;
Let romance lead you
On, for I need you!
If pads impede you
Fling them far away!

[*Terrific musical climax.* SADIE *and* HOWARD *vehemently fling one pad away each, one of them being caught, in self-defence and indignantly, by* BASIL, *who throws it off into the wings.*

HOWARD *then kisses* SADIE *and marches up-stage to the wicket.*

(*Music*)

SADIE *goes towards her seat, down-left, but on the way she and* BASIL *suddenly see each other. They stop and stare, registering intensity.*]

SADIE (*glances up-stage, then back to* BASIL, *dazed*). Hell! Have I made a mistake? (*passes on, still dazed, to her seat, down-left*)

[*Meanwhile* HOWARD *is taking 'guard', etc. The score-board is illuminated and gives the following information:*

Batsman – HOWARD
Score –
Bowler – ENDIVE
Father's name – LORD FENNEL
Clubs – CARLTON *and* BUCK'S

HOWARD *flourishes his bat, there is a sharp crack, fielders relax and* HOWARD'S *score at once leaps up to* '10'.

During the following the game proceeds quietly at the back, HOWARD'S *score leaping up by tens and fifteens.*

Enter, down-left, three LADIES OF LORDS.]

FIRST L.L. (*without looking towards the field, hearing the applause*). Oh, my dear, has something happened?

SECOND L.L. My dear, what *could* happen? They seem to do *nothing* but drink lemonade.

THIRD L.L. It's *too* stupefying.

FIRST L.L. And yet the *moment* one relaxes somebody gets out or something and one misses the *real* event of the season.

SECOND L.L. Oh, *darling* – there's *Basil!* (*calling to the Camrow captain*) '*Basil* darling!'

[BASIL *turns and, self-conscious, motions them with his hand to be quiet.*]

SECOND L.L. Oh, *darling,* don't be *pedantic!* I *only* wanted a *cigarette!*

[*All, yawning, turn front.*]

All three. Ladies of Lord's,
Easily-boreds,
And frantic from sitting like sardines
Sucking hot sweets
And ignoring the feats
Of our embryo Hobbses and Jardines,
Ladies of Lord's,
Oh, how we suffer,
Sitting on boards
And growing no tougher!
We don't understand what it's all about –
Why do they keep throwing that ball about?
Every half-hour they have drinks taken out,
But nobody'd care if we *died* of the drought.
Ladies of Lord's!
It's treason to state it,
But, oh, how we hate It,
The Ladies of Lord's!

Ladies of Lord's,
Mortally-boreds!
It's all very well for our brothers.
Maybe it's fun
To run round in the sun;
They don't have to sit next to their mothers.
Nobody cares,
It's all very tiring;
Everyone stares
At young men perspiring.
It's a game that develops the character
(As the schoolmistress said when they

barracked her),
But, though it is good for our brothers, no
doubt,
It seems to bring all that is worst in us out!
Ladies of Lord's!
It's treason to state it,
But, oh, how we hate it,
The Ladies of Lord's!

[LADIES OF LORD'S *exeunt* – R.

A waiter brings on to the field from the pavilion a tray full of glasses, with a jug of lemonade. The players bound towards him and pose with glasses round him.

During this, SADIE *(who has formed a passion for the handsome* BASIL*) goes to him.*]

SADIE. Are you really Basil Mayhew?

BASIL. Yes.

SADIE (*intense*). I might have known.

BASIL. Tell me, is it true that you will marry him if he makes a hundred?

SADIE. It was. Do you think he will?

BASIL (*grimly*). Not if I know it! His late-cuts poison the air!

SADIE. Oh, Basil, since I have watched you in the long-field I have understood cricket at last. (*holding out the bat*) Will you teach me?

THE CRICKET LESSON

[SADIE *makes passes with her bat;* BASIL, *gesturing with an imaginary bat, shows her what to do.*]

BASIL. No, Miss Sadie, that's unsound;
Bring that left elbow more round!
No, not like that!

Excellent! you have it pat.

[SADIE, *miraculously, knows the whole art already.*]

All our lives we will be two good cricketers
In our cosy little flat,
Pillars of the Church and season-ticketers,
Joined together by a bat.

SADIE (*speaks*). When may I bowl someone, please?

BASIL. Not until you are confirmed and have a permit from the Foreign Office.

SADIE (*sings*). Something so deep in my soul
Tells me that I'd like to bowl.
(*Waltz*)
I'll play games with you
Whenever you've no dames with you;
You'll be the bat – I the ball,
And you can hit me anywhere at all.

Then I'll bowl to you,
Surrender my whole soul to you –
All the common world will seem
Players in a distant dream –
You and I will be a team
Of two.

[HOWARD, *up-stage, observes the end of this affecting scene with dismay, but the Lemonade Interval is over, the fielders return to their places, and* HOWARD, *with a long lingering look, goes back to the wicket, i.e.* OFF, *up* R.

The players (and SADIE*) return to their places.*

HOWARD'S *score is now eighty-two.*

There has been an over, and HOWARD *is now batting* OFF, *i.e.* R. *We therefore see the* SECOND

BATSMAN *and the* UMPIRE; *and we now see the* BOWLER *run on from* L., *bound into the air and fling the ball into the wings. There is a crack, applause, and* HOWARD'S *score leaps up to ninety-nine.*]

SPECTATORS (*in unison*). Ninety-nine!

[BASIL, *now down-left, is in a fever of tension. All lean forward eagerly.*

(*Chord*)

The BOWLER *bowls, there is a crack, the* SECOND BATSMAN *runs off, and* HOWARD *runs on; but he halts and, like everyone else, gazes skyward. He has struck the ball very high into the air and it looks like falling in* BASIL'S *neighbourhood.* BASIL *shows that he is aware of this by dodging anxiously about.*]

(*Music*)

MELODRAMA

As the ball approaches –

BASIL. See the ball!
It must fall.
Clinging fingers, play your part!
Happiness is near
If you grip – grip it with a will:
It may disappear
Like the whip-whippoor-whippoor-will.

[*The ball comes into view, descending slowly at the end of a string.*]

SADIE (*rising*). Give romance
Every chance –

Catch it bravely, though it smart.
Tra-la-la-la, *etc.*
Both. Love is all!
Hold the ball,
And you hold {my / her} heart.

[*The ball halts in mid-air.* BASIL *and* SADIE *turn front and sing to the audience, supported by all the Lord's audience and players:*

See the ball! *etc.*

Finally BASIL *turns up-stage, the ball descends and he catches it. Applause. Sensation.*]

FINALE

But HOWARD, *who all this time has been running runs, now bounds down-stage and, gracefully, elegantly, but none the less forcibly, strikes* BASIL *on the head with the little white bat.*

BASIL *falls to the ground and lies on his side, facing the footlights, dead, but holding up, tightly clasped against his chest, the fatal ball.*

SADIE *runs to him and kneels at his side.*

The CROWD *cluster behind.*

TABLEAU

But the picture is broken up by the UMPIRE *(bowler's end), who thrusts his way through the crowd (centre) and inspects the body (or rather the ball – the only thing that interests him). Assured that the ball has not touched the ground, he rises to his full height, points a majestic finger to heaven and says in a great voice –*

'OUT!'

(*Very loud music*)

FULL COMPANY

Fling away – all fettering things, *etc.*

CURTAIN

XXIX

PRIVACY

> 'A sightseer from a London coach told me, "I have been to Ferring every Sunday for the last three weeks. I shall continue to come every Sunday until I see Mr Thomas in the grounds." '
>
> 'This afternoon a motor-coach arrived from Yorkshire.'
>
> *Daily Paper*

But what sort of Britons or beasts are these? Where is the celebrated British sense of fairplay, reticence, reluctance to hit a man when he is down, and all the rest of it? And where is that old legendary place, the Englishman's castle?

> 'Throughout the afternoon there was a stream of cars to Ferring. The beach was packed with sightseers, who took picnic meals and sat eating them at the end of Mr Thomas' garden within full view of the house.'

The victim, I suppose, may think himself lucky that there were not Autogiro Expeditions, enabling the ghoulish, the bat-witted, and malignant to hover over the house and peer down the chimney.

It is time that we had a Law for the Defence of Privacy. If a citizen is suspected of 'loitering with intent to commit a felony' he can be whisked away by a constable without a warrant. We may soon have to grant the same sort of powers in a case of mass-loitering with intent to commit a breach of taste or a private nuisance. The law is vigilant and firm to protect property or to prevent the obstruction of traffic. If any one, for example, had held up that 'stream of cars' for so much as two minutes, grim things would have happened to him. There is no good reason why Privacy should not be as well protected as Property or Traffic.

The moment is opportune. I have been writing about the reform of the law of libel for many years; and at last the 'serious' people are beginning to think about it. A draft Bill has been publicly discussed, good so far as it goes. It would discourage the bringing of 'gold-digging' or semi-blackmailing complaints of libel against the Press. It does not go far enough: it does little, for example, to relieve the particular grievances of authors; and one legislator, at least, could not support a measure which left Grub Street defenceless at so many points. But that by the way.

The Bill proposes that, except in certain cases, the plaintiff in a libel action must prove 'actual damage'; and the basic assumption is that unless one can prove material damage or loss of professional or sexual reputation one has no right to complain of what is publicly said about him (or her). All very well, if you are dealing with a genuine, professional, gold-digging plaintiff. But might it not take us a little too far along the path of freedom?

It may be that we have gone too far already. Is it never the case that a man may justifiably complain of things which are said about him, though every word is true and none of it is libellous? It is not libellous to say that Mr — has taken a house at —, that he wishes to remain there in quiet seclusion, but that it is easy to see into the garden from the road. It is not libellous, but it is heartless and cruel, and, by every decent standard, offensive.

We now condemn the coach-loads of peeping asses: and soon – when they have ceased to be 'news' – the daily papers will condemn them too. But who began it? Who thought it important to publish photographs of a certain house? Who printed the kind cartoons with that house in the background? Who sends those clouds of reporters (and they can but do as they are told) to infest the doorsteps of bereaved families or citizens in trouble? Who announces that 'Mrs — is most anxious that her whereabouts shall remain secret. She is here at the Splendid Hotel'? The very people who complain that the 'Freedom of the Press' is being foully diminished by the law which permits the bringing of bogus libel actions.

They may be right. But the Freedom of the Person is important too. The citizen who can technically complain of libel, and obtain damages where no damage has been done, may have too great rights – I am not sure. But the citizen who cannot complain of libel – as in the preceding paragraph – who can only say that his private life and feelings have been cruelly sacrificed to the great god 'News', has neither right nor remedy.

And so I suggest a reasonable compromise: Let the 'Freedom of the Press' (which, by the way, is not recognized by the British Constitution, and never has been) be protected, where proper, from the heartless private citizen in the domain of libel. But let a new right, the Right of Privacy, be erected and protected by the same measure.

It would not be an absolute right: that would make things too difficult. It could only be insisted upon, perhaps, after notice, and only enforced at law upon the *fiat* of the Attorney-General. But it should be there in the background: so that at last the harassed victim could say, 'This is a gross invasion of my private life; and if I cannot repel it I will punish it. Therefore let these reporters disappear from my door: and let these garden-gazers be dispersed as common loiterers.' If this can be represented as a dangerous curtailment of freedom I shall be sorry, but I shall be surprised.

And there is another thing. I have recently learned (expensively, from 'counsel') that no Briton has any rights in his own name. That is, he cannot complain (unless anything libellous is said) of the use of his name in the advertisement columns or anywhere else. If an aeroplane were to pass across London towing the message that 'The Archbishop of Canterbury uses — Soap' his Grace would have no remedy (supposing the assertion to be true). A certain famous amateur golfer was only successful in a suit about a similar affair because he was able to show that the advertisement complained of might throw doubts upon his status as an amateur golfer. All this is odd. It is fair to add that most advertisers carefully avoid such offences, since good taste must be part of their appeal. But queer things have happened, and may happen again, and here is another point for those who frame the new Law of Defamation and Privacy.

Who is to do that? In the old days one would have said 'The Government'. But some of the questions to be answered will be difficult and even 'controversial': so we must not expect anything from the Home Office yet. Meanwhile, I hear that there are many great brains not wholly occupied at the Temple today, and I suggest that my much more learned brethren direct their minds to this novel but not un-English conception – the Right of Privacy.

XXX

MR MAFFERTY DEFIES THE UDC

'Are you the Bathin' Inspector?' said Mr Mafferty. 'Are you the Shore Inspector of the Urban District Council of the fine town of Bugton-by-the-Sea? Is it yourself is strollin' the shore to see no man swims in the ocean before two o'clock of the afternoon, an' it Sunday? It is so? Then let you take a small piece of a walk with me across the beach from this place to the margin of the sea, for it's meself will be takin' a great swim this moment, though it's no more than the noon of the day.

'Regulations, is it? An' will you tell me now who made them regulations, Mr Inspector? You will not at all, for I'll tell you meself. 'Tis about six or seven corpulent gentlemen will never be fifty again, an' wouldn't swim in the sea if you gave them the Crown Jewels itself. 'Tis a few round old gentlemen has made money at the shopkeepin', an' you've made them Councillors by reason of the fine heads they have on them for figures, an' the fine talent they have to be runnin' the trams an' organizin' the drains. There's old Mr Withers that sells the hosiery, an' he an expert on the town sewers; there's Mr Mudd is an ironmonger an' understands the water-supply; an' there's old Mr Egg is blind an' deaf, but makes great speeches about the electric light. It's grand old fellers they are, surely; an' you've put 'em in charge of your sanitation, an' your education, an' your recreations, an' your arts, an' your libraries, an' the way you dress, an' the morals of your young. It's not meself would be complainin' of that, for there's no man livin', I'm thinkin', is better able to say what kind of a play is fit an' proper to be played in Bugton than Mr Mudd himself, an' he an ironmonger disapproves of the theatre. An' why wouldn't Mr Egg set his face against music in the park, an' he not able to hear a note of it, the poor old fella? There's nothin' they can't do on the land, them gentlemen; but will you tell me now what right they'd have to be rulin' the sea as well? It's the Public Health Acts, is it? Well, them's fine pieces of legislation, surely, an' it's not meself would be liftin' the tip of a finger to be injurin' the public health. Maybe I'd cause a pestilence, an' I enterin' the sea. Maybe there'd rise up a great commotion among the fish, the way the food of the town would suffer. But after two o'clock, you're tellin' me, there's no more danger. Well, it's twelve itself now, an' I'll risk it. I'm goin' into the wide sea, Mr Inspector, an' let you stand there an' inspect.

'Sunday, is it? Well, I've been to church, Mr Inspector. An' if I'd not been to church at all will you tell me what call has Councilor Mudd to be keepin' me out of the English Channel? Will you tell me what way it concerns Mr Egg if I go to church at the risin' of the sun or the fall of night, at the noon of day or no time at all? Is Mr Withers, that runs the drains, in charge of religion as well? Is it himself is to lay down me hours of worship an' meditation, by reason of the great knowledge an' capacity he has for managin' the sewers? An' if that's the way of it does he think he'll draw me into church or chapel by keepin' me out of the sea before two o'clock in the afternoon, for it's the contrary altogether.

'I've no wish at all to be enterin' the ocean, Mr Inspector. It's a quare, grey, cold-lookin' kind of an ocean, an' it heavin'. It's a poor foolish thing, I'm thinkin', for a man to leave the warm land an' trust himself to the water, with the stones tearin' the flesh from his feet an' the great waves dashin' the wind out of his body. I'd sooner sit here, Mr Inspector, an' think holy thoughts under the arch of the sky, an' humble me heart before the thunder of the ocean. There's many a man, I know, can't rouse himself to a solemn reflection without he has a great crowd bawlin' a hymn behind him. But it could be, Mr Inspector, it's meself would come as quick by a holy thought an' a humble heart in this place as Councillor Withers an' Councillor Mudd, an' they preenin' an' poutin' like two prize pigeons in the Council pew.

'I've no wish to take the water at all, I'm tellin' you. There's no man livin' dislikes the swimmin' more than meself. It's a tirin' exercise an' makes the hair sticky; I'll have the ocean up me nose an' the salt sea in me ears the way I'll not hear nothin' for a week of days. I'll be pantin' an' puffin' as the high waves strike me, an' in dread of drownin' at the latter end. It's a poor unhappy creature I'll be from the time the water comes lappin' at me knees till the time I'm out of it entirely, I'm destroyed shiverin' at the sight of the sea only; I've not gone swimmin' since me twentieth birthday. But as soon as me eyes fell on your crazy notice to say there's no swimmin' lawful before two in the afternoon of Sunday, it's the great longin' rose up in me heart to be swimmin' in the sea this day. An' it's a pity now I'd not be seein' that notice before, for you'd have heard the noise of me swimmin' from the break of mornin' till the present time, splashin' an' kickin' an' cryin' harsh curses on Councillor Withers an' Councillor Mudd an' the whole museum together. It's a kind of an ache an' madness is in me mind to be plungin' into them waters an' defyin' the Urban District Council from this hour till the fallin' of the dew. Isn't it a British subject I am, an' we rulin' the waves? An' is it such as Councillor Withers is to be takin' away me birthright an' shuttin' off the public ocean from a son of the sea?

'Holy Bugton! *Balmy* Bugton, that puts them great advertisements in the papers to be drawin' the Americans to Bugton, an' the French besides, an' it wonderin' why they don't arrive at all. It's a wonder, surely. You'd think the whole world would be flockin' to Bugton to see the fine English haunt of pleasure an' fun, where a man can't put his nose in the ocean on a Sunday mornin' without the leave of Councillor Mudd an' Councillor Withers that understands the drains.

'But what's the use of talkin'? I'll be swimmin' now, Mr Inspector. Stop me, is it? Arrest me, is it? I wouldn't say you'd be doin' that. Maybe you'll keep me from undressin' on the beach by reason of your loathsome by-laws: an' maybe you'll keep me from undressin' in a municipal hut by reason you have the keys; but will you tell me now how you'll keep me from walkin' into the ocean in me clothes, an' it me Sunday suit? For that's me intention, Mr Inspector. Me blood is up, me soul's alight with the blazin' fires of a holy indignation, an' if you brought the Bugton Fire Brigade, an' the 10th Dragoons, an' the Flyin' Squad, an' the Manchester Watch Committee, an' Councillor Mudd himself, an' they kneelin' on their knees before me, they wouldn't stop me from steppin' into the English Channel an' swimmin' about in a derisive manner to show the contempt I have for the whole battalion of you. An' if you've annythin' more to say on this subject, Mr Inspector, let you follow me into the water in the grand uniform you have.'

With these words Mr Mafferty removed his hat and walked slowly into the sea.

XXXI

OUTSIDE BROADCAST

It is Mr Mervyn Flute speaking, and I am at one of the microphones which have been established at the Abdul Turkish Baths in London on the occasion of the centenary celebrations, to which a number of well-known people have been invited. A hundred years ago today, in the year 1829, the Abdul Turkish Baths were opened for the first time, and this is therefore the centenary of these baths, and a number of distinguished citizens have been invited to be present on this occasion, which is the hundredth anniversary of the opening of the Abdul Turkish Baths in London, and which –

'I don't know how many listeners know what a Turkish Bath is like, but in case there are any listeners who have not had a Turkish Bath I must explain that a Turkish Bath is not like an ordinary or, if I may say so, Christian bath. A Turkish Bath is not so much a water-bath as a hot-air bath; indeed, many Turkish bathers do not enter the water, in the strict sense, at all. The principal thing about a Turkish Bath is the production of – well, I am not sure that the word I am going to use has ever passed through this rather delicate microphone before, and as a matter of fact there is another word which in a sort of way conveys what I want to say, and that word is the word "perspiration" – This is Mr Mervyn Flute and I am here with Major Hallam at one of the microphones which have been set up in the Abdul Turkish Baths on the occasion of the centenary celebrations of these baths, and I was just saying that the prime object of a Turkish Bath is the production of what, for the want of a better word (and really, if I may say so, there *is* no better word) can only be described by the fine old British word – what do you think, Major Hallam, dare I say it?'

'I should risk it, Mervyn.'

'Well, sweat! There, I have said it, and I hope that listeners will forgive me. Well as a result of sweating, or perhaps I should say a cause of sweating, the pores of the skin are opened and certain beneficial results follow, among them being, for those of an adipose tendency, a certain reduction of – However, I do not wish you to think that all those who take Turkish baths are of an adipose tendency; certainly not tonight, when many well-known people have been invited, including a number of literary gentlemen who are of an exceptionally spare and athletic build, and as a matter of fact one of the great features of a Turkish Bath is that people of any size can obtain benefit from their bath at the Abdul Turkish Baths, which are celebrating their centenary this evening; at the same time, in view of the festive season which are we now enjoying and in which the pleasures of the table are perhaps – well, as I was saying, it is perhaps fortunate that the centenary celebration of these Baths, at which any tendency to over-consumption can be so delightfully counteracted, have coincided with that other season of which I have spoken, and which – As a matter of fact I see many well-known members of the Lucullus Club here tonight. I think Major Hallam will support me there?'

'Yes, there are a large number of well-known people here to-night. I can see Lord Castlerosse. No. Yes. What do you think, Mervyn? Is that Lord Castlerosse?'

'It's difficult to say, Hallam, without the clothes – '

'Yes. Well, it's really an amazing sight. I really think it's one of the most astonishing sights I've seen. Don't you think so, Mervyn?'

'It's a very remarkable sight certainly, Hallam. Perhaps Major Hallam will take over now?'

'Yes. Well, if listeners will look at the sketch-map of the Baths with which they have been provided they will see that it is divided into numbered squares, these squares representing the various "rooms". We are now in the first room, or *tepidarium* (Square 2), which has a temperature of 110 degrees, and where the bather begins the gradual process as a result of which he will ultimately sweat. I should mention that the bather wears nothing but a white towel about his middle, and it is really very interesting to see the many distinguished people who are here tonight dressed in this way. Now I can see Mr Maurice Baring, the Bishop of London, Mr A P F Chapman, Mr Maxton, Mr C B Cochran, the Italian boxer Camera, and the President of Balliol, which is one of the better known Cambridge Colleges.'

'Oxford.'

'Thank you. Mr Flute has reminded me that Balliol belongs to the sister University. I must apologize to listeners. Well, placed round the *tepidarium*, but at a slightly higher level, are the various "hot" rooms, each hotter than the one before (Squares 3 to 5). These rooms have glass sides, so that from where we sit the distinguished persons in them have the appearance of very large red fishes moving slowly about in the tanks of an aquarium. I can see Sir Eric Geddes in the third hot room (Square 4). Lord Castlerosse has just entered the *tepidarium*, wearing his towel with an air.'

'That can't have been Lord Castlerosse we saw before.'

'No, Mervyn. I slipped up there. I should mention perhaps that the unaccustomed bather sometimes finds it difficult to sweat, and in the absence of sweating a heaviness of the head and danger of taking cold ensue. In this case the bather is instructed (in the Directions for Sweating) to take copious draughts of water, to pour tepid water over the head and await the free outburst of perspiration. I observe that the Bishop of London and Mr Bernard Shaw are thus engaged at this moment.

Mr Maurice Baring is an old hand and has already passed on to the next room (Square 2 to 3), sweating gracefully as we should expect. One rather interesting phenomenon to be observed from this vantage-point is this – as the bathers progress from room to room the bodies gradually change colour: here in the *tepidarium* the bodies are pale cream with a dry matt surface; after a short period in the next room they are pink, and a faint gloss begins to appear; in the third room they grow red and shiny – and so on. It is really very interesting to watch this transformation (which can only be compared to the approach of dawn or the rapid ripening of an apple). It is really an amazing sight. And now I will hand over to Mervyn Flute.'

'Well, the Lord Chief Justice has just come in. I can see Mr Priestley, who is now, as it were, swimming into the fourth room (Square 5), where the temperature is very high indeed. Mr Priestley appears to have solved the problem of perspiration. Mr Shaw, on the other hand, is still pouring tepid water over his head. A literary critic, I dare say, might find something instructive in the different reactions of these two great writers, comparing them with the easy exuberance of Mr Priestley's writings and the somewhat inhuman frigidity of Mr Shaw's. That, however, is not the business of this observer. I am Mr Mervyn Flute and I am at the Abdul Turkish Baths. Mr Maurice Baring is now rose-pink. Mr James Douglas has moved into the second room (Square 3). The Bishop of London has given up the tepid water and, on the advice of Mr Baring, has gone into the Russian Steam Bath (Square 7). This is a small compartment where the bather sits in a cloud of Russian steam; and very often this produces a free outburst of perspiration when all else has failed. Mr Shaw has followed the Bishop of London. The Lord Chief Justice is sweating well. Mr Jack Hulbert is sweating beside him (Square 2). Mr Camera is bright-red (Square 4). Lord Rothermere is sweating slightly. Maurice Baring, a very rapid bather, has finished the final stages and gone to the shampooers (Square 10).

'I have now a rather important announcement to make. I expect you have all been feeling a little anxious about Mr Bernard Shaw and the Bishop of London. As I told you before the bather who fails to perspire runs a risk of cold or even pneumonia. And I am sure you will be glad to hear that both the Bishop and Mr Shaw have now come out of the Russian Steam Bath and are sweating satisfactorily. Very possibly some of you heard the low murmur of applause which ran round the *tepidarium* when it was seen that these two valuable citizens were out of danger. I am now going to the hottest room of all (Square 5). One minute, please.

'I am now at Square 5, where the heat is very hot – about 250 degrees. On my way here I passed Mr Shaw and Mr Louis Golding discussing boxing with Mr Carnera. Mr Golding was very red indeed. Generally in the hot rooms there is absolute silence, but both Mr Shaw and Mr Golding seemed to have a good deal to say. Looking about me, I can see some very distinguished bodies recumbent on the couches – Mr Priestley, Mr Cochran, Mr Hermann Finck, Lord Birkenhead, Lord Castlerosse, the Archbishop of York, Mr Hugh Walpole, and Mr Tom Shaw. In this room there is no talking and nothing is to be heard but the panting of the various bodies. Lord Rothermere has just cautiously entered the room. Lord Rothermere has now gone out. Now Major Hallam will take you to the shampoo room (Square 10).'

'It is Ivor Hallam speaking, from the Abdul Turkish Baths (Square 10). Here the bodies are laid upon seven marble slabs and thoroughly soaped, massaged, and rinsed. Perhaps you can hear the sound of splashing water and the rhythmic movements of the shampooers as they massage the chests or slap the livers of the bathers. Mr Shaw (Bernard), Mr Hulbert, the Bishop of London, Mr Priestley, the Lord Chief Justice, Mr George Robey, and Lord Rothermere are now lying on the slabs. What you heard' then was the final slap which the shampooer (a powerful ex-sailor) administered to Lord Rothermere's liver. Mr Shaw's

(Bernard's) shampoo is nearly finished. The Lord Chief Justice looks a size or two smaller. Lord Rothermere is being hosed with a hose. After the hose the bather is led to a cold plunge-bath, the far end of which is in the *frigidarium*, where the bather lies wrapped in towels till it is time to dress. The plunge-bath is optional, and Lord Rothermere has decided to walk round. Mr Bernard Shaw is now approaching the plunge-bath. It will be very interesting to see if this well-known writer takes the plunge-bath or walks round. Mr Shaw is now standing ready for the plunge. Mr Shaw has plunged.

'I am now in the *frigidarium* (Square 1), where refreshments are served. The Lord Chief Justice is weighing himself. Lord Rothermere is enjoying a cocktail. Good night, everybody, *good* night!'

XXXII

TOMATO JUICE

(*A Song of the Sea*)

Life is a most extraordinary thing.
I sit and see the coast of Spain go by,
And watch the circling sea-birds on the wing;
The sun is o'er the yard-arm and I cry,
'Steward, it is the moment for a can –
But not of beer. Bring something soft and cheap;
For England's far, and I'm a better man;
Bring me the best tomato-juice you keep.'
And here is news to make the Devil grin –
Tomato-juice is twopence more than gin!

Ozone is in my lungs; and in my soul
Ozone is present. I would drink a toast
In some demure and unfermented bowl
To Nancy Astor and the healthy host;
For they are right: and always I will be
Unalcoholic as a heather-bell.
I will take naught but vitamins and tea,
Preserve my liver and my wealth as well.
But, oh! sobriety's as dear as sin –
Tomato-juice is twopence more than gin!

Tomato Juice

If there is anything that I desire
   It is a beaker of tomato-juice –
With Worcester sauce, a dash of it, for fire –
   Anti-scorbutic, purifying, puce.
And if these ladies – as I think they do –
   Expect refreshment of a liquid kind,
I would delight them with tomatoes too
   And put the Demon Alcohol behind;
But I have duties to my kith and kin –
Tomato-juice is twopence more than gin!

So, Steward, bring them Sweet Martinis all!
   Life is a most extraordinary thing:
False values everywhere the saints appal,
   The good men suffer and the wicked sing.
Whenever I determine to be good
   I know that some misfortune will befall.
I am a martyr, much misunderstood;
   So, Steward, mix a cocktail for us all.
But what a ship! How can the angels win?
Tomato-juice is twopence more than gin!

XXXIII

COMPLICATED SPELLING

I see with some dismay in a letter to *The Times*, signed by many great men, that I may have to lern to spel again. The great men wish for a Committee to be appointed to consider the simplification of our spelling, because it is inconsistent and 'difficult'. They are sorry for the poor British children and the poor grown-up foreigner. They do not seem to be at all sorry for me. It will be just as tiresome for me to learn the new spelling as it is for other people to learn the old one. Indeed, now that I have bought a book on the subject and warily nibbled at it, I am sure that it will be worse.

The simple-spellers are, I think, a little deceitful. They lead us up the garden path so plausibly. They complain that the student has to learn *two* English languages. (Well, for that matter, the singer has to learn two lots of notes – one written and one sung.) How absurd, they say, that 'tough', 'though', 'through', 'trough', and 'bough' should be pronounced in five different ways! Why not spell them 'phonetically'?

Well, that sounds well enuf – at first. One thinks of 'tho' and 'thru' (and one particular one dislikes even those). And 'tough', I suppose, will be 'tuff' (if one has only the old alphabet to play with), and 'cough' 'coff', and 'bough' 'bow'.

But difficulties arise at once. If we are to spell phonetically – that is, according to the sound – we must assume that everyone pronounces the same word in the same way. But they don't. Take 'tough'. Many excellent citizens in the North do not say 'tuff' as we do; they say 'tooff'. And many English-speakers in North America say 'terf'. So that a triangular correspondence, phonetically spelt, on the subject of toughness would end in the wildest confusion. As things are, these three corners of the earth can discuss toughness and rough stuff with perfect understanding. Surely it is the great merit of our spelling that people all over the world can attach the same meaning to a written word though they utter it quite differently? Different musicians, coming upon a high C in a song, will sing it differently – some true, some sharp, some flat. But they all mean the same thing. Now, there are many composers who cannot sing correctly. But if they all wrote a different sort of C, exactly as they would sing it, what chaos would cover the world of music! And what, by the way, a beautiful analogy!

We say 'water'. The North-American says 'wotter' – or something like it. Simplified or phonetic spelling, it is suggested, might make the English tongue an international tongue. On the contrary, it would produce the conditions of Babel even in the English-speaking world.

The answer of the reformers is that by degrees, by the dictionary, and by the BBC we shall teach everyone to pronounce everything in the same way. Which appears to me to be a conception as improbable as it is deplorable.

I do not even agree that 'ruff stuff' will be easier to learn. For all the foreigner knows, that may mean the stuff of a ruff, and we shall have to put horrible little dots and things to distinguish between the ruff you are and the ruff you wear.

And how should we distinguish between the bow of a tree and the bow of a gentleman?

Further, it is not true that we say 'rough' precisely as we say 'ruff'. Get a good actor to say 'a rough ruff'– say it yourself, brother – and you will agree. 'Cough' does not truly rhyme with 'toff', nor 'would' with 'wood'– though in an operetta or revue we may pretend that it does.

Say seven times –

'I would not saunter through that wood.'

Now say –

'His wood is better than my wood.'

The second words in these sentences are *not* pronounced in the same way; and therefore it is a good thing that they should not be spelt the same. Even the much abused 'ough' can be not merely defended but applauded by those at least who value the subtleties of sound and language and object to an excess of planning and simplification.

But the simple spellers are not so simple as they seem. We have assumed so far that they will retain the same alphabet with which our feeble and foolish race has survived so many centuries and combated so many perils; and some of them, those, for example, who want a Committee, proclaim that this is their intention. But others, evidently, have perceived the difficulties discussed above. For, according to the published book which I have bought, our spelling can be only simplified by making it much more complicated – that is, by adding to the alphabet numerous new signs and symbols most of which look like bacilli, and to these eyes at least are loathsome.

The author of the book before me is modest and proposes only to add 'nine or ten letters' to the ABC of everyday use; and most of these are made by putting lines through old letters or decorating them with dots or squiggles – as *d* ('dhee'), *ơ* or *ö* ('ur̊'), *b* ('thee') and *z* ('zhay'). But even he has one repulsive thing which looks exactly like the beginnings of diphtheria or tuberculosis and is called a 'surd vowel symbol'—9̄o. Ugh!

It is solemnly proposed, I gather, that for the benefit of the foreigners and the establishment of a World Tongue not only our time-tables but our treasures of literature are to be 'translated into the new spelling'. And the works of Shakespeare will look like the bottom of a pond in spring-time or a small piece of old cheese under the microscope. I hate to be obstructive, but here is the opening passage of the Prelude, to Milton's *Paradise Lost,* done in the Lepsius alphabet, whatever that may be:

Here is the same passage in 'Mr Immo Allen's phonetic spelling'. It is less rich in bacteria, but alarms me almost as much:

"Ǫ̆v mạn'z fọ̄rst dĭsọ̄bīdyĕ̱ns ạnd δĭ frūt
Ǫ̆v δạt fọ̄rbĭddĕ̱n trī, hūz mọ̄rtăl tẹ̄st
Brọ̄t deϑ ĭntŭ δĭ wọ̄rld ạnd ọ̄l auọ̄r wọ̄
Wiδ lọ̄s ọ̆v Īdn, til wọn grẹ̄tọr Mạn
Rẹ̆stọ̄r ọ̆s, ạnd rĭgein δĭ blĭsfūl sīt:
Siṅ, hĕ̱vnlĭ Myūz, dạt ŏn δĭ sīkrẹ̆t tŏp
Ǫ̆v Ō̱reb ọ̄r ọ̆v Sainai dĭdst inspaiọ̄r
Δạt šĕpọ̄rd hu fọ̄rst tọ̄t δĭ čọ̄zn sīd
Ĭn δĭ bĭgĭnnĭṅ hau δi hĕ̱vns ạnd ọ̄rϑ
Rọ̄z aut ọ̆v kẹ̄ōs;..."

And here it is in the crude old-fashioned spelling of the author's lifetime (the edition of 1667):

"OV Manz fæ.st diswbi.di'ns d y fru.t
V yat f'bidn tri. 'u.z mo.tl te.st
Bro.t Deh intu y uæ.ld d o.l au' uw
Uiy lo.s v I.dn , til uæn gre.t' Man
Risto'r 's d ri.ge.n y blisf'l si.t—
Siq 'Ev'nli Miu.z , yt on y si.krit top
V O'reb o'r v Saineai didst inspai'
Yat cep'd 'u fæ.st to.t y tcwzn si.d
In y biginiq 'au y 'Evnz d Æ.h
Rwz aut v Ke.os:"

Of Mans First Disobedience, and the Fruit
Of that Forbidden Tree, whose mortal tast
Brought Death into the World, and all our woe,
With loss of *Eden*, till one greater Man
Restore us, and regain the blissful Seat,
Sing Heav'nly Muse, that on the secret top
Of *Oreb*, or of *Sinai*, didst inspire
That Shepherd, who first taught the chosen Seed,
In the Beginning how the Heav'ns and Earth
Rose out of *Chaos*;

It may be that I speak ignorantly of this great reform, and a committee of inquiry might usefully instruct us all. Meanwhile, rather than relieve the foreigner and the British child in the manner suggested, I shall cheerfully continue to see them suffer.

The foreigner indeed! At least we do not compel him to learn the sex of a table or distinguish the sexes of a garden and a pen.

XXXIV

PAINTING THE BOAT

We are painting the boat. We are happy. We do not care if it snows. This is fortunate, for it feels like snow.

A criminal north-easter hisses along the foreshore and bites through my back. I am standing deep in mud and my sea-boots leak. My feet are falling off. It is the Spring. It is going to snow. The tide is crowding in and soon I shall have to clamber aboard. No matter. For then I shall have an excuse to thaw the frame before the stove. And if it snows I shall have an excuse to paint something in the cabin. We swore that this year we would paint only parts of her exterior, for the sake of respectability and to comfort all those good watermen on the tideway who remark politely that she could do with a coat of paint. For she is crumbling, the poor old boat, and this must be her last year of active life. Nevertheless, once one begins painting a boat it is tempting to continue, it is difficult to stop, it is *impossible* to stop. And so I do not care if it snows.

Meanwhile here I am defying the Spring and slowly covering her long port flank with good white paint. It is a pitiful task, for at this close range, necessarily confronting every inch of the old lady, I can no longer ignore her imperfections, her horrid wounds. A longshoreman, passing behind me, says, not so politely as I should wish, 'Take care you don't put the brush through her'. 'Too right', as the girls of Melbourne used to say.

'Too painfully right'. When I scrubbed this same port flank, making ready for the painting, I had to stay my strong hand here and there because great flakes of rotting timber were falling from her aged side, great cavities and craters were appearing, and I was afraid that suddenly I might find myself peeping through into the ladies'cabin. And now, true enough, I feel that if I paint too fiercely the brush may penetrate into the larder or the lavatory through this tender spot. But I will be gentle, I will thrust putty into the wound and splash paint over the putty and hope for the best. Where is the putty? As I expected, the putty has fallen off the bucket into the mud. Never mind – I am painting the boat. Let it hail.

Even her wounds, her tender spots, her large areas of flaking and crumbling and of simple non-existence seem noble and inspiring as I plug them with putty and try to comfort them with paint. For I can remember nearly all their histories. This nasty little place now, that was Gravesend, Easter Monday, last year, when that incapable youth in a motor-boat brutally rammed her in mid-belly, putting me aboard. And very nearly sank her, the silly adolescent, a few yards only from the pilots' pier. What agony, what rage, what a terrible dent in her side – and yet how polite we all were! But we brought her home from Gravesend through a hostile wind and had her side straightened and patched; and here she is, still afloat, with this honourable wound-stripe through which the rain trickles slowly into the port lady's bunk. Never mind. A little putty and a lot of paint. It is her last year of life.

And here is the crack she had one summer night from a moored lighter in the Chelsea Reach. Still nearer to sinking then. But that, I confess, was my own fault, for I was exchanging unintelligible abuse with the pilot of a collier, and in the thrill of altercation neglected my navigation. Never mind. Now, when we pass, the pilot and I wave hands and blow kisses. Let us paint the poor wound; it will never be painted again.

And here is the place where she was biffed in the blackness of the tunnel at Blisworth, on the Grand Union Canal, travelling to Birmingham. It was 7 a.m., many years ago, and I had hay-fever badly; and while I sneezed she met something. Ah, those were days! Never mind. There is white paint in my eyes and white paint in my hair; but her port flank, shattered or sound, is white and glorious again. Here comes the hail.

Outside it is still hailing, or maybe worse, for it is pitch dark within the vessel. But at least it is warm; and all the family are huddled together, like Noah's brood, each with a paint-brush itching in his hand. It has hailed too long, for – I knew it would happen – we have begun painting the interior. I said we would NOT paint anything inside; everything was smart enough inside; she was doomed; it was a waste of paint and trouble and – But everything is being painted now. It began simply enough with my upsetting a pot of blue paint on the floor; I naturally painted the cupboard blue. It was then clear that the shelves would have to be done as well, for they looked dingy above the brilliant cupboard. The family started on the shelves; and, since it was still hailing, I did the table and a chair. The family retaliated with the bedposts and the coal-box. Everything is blue now. It is impossible to stir without touching blue paint. One breathes blue. But I slipped away to what we call the engine-room and painted the fly-wheel of the engine green. And this, I think, is the most beautiful spectacle of all.

It has stopped hailing. The Arctic blast has abated. I creep out, feeling a little guilty about the cupboard and the fly-wheel, to admire the pure white port flank of the boat in the treacherous and anaemic sunshine of the Spring. Alas! while our backs were turned, small boys have passed along the foreshore and carelessly flung stones into the mud, so that the pure white flank is speckled with horrid mud. Never mind. That can be removed. We are painting the boat. And now there is all the finicky, top-of-the-table work to be done, the little squiggly bits, where green trespasses into white, and blue drips horribly on to green. What anxiety, what toil and care! But how important! What do the Budget and the Polish Corridor matter? We are painting the boat.

For six days we have been painting the boat; and every day some new and unsuspected area appears, insistently demanding paint. We have not the heart to refuse, for this is the last time. She does not keep the rain out now; she will hardly keep the river out through another winter. She is doomed. And so we cannot say, 'That can wait till next year'. It is now or never. Nor will we say, 'She is not worth it'. She is worth anything. For she was born in that great grim year 1914, and has seen many adventures and travelled to Birmingham of the one part and Gravesend of the other part. She shall have all the paint she asks, though we know it to be but a funeral garment. There is paint in my ears and in my hair. I have a fear that one morning I shall wake and find that the family have painted the anchor. Last night I dreamed that I had painted the carburettor. I smell of turpentine. There is paint in the bathroom and paint on the drawing-room chairs; and all the family have chilblains. Never mind. We have painted the boat.

XXXV

UTOPIA

In Utopia, Perfect Place,
  Everything's exactly right;
No one's virtuous or base,
  There is neither Day nor Night.
But where everything is right
Nothing's left for which to fight –
It's beautiful, we own, but boring.
No one's wept for quite a while.
What is more, we do not smile;
We could have no cause for chaff;
For the things at which you laugh
Are the things that other people are deploring.
So in less enlightened lands the happy populations grins
At the elderly pedestrians who tumble on their chins:
But that couldn't happen here, for we have no banana-skins.
It's beautiful – but boring.

We have neither rich nor poor,
  Neither tempest, cold nor rain;
At an even temperature
  Every season we remain.
Most of us by now forget
How it felt to have a sweat:

It's beautiful, we own, but boring.
We have lost the pleasant itch
To be even with the rich;
Free of passions, free of crimes,
Life is rather like *The Times*.
We've eliminated Sex and Sin and Snoring;
And when anybody dies – it seldom happens, I may say –
We increase the population in a cleanly simple way
By putting capsules in a cylinder and pressing Button A –

It's beautiful – but boring.

Nothing happens that is new,
Nothing happens that is wrong;
So we've nothing left to do
And the days are rather long.
Nothing happens that is bad,
So no scandal's to be had;
It's beautiful, we own, but boring.
Flesh is wholly in control,
One is just a lump of soul,
In an Art-and-Craft chemise,
Playing harps in minor keys,
And no avenue remains that's worth exploring.
Since we've sublimated Love, it doesn't matter what we wear;
And no bishop here complains that girls are dangerously bare;
They could go about with nothing on and nobody would care –
It's beautiful – but boring.

XXXVI

'TRAINS, DRUNKENNESS IN...'

I should like to translate the first few thousand pages of the Licensing Commission's Report into French, gather together a few hundred Frenchmen, have the Report read to them, and watch their faces. How they would laugh! It would be the final proof that the English are insane.

One does not expect poetry from a Royal Commission on Licensing, and I doubt if the Rev. Henry Carter has even heard of 'beaded bubbles winking at the brim'. For these earnest philanthropists there is neither beaded bubble nor golden wine: there are only 'alcohol'and 'intoxicants'. When the Report is read to the French it will be fun to substitute for these alarming (and question-begging) words the names of some specific beverages, thus:

> '*Liebfraumilch* 1921 is freely described as a "stimulant."
>
> In point of fact...its action is almost entirely narcotic... *Veuve Clicquot* when taken into the stomach is absorbed into the blood stream. Its immediate action is on the central nervous system: and the degree of strength of this action is dependent on the level of maximum concentration of *Veuve Clicquot* in the blood... *Vin ordinaire* selects first the delicate nerve centres of the brain, retarding and sometimes paralysing the action of the higher inhibitory

controls... *Lager beer* is thus definitely a drug, in that its effect is to modify, for the time being, the action of parts of the mechanism of the body... Like any drug, moreover, *Crême de Menthe* becomes poisonous when used in such excessive quantities,'etc., etc.

Can you not see the eyes of the Frenchmen goggling?

But if the Frenchman examines the book at all seriously, as that serious (though 'alcoholic') nation is quite likely to do, they will soon cease to laugh. For they will conclude that Great Britain is in a really bad way, a far worse way than even perfidious Albion deserves. Suppose that they glance through the Index and come suddenly upon these adjacent and horrifying items:

Methylated spirits, drinking of, para. 787.
Trains, drunkenness in, para. 802.

'*Mon Dieu!*' I hear the Frenchman say. 'The English they drink methylated spirits and get drunk in trains!' Visions of our statesmen and ambassadors swilling methylated spirits and paraffin will pleasingly explain our queer foreign policy; but

'Trains, drunkenness in,'

is more startling. For there are still a few bold Frenchmen who travel to this lunatic land. With trembling hands the Frenchman turns the pages to find out what the English do when they get drunk in trains. And what does he find? The first thing he finds is that the English do *not* get drunk in trains at all. Nothing about orgies in the guard's van, or debauches in the corridor – only this:

799. We have received no complaint from any quarter that the service of drinks outside the restaurant car has led to abuses of any kind...

802. ...as we have indicated, we do not believe that the service of intoxicants in railway-trains involves risk of excess...

No suggestion is made that any Briton has ever got drunk on a train with alcohol supplied from the restaurant-car; indeed, the Report goes out of its way to record the suggestion that 'such drunkenness as may be observable from time to time in railway trains is almost always to be attributed' (*Mon Dieu!* what charming language!) 'to the effects of liquor which has been consumed by passengers before entering the train...'

And yet there is a page and a bit devoted to the frightful illegality, anomaly, privilege or what-not, by which the lawless Briton can get a lager beer in the restaurant-car outside 'permitted hours', and can even get one (if the bell is answered) in his own compartment, though strictly (para. 798) 'the excise licence does not cover sales outside the restaurant-car'.

And in spite of the assurances in paras. 799 and 802 that all is absolutely well the Commission think it necessary to recommend *new restrictions* – 'certain definite hours should be generally prescribed for the sale of intoxicants in passenger-trains', and excise licences should be issued to cover the compartments as well as the restaurant-cars.

O Bedlam! A small thing, you think, my friends. So it is. It is as a straw in the hair, and it shows which way the mind of our governors blows. This 'Trains, drunkenness in...' page is the most illuminating in the whole Report. The only point of regulations and restrictions is (or was) to prevent abuses. But some of our rulers have got themselves into such a state of mind that they must have regulations, even when they themselves can discover no abuses. They can leave nothing alone. If they see us doing anything in our own way at our own time, without reference to any Statute or Order in Council, they perceive a vacuum, and, like Nature, abhor it.

Another significant straw in the hair is the last and thirty-ninth chapter. Here are four pages dealing with the vital social problem of 'Billiard Licences'. Billiards, as we all know, is an obscene game, and by an Act of 1845 may only be played in a public place with a justices' licence, within stated hours, and not at all on Sundays or Christmas Day. And on Sundays, in the case of a fully licensed public-house, the billiard-room must be kept closed.

The law of billiards is immensely complicated, and many publicans have given up their billiard tables because it drove them mad – also, as even the Commission discovered, because on Sundays they could not afford to lose the use of their largest room.

So here the Report makes one of its rare concessions and recommends that 'it should be made lawful to keep open the billiard-room in licensed premises on Sundays and Christmas Days, *provided* (my italics) *that the billiard table is kept covered up throughout the day'!*

'Formidable! Incroyable!' cries the bewildered Frenchman. Surely in the year 1931 you would expect a number of responsible Commissioners to say, 'What in the world is all this bilge about billiards? What is this drivelling Act of 1845? Sweep it away! Billiards is no more an act of indecency or danger than golf or lawn-tennis, and should be lawful at any time.' Not a bit of it.

What the Commissioners do say is this: *'It seems to be generally admitted'* (by whom?) *'that the hours allowed by the Statute for the playing of billiards are too long; and it is clearly desirable that the law in this respect should be amended...'*

Well, billiards bores me as much as beer bores the Rev. Henry Carter, so I have no prejudice in the matter: but it is another of the frightening little corners in this Report which every citizen should study, together with 'Trains, drunkenness in...', and 'Snugs and partitions, elimination of, para. 207' (why in the name of Carter should snugs and partitions be 'objectionable features'?): and the burning question of pianos ('while the provision of a piano for impromptu performances by customers has been held not to carry with it the necessity for a music licence, the position is different when the performance is given by the licensee or his wife...'!): and dancing ('we wish to record also that we recognize a certain danger in the service of intoxicants in rooms in which dancing is actually going on'). *What* danger, O men with loathsome thoughts? Have you ever been to the Savoy, or Berkeley, Hotel, and, if so, what hideous peril did you see?

These small, foul sentences, even more than the major proposals, betray the minds of our Commissioners, and they alarm me.

Mind you, this Report might be worse than it is. In their patronizing, pedagogic manner the Majority do make a few minute concessions to liberty. And some of their remarks on improving the public-houses are admirable, though even there they have failed completely to touch the root of the matter, the licensing system and the licensing justices.

But, in general, the Report is based on the assumption that the Briton is a wild beast and the beer-drinker a sort of criminal on ticket-of-leave.

Therefore it is wrong, I think, to dismiss this Report as a passing jest. We poor, ordinary citizens must realize that above us there is this remote and monstrous race, who see nothing in a glass of wine but 'alcohol' and cirrhosis of the liver, and wish to see all 'licensed premises' in London closed at 10 p.m. They are of the same breed as the licensing justices who, from the Bench, make the following pronouncements:

'Although not illegal, the Bench are determined to set their face against dart-playing on Sundays.'

> 'Music combined with the sale of intoxicating liquor is an abomination.'

'We must lay down a hard and fast rule that if houses make use of music in any form it is presumably to attract custom; and that would be one factor in the consideration of redundancy.'

In other words, if a pub seeks to 'improve' itself and provide something more than 'alcohol', it may lose its licence.

Mon Dieu!

XXXVII

MR MAFFERTY TELLS A SEA-STORY

'I'm wonderin',' said Mr Mafferty, 'I'm wonderin' what's become of me old friend Admiral Fallow, because it's twelve years to a day he was insulted on the high seas by a common fireman in a quare unnatural kind of a way, an' he an Admiral itself an' not able to answer back.

'When I was fightin' for your quare country,' continued Mr Mafferty, 'in the Shetland Islands an' them parts, I was Colonel of a small kind of an armoured yacht that did be huntin' for submarines when we weren't chasin' the sailors out of the places of refreshment. One night the Admiral comes aboard, an' he a retired officer of eighty, or maybe more, an' he says, "Mafferty, let you be gettin' up steam, there's a submarine lurkin' in the neighbourin' waters", an' he in a grand state of emotion. So I fired a gun the way the crew would be hearin' it in the nine places of refreshment ashore. And when I heard a gintleman undertakin' to cut out another gintleman's lights and liver on the quay I says to the Admiral, "All aboard, Sir," because I knew that would be Fireman Flood, an' he the last aboard always. So we steamed out into the black night, the Admiral an' meself on the bridge an' peerin'this way an' that for the dirty submarine. An' presently I heard a voice come up from the stokehold, through the ventilator, you understand, which was just behind us, an' it singin' "Nearer, my God, to Thee". So I said to meself, "An' what for would Fireman Flood be conciliatin' the

Admiral?" because the Admiral was one of them hymn-singin' sailors; but I'd never heard annythin' of that kind against the Fireman before. "Do you hear that, Mafferty?" says the Admiral, as pleased as Punch. "I do, Admiral," says I, an' "It's quare an' gratifyin' ", says he.

'Well, it was a still quiet kind of a night and presently I heard the same voice talkin' to itself below, an' it as clear as it might be me own voice talkin' to you at the present time, an' it says, "Good-mornin', Admiral Beatty. – Good-mornin', Admiral Jellicoe. – How are you, Beatty? – I'm fine, thank you, Jellicoe, an' how's yourself? – I mustn't grumble, Beatty; but look here, Beatty, I've got a small kind of a job for you. – Pleasure, I'm sure, Jellicoe. What is it? – Well, I want you to go up to the Shetland Islands, Beatty, an' you'll find up there a stinkin', blinkin', gollopin' son of a cross-eyed parson called Admiral Fallow. An' *all* I want you to do, Beatty, is to cut out his perishin' lights an' liver. – Oh, how's that, Jellicoe? – Well, Beatty, he's the kind of an unpronounceable interferin' fishwife that drags poor sailors out of the pubs an' sends them to sea on a dark night, an' that's the way of it, Beatty. So what I want you to do, Beatty, is to go up to the Shetlands, Beatty, an' cut out his perishin' lights an' liver, see? – Oh, well, if *you* say so, Jellicoe, I'll do it at once. – Good-mornin', Admiral Beatty. – Good-*mornin'*, Admiral Jellicoe."

'Well, the Admiral comes across to me an' he says, "Did you hear that, Mafferty?" an' "Never a word," says I; and there's maybe five minutes' quiet. Then the furnace-door bangs an' the voice comes up again, quare an' cheerful in tone, an' it says, "*Good*-mornin', Admiral Jellicoe. – *Good*-mornin', Admiral Beatty. – How's your family, Jellicoe? – Satisfactory, thank you, Beatty. Have a beer? – Well, I don't mind if I do, Jellicoe. What's yours? – Mine's a bitter, Beatty. But look here, Beatty, how about that little job? – What's that, Jellicoe? – Well, didn't I tell you to go up to the Shetland Islands and find an old bollard called Admiral Fallow? – I believe you did, Jellicoe. Must have slipped my memory. – Slipped your memory, did it, Beatty? That won't do. – Have another, Jellicoe? – Well, perhaps I will, but you can't get out of it that way, Beatty. You do as I tell you, there's a good lad. All you've got to do is to go up to the Shetland Islands and you'll find there a perishin' old freezer called Admiral Fallow, d'you see, Beatty? An' I want you to cut out his lights an' liver for me. – All right, Jellicoe, if you make a point of it, I will. – Well, good-mornin', Admiral Beatty. – *Good*-mornin', Admiral Jellicoe." An' every time the Fireman comes to the lights an' liver you'd hear him open the furnace-door and let fly his shovel as if the Admiral himself was on it.

'Well, the old man comes across to me again, shakin' like an aspen on the hills of Kilbog, and he says, "Did you hear *that*, Mafferty?" "I wouldn't tell you a lie," says I; "it could be that I might be catchin' a word or two here and there." "Well, what will I be doin'?" says he. "I wouldn't be noticin' it at all," says I; "the gintleman below don't know that he's to be heard above, an' it's beneath the dignity of a fine officer like yourself to be overhearin' the private talk of a fireman, so it is, an' you commandin' the great fleets in your time. But it's meself that will be sayin' a word in season to the Chief Engineer, the way the gintleman will be keepin' his soliloquies to himself from this day to the world's end."

'So I says a word to the Chief Engineer, an' he goes below an' he whispers to the Fireman, "Will you keep your perishin' mouth shut?" An' the Fireman says, "I never opened my mouth, Sir, except to sing a hymn; but I won't sing no more if you say so, Sir."

'Well, then there was quiet for maybe ten minutes, an' the Admiral came back near the ventilator again as calm as you'd wish. But presently it was "*Good*-mornin', Admiral Jellicoe. – Good *mornin'*, Admiral Beatty. – How are you, Jellicoe? – My cough's bad, Beatty. – Oh, I'm sorry to hear that, Jellicoe. Hot, isn't it? – It's perishin' hot, Beatty. And talkin' of that, Beatty, how about that old freezer in the Shetland Islands? – Which one, Jellicoe? – The one that drags poor sailors out of the pubs an' sends them to sea on a dark night. – Oh, you mean Admiral Fallow, Jellicoe? – That's who I mean, Beatty. – Well, don't you worry, Jellicoe, I've done what you said. – What, you've cut out his perishin' lights an' liver, have you? – Yes, Jellicoe, I've cut his perishin' lights an' liver out. – Well, I'm glad about that, Beatty. – Yes, I thought you'd be pleased, Jellicoe. – So you went up to the Shetland Islands an' cut out his perishin' lights an' liver, did you? – Yes, Jellicoe, that's what I did. I went up to the Shetland Islands an' I found the old rumbletummy, an' I said, 'Good-mornin', Admiral Fallow.' 'Good-mornin', Admiral Beatty,' he said. An' I said, 'I've got a message for you from Admiral Jellicoe.' 'What's that, Admiral Beatty?' he said. 'Well, he says he wants me to cut out your perishin' lights an' liver.' 'How's that, Beatty?' he said. 'Well, the fact is, Admiral Fallow,' I said, 'Jellicoe says that *you're* the old freezer who drags poor sailors out of the pubs on a dark night an' sends them to sea. So now I'm goin' to cut out your perishin' lights and liver, you see.'– An' what happened then, Beatty? – Well, then I cut out his perishin' lights an' liver, Jellicoe. – Oh, you cut out his perishin' lights and liver, did you? That's a good job, Beatty. – Yes, I knew that's what you wanted, Jellicoe. An' then I said, 'Good-mornin', Admiral Fallow.' 'Good-*mornin'*, Admiral Beatty,' he said. – Well, I'm pleased about that, Beatty. Have a beer? – No, I don't want a beer, thank you all the same, Jellicoe. – You're welcome, Beatty. An' now you've cut out that old freezer's lights and liver, I think you ought to have a beer. – Oh, well, Jellicoe, if you insist–" – "I'd rather you had a beer, Beatty, because I want to hear how you cut out – "

'Well, so it went on,' said Mr Mafferty, 'like the Shannon river, for ever an' ever, an' all the time the old man was pacin' an' pacin' up an' down the bridge the way you'd think he was a caged lion, an' meself gazin' into the black night pretendin' I was a deaf man. An' at last he exploded in a grand passion, an' he says, "If this doesn't stop, Mafferty," he says, "you'll lose your ship." So I put my head into the great ventilator-shaft, an' I was just framin' a quare kind of a caressin' message on my lips to Fireman Flood, when the torpedo struck us.'

'What happened then, Mr Mafferty?' I said.

'We was all drowned. Ivery one of us,' he said.

XXXVIII

GORING AND GOBBLE

I am so bored with Gobble and with Goring,
   And all the vetotalitarian *corps*:
It's hard to say if Gobble is more boring
   Or whether Goring is the bigger bore.
I only know that Goring's always roaring
   And shouting seems to be what Gobble's for:
I know the name of Goring sets me snoring,
   And Gobble makes me want to go to war.
I have no doubt that Gobble will ultimately wobble
   And be returned, alive or dead, to store;
I even hope that Goring may become so very boring
   That someone has to show the man the door.
But then – where are we then? – there are swarms of silly
      men,
   And Himmelbaum and Slump will take the floor,
And Himmelbaum will thump all the drums in aid of
      Slump
   And Slump may be an even *bigger* bore.
It's sad to think that Science, nobly slaving,
   Has made it much more easy than before
To ascertain how every one's behaving
   And disseminate the news from shore to shore,
And the one result (except for cricket scoring)
   Is that any ass can propagate a roar,

Goring and Gobble

That Gobble can be cosmically boring
   And we can't escape from Goring any more.
I think it's time the Press began ignoring
   The kind of information I deplore.
Well, does it matter what was said by Goring
   Or what uniform it was that Gobble wore?
But, all the same, each morning finds me poring
   O'er the news concerning one or other bore,
And the avenue which I am now exploring
   Is familiar, I dare say, to many more.

XXXIX

BREAD

Wheat, I see, is giving trouble. But wheat is always giving trouble. Either the people are not getting enough wheat or the wheat-grower is not getting enough for his wheat. Sometimes both. Good statesmen are always worrying about wheat. And at the back of their minds there is always, I believe, a gigantic error – the belief that *bread is a good thing, and that above all things the people need bread.*

The people do not need bread.

I am not going to say (as Dr Hay does) that bread is wholly redundant; but to say, as my encyclopaedia says, that 'bread is the chief food of civilized peoples', is to say that which is clearly wrong.

Every class is agreed about this, though I am the first person who has the courage to express the truth. Begin at the nursery. The pampered child of the rich does not want bread; he wants jam and cake. And when he is ordered to eat two slices of bread before passing to cake he does so with reluctance – and rightly.

Nor does the child of the poor want bread. Invite some slum-child into your house, offer him a nice hunk of bread, and see what he says.

Nor does the indigent adult want bread. He wants fried fish and sausages and a steak and vegetables and beer. Offer the next poor tramp who calls at your door a nice half-loaf and see what *he* says. No doubt, if he is really starving and you have nothing more to offer, he will wolf the bread. But in those circumstances he would wolf Brazil-nuts and potato-skins. We should not on that account say that Brazil-nuts or potato-skins were the chief food of civilized peoples. It is an obvious blunder to assess the value of a foodstuff to the civilized world by reference to the willingness of a starving man to eat it. We must assume that in the civilized world the great majority of the people are not starving, which happily is still the case.

For a fair test go to any public eating-place and see the proportionate part that bread plays in any given meal. It is amazingly small. Bread, you will find, is the only food left behind on the tables and plates (except some little heaps of mustard and salt). Indeed, I should describe bread not as 'the staple food' of Man but as the Principle Condiment of Man. It is an effective adjunct to almost every food. It is (in the form of toast) the perfect platform for an egg, a mushroom or a kidney. It is excellent (crumbled) as the decent covering of a sole or as companion to a grouse. For such purposes as the mopping-up of delicious gravy its value is undeniable. It is a useful ingredient in a sauce or a fishcake. It serves as the machinery of a sandwich or the basis of a primitive poultice. But a platform, an ingredient, a gravy-mop, a poultice – how can such an article be described as our chief food?

Note at the end of your next picnic what food it is you throw away or give to the birds. The bread. You do not throw the cold tongue and ham, the potato-salad or galantine to the birds. You pack them up carefully and take them home.

Cast your bread upon the waters and after many days it will return to you. Nobody wants it. But cast a case of kippers or a barrel of beer on the waters and see how soon they return to you.

What is the traditional thing that (besides the shilling) the angry father cuts off his erring child with when he turns her out of the home? A crust of bread – the most contemptuous form of nourishment that he can think of.

Bread, in short, has no independent existence of its own. By itself it is just the dullest thing you can eat. You cannot persuade the rich to eat it at all unless it is done up or disguised in some fancy fashion as French rolls, or toast, or bread-crumbs, or soup-billets, or prepared in some patent way that is alleged to do them good. And the poor won't eat it if they can get anything better.

In a world, then, the main purpose of which is to raise the standard life of the poor to the level of the rich it is absurd to go on saying that bread is the really important food. And any one who is still surprised about the wheat-trouble is merely showing his ignorance of modern tendencies.[1]

There was once a similar tradition about land. Certain political parties existed for decades on the assertion that the Land belonged to the People, that the People wanted the Land, and the Land ought to be given to them. I have often challenged persons holding this creed to go into the Bethnal Green Road and offer the first twenty citizens they saw nice pieces of land to look after and live on. It has never been done. The last thing the People want is Land. They want cinemas and greyhound-racing, naps in the morning and winners in the evening. There are few places in which there is so much land as Australia, but more than half the population are huddled together in a few towns at the seaside where the cinemas are.

In the case of bread the cause of all this loose thinking is the longevity and power of words. Things change, but expressions remain – old phrases about 'our daily bread', 'the bread-winner',

1. Today (three years later) I am supported, I see, by the League of Nations: 'In Europe especially, partly because of the increased availability of protective foods, the consumption of cereals has tended to diminish, except under conditions of heavy manual labour or because of limitations in income' (*Interim Report of the Mixed Committee on the Problem of Nutrition, 1936*).

and so on. They date from times and stages of civilization when bread was really important because most people could get very little else. I have no doubt that among certain remote and backward tribes bread is still 'the staple food'. I gather that it is in Russia. But in the civilized world bread is only one of many foods equally important. A man who won nothing but bread for his family today would be locked up for neglecting them. We ought, in short, to speak of the eggs-and-bacon-tea-milk-and-sugar-sausage-and-mash-kipper-meat-and-two-veg.-fish-and-chip-beer-butter-and-bread-winner. That shows bread in its right proportion and at once illuminates the whole wheat problem. The people have grown out of bread, but the poor farmer away out in the Middle West has not yet discovered it. The only solution, therefore, if we want to keep the wheat-farmer going, is to force the people to eat more bread. Among ourselves we can do a certain amount in a voluntary way. If every householder bought an extra half-loaf every day and gave it to the birds it might ease the wheat-problem. Probably there would be a sad outbreak of mortality among the birds if they ate all the bread, but I have noticed that even the birds soon tire of this food (yes, even swans); so perhaps they would survive. But then, the doctors and nutrition experts inform us now that we eat too much bread. It is *not* a good thing. The staff of life is dangerous. Read this:

> 'It is not the staff of life, and in its refined form it is verily the staff of death, for its use in this form, white, denatured, emasculated thoroughly, is one of the surest and the quickest roads to acidosis, the fatal alkalin deficiency that is the great cause of disease.
>
> 'Whole grain can be used, even to some advantage, by the labourer, if taken in such combinations as will allow it to digest without the usual fermentation, but it is *never necessary* even to the labourer, and to the desk worker it is

a continual and immediate source of danger.' (*Health via Food,* Dr W H Hay.)

So, you see, I am right. It is all very difficult.

XL

BRITISH MOTHER'S BIG FLIGHT

(From *Streamline*)

SCENE: *A studio at Broadcasting House. Curtains. A microphone. A switch somewhere, and a red lamp.*

An ANNOUNCER, *almost excited, enters and presses a switch. Red light. He goes to the microphone.*

ANNOUNCER: This is British National. Tonight we have rather a special surprise for you. Miss Gladys Potts is going to tell you about her magnificent flight. I'm not going to say any more – I'll just introduce you to Gladys – Great Britain's Best Ambassadress!

[*Enter* GLADYS. *She carries a baby. She has just landed and is in flying kit. She is very shy, staccato, and incoherent. When in doubt she always refers to her beloved engine. But perhaps she is not quite so stupid as she seems, for gradually we become aware of the make of her engine, her fuel, oil, and other important matters.*]

GLADYS: Ladies and Gentlemen, I don't know what to say. The engine was wonderful. Of course it is wonderful to be the first mother to fly to the North Pole with her baby. But I never thought people would make such a fuss of me. I'm sure any of you mothers would have done the same. And I hope before long every British mother will be able to fly to the North Pole with her baby. The engine was wonderful. I hope none of you think I did it for the publicity. I just couldn't believe my eyes when I saw my name in the papers – and everything. I dunno – I just had to do it. I felt I had to strike a blow for British motherhood – and the British carburettor – and everything. The engine was wonderful. Lord Merridew's been ever so kind. Baby was fine. Of course I used MERRIOL lubricating oil. (*The* ANNOUNCER *appears and puts his finger to his lips, shaking his head warningly. No advertisement is allowed.*) Now perhaps you'd like to hear what it felt like to be over the North Pole – just a British mother alone with her baby. Of course we couldn't *see* the North Pole. We were flying blind – clouds and everything. But somehow I just knew we were there. And – I dunno – I got a sort of lump in my throat, thinking of mother, and England, and everything, and I held baby over the side, and I said, 'There, Tiddles, you'll be able to tell your children you were the first baby to be sick over the Arctic Circle'. (*rapidly*) Then I shut off my 365-horse-power-Merry Watson-engine (*the* ANNOUNCER *appears, frowning, but he is too late, and she makes a face at him*) and sent up a little prayer for the Old Country. After that we came back. I shall never forget the first sight of home. We flew over the white cliffs of Kent, and there was Mr Noel Coward jotting down a new play. The engine was wonderful. (*modest*) I dunno, I hope perhaps my flight may lead to a regular mail-service to the Pole. There's nothing up there – no aerodromes – nothing. I mean, if Great Britain doesn't do something other countries will step in – though, of course, none of them have got a carburettor like my patent Merridew self-fertilizing carbu – (ANNOUNCER *appears, looking real daggers now, and she stops*). Well, about my plans. Baby and I have had a lot of offers. Of course, I'd much rather stay quietly at home with hubby and mother – but I've got to think of baby's future. I dare say I shall write for the papers. I want to do my bit in making British mothers air-minded. I dare say next year I shall do another flight. I don't think any mother has flown to Australia upside-down yet – and Lord Merridew thinks that's a record Great Britain ought to have. Anyhow (*louder, rapid, and defiant*) you can take it I shall go on using BRITISH MERRY SUPER FUEL, MERRIOL LUBRICATING OIL, THE MERRIDEW carburettor, and the MERRY MERRY Mother's Biplane – price £175 with – (*The* Announcer *rushes in shaking his fist, and presses switch. The red light goes out. Having got her point she makes an ironical curtsy to the Announcer. Blackout.*)

XLI

THE COMMON COLD

The Common Cold! The Common Cold!
The doctors really must be told
It's really time that they controlled
The horrors of the common cold.

I love the doctors – they are dears;
But *must* they spend such years and years
Investigating such a lot
Of illnesses which no one's got,
When everybody, young and old,
Is frantic with the common cold?
And I will eat my only hat
If they know anything of *that!*

Mark with what long and patient care
The doctor studies what is rare.
He cannot do too much for you
If you have something strange and new,
Nor can he quite conceal his bliss
If it should chance to end in-*is*.
Moreover, if the thing's obscure
He may be slow but he is sure.

He knows the perfect pill or paint

The Common Cold

For every tropical complaint,
Which is not likely to occur
In Battersea or Westminster.
But there are fortunately few
Who suffer from the strange or new;
I do not know a single case
Of Indian Itch or Persian Face,
Nor do I think that I have met
A man with sleeping-sickness yet.

But all of us have *one* disease –
We all sniff, snuffle, cough, and sneeze.
The common cold! The common cold!
If all the populace was polled,
A large majority, I'm told,
Would register a common cold.
This is the universal plague,
And here I find the doctor vague:
To *poly*- this and *poly*- that
He plays a straight and pretty bat,
But when it is the common cold
The man is absolutely bowled.

And you would think that Harley Street
Would be ashamed of this defeat;
You'd think, I say, that here and now
The Street would vow a holy vow –
'Whatever any doctor's at
We will desist from doing that,
No more inquire the cause of twins,
And stop inventing vitamins,
And drawing teeth and drawing fees
Till we have done for this disease;
We will not sleep, we will not eat,
Nor shave the face nor wash the feet,

Nor shall our boots be heeled and soled
Till we have killed the common cold.'

But if, in fact, you chance to meet
A specialist in Harley Street
And say to him, 'Look here! Behold!
I have – *again* – the common cold,'
The gentleman will only stare;
He really does not seem to care.[1]
He then remarks without remorse,
'Oh, well, the thing must take its course.'
But I reply with frank chagrin,
'Why must the blasted thing *begin*?'

The Common Cold! The Common Cold!
The doctors really must be told
It's really time that they controlled
The horrors of the common cold.

1. But this is not quite fair to Dr W H Hay, who says plainly that the chief cause of the common cold is improper eating, and that those who eat according to his system will not suffer (*Health via Food*, Harrap).

XLII

THE FATHERS' MATCH

No, Mr V, I shall *not* describe the Fathers' Match for the School Magazine.

Is it not enough that, year by year, we consent to suffer thus? Must we as well be, so to speak, our own agonometers? Would you invite the condemned gunman to record his impressions of the final ceremony for the pleasure of the *Police Gazette*?

And this year there is more cause for decent reticence than usual. It was not merely that we were dismissed first ball (that had happened before, though not for about five years); it was not merely that our Fathers' Match average was brought down to about 7 (it began at 0); it was not merely that, as usual, the Boys seemed to have 15 men in the field and we were brutally caught by the fifteenth boy (there is a precedent for that). No, no; the wound lay here – that this was our first appearance as a Grandfather in the mere Fathers' Match, and this was the occasion they chose on which to have us caught by some sort of illegitimate slip off the very first ball bowled in our direction.

There is, there could be, no excuse for this behaviour. We were, we think, the only Grandfather in the team. One or two of the Parents looked older (we thought), and even more circular in the region of greatest circumference; many had less hair; each had contributed his modest quota to the next generation. *But not one of them had done anything about the next generation but one.*

That takes it out of a man, say what you like; and we expected that some sort of concession would be made. Every allowance is made for the supposed immaturity, the quite mythical inferiority of the Boys. If a spherical Father scores so many as 20 he must retire at that enjoyable point; but a great big athletic boy may go on batting into the 60's. Moreover, the round-tummies' team are always put in to bat first. This is not a compliment, as the school pretends, but a conspiracy. In the tricky morning light, before the haze is off the sky and the aged London eyes, the Boys cruelly tease and toy with the batting ancestors, and dismiss the last one punctually at five minutes to lunch. They are then taken indoors, stupefied with sherry and gorged with salmon and strawberries. After this they are herded back to the field and made to run about in a comatose condition – which is not good for fathers. By this time the sky has cleared, and the light, though blinding and brutal to the fielders (especially to that parent who has been posted at the dangerous and degrading place called 'point'), is very favourable to the batsmen. Also a little breeze has risen, the deadly pollen moves about the meadows, and any grandfather who has hay-fever begins to sneeze.

Though the Ancients bat 14 a side they may field only 11 (another injustice): and when any father shows the smallest sign of spirit or mobility he is sent off the field and ordered to swim in the delightful river on the square-leg boundary. Swimming, it is well known, impairs the 'eye' and exhausts the reserves of power. After the swim the Father is placed at long-stop or point, and the Boys deliberately humiliate him by snicking in his direction unchristian twisters which spin across his front and whizz away past his left ankle. (There should be no 'point'in a Fathers' Match). If the Fathers still make a show of resistance a Tea Interval is declared; and thereafter, if not before, the Boys have no difficulty in gaining the usual victory by six or seven wickets.

Well, as a mere Father, we have long accepted all this unfairness; for there may be a little in the theory that if the Fathers were treated in Christian fashion they would sometimes win. But we did think that there would be some sort of special rules for a grandfather, who, *ex hypothesi,* must be as defenceless as a boy.

But no. We batted 12th; and the moment they saw us totter from the pavilion they brought back that enormous and Machiavellian bowler whom we had distrusted from the first. We never believed that he was a real boy; and his first devilish delivery proved him to be an impostor. Perhaps after all we should have worn the spectacles. We wear them for yachting now; but we had never batted in spectacles, and, somehow, it seemed a sort of turning-point. And there were our Young, standing close to the pavilion. The Young, we knew, are severely critical of Mother's wear on these occasions, and it might be that the Young would have something to say about a Father who batted in spectacles. We borrowed pads too large for us, and a bat too small: we bound great lumps of rubber to our hands, and marched out filling the lungs and slashing the air with the bat which had just hit a six. But we left the spectacles behind.

No doubt it was the spectacles. Not that we would belittle the ball. It was cunningly 'flighted'. It seemed to swerve a good deal. Eye-witnesses of the scene admitted that the break was tremendous. The bowler's umpire thought that few grandfathers could have got the bat to it at all. This one did – but only just. As the ball spun past us towards this seventh (and illegitimate) slip, we could hear the sound of its spinning, the malignant hiss of incredible rotation. How that boy held it we shall never know. What a catch!

And, by the way, we have not mentioned the light. There wasn't any. So far as there was light, it was a fiendish light. There had been a sort of blight or haze about all the morning, and while we took guard all the dingy corners of the sky seemed to crowd up into the centre, forming a thick and bilious kind of canopy immediately over the wicket. Imagine that. Imagine some unusually dense and lofty trees behind the bowler's arm. Out of this murky background imagine a rather dirty ball (small size) snaking and zigzagging and spinning unnaturally. Remember about the spectacles. And you will then have some vague impression of the conditions.

When the incredible occurred and those small fingers gripped the red-hot whizzing sphere, we thought that at least the captain would say: 'Oh, trial ball, Sir!' or 'Oh, I say, fair-play for grandfathers!' But the general expectation seemed to be that we should return to the pavilion. Accordingly, in some surprise, we began the longest walk in the world.

The Young, mercifully, had left the field for lunch.

It may be that there are spiritual lessons to be drawn from the Fathers' Match. It is, without doubt, on this day, and not on New Year's Day, that the truly valuable discoveries and resolutions are made, concerning, for example, the size of the stomach, the volume of the wind, the choice of diet, course of abdominal exercises, and so on. But we do not think that any of this is suitable for the School Magazine. Nor can it be desirable to record very loudly the fact that once again the Boys have won.

Which things being so, we decline to write a word about the Fathers' Match.

XLIII

PLEASANT SUNDAY MORNINGS

(1) WITH MR J L GARVIN

The tide of human affairs sweeps on with a momentum not to be arrested even by the *Observer.* Yet here, as in Nature, there is vouchsafed from time to time a salutary pause while the waters hang betwixt ebb and flow. Here is the opportunity natural for the shifting of moorings, the readjustment of uncertain anchorages, the tautening, loosening, and renewal of ropes. We write this week at political slack-water. If Ministers waste this Heaven-sent interval in the old bickerings and narrow animosities, the country will suffer for a generation. When we speak of the tide we forget too often that the ebb has its virtues as well as the flood. The Ship of State must journey down the river as often as up. Shakespeare himself fell into error here. Events may prove that for this old island it is the tide taken at the ebb which leads out to fortune.

(1) 'REVISE – REVISE!'

During the next few months we shall return again and again to this inspiring parallel. It may be that we shall have to envisage a drastic reshaping of all those preconceived notions on which the national life is built. If this is so we shall fearlessly face the issue, though it exposes us to the slings and arrows of outrageous calumny and runs us into four columns instead of our ritual three. It has never been the habit of this journal to cling to obsolete fetishes to gain the applause of Mandarindom. Where there is no revision the people perish.

Front things to the front. With no more delay than is imposed by the practical necessities of the case the fourth stump must at last be added to the wickets of England. That we have escaped ultimate disaster for some centuries with no more than three is the argument of indolence and blindness. The fourth stump is as needful and natural to cricket as the fourth wheel to a carriage. In an age more and more tending towards symmetrical form in every branch of life, what other nation would have tolerated so long the illogical and angular arrangement of the threefold wicket? As well fetter the modern impulse to speed by insisting on the tricycle as the ideal design for a vehicle. As well have three batsmen.

Odd numbers are an offence to the new era of social cohesion, scientific standardization and international equality. Partnership, not particularity, is the note of the time, politically. Odd man out is a game for children and savages. In art and science as well we move always to what is level and even. A three-shilling piece is at this date an impossible conception. The fourth stump must come. So much is moon-bright.

The Sequel – and a Moral

Consider next the inevitable sequence of events. At once the national game takes to itself new life and meaning. From the giving of guard to the drawing of stumps a new technique and practice are born. With four targets for the attack instead of three the bowler is thirty-three per cent more dangerous, and the striker thirty-three per cent more vulnerable; the difference in power representing sixty-six per cent on a division. At once there is an end of the drawn match, the prolonged negation of our present experience. Every contest is pushed to a quick and certain conclusion; and meanwhile bowler and batsmen alike must think out a fresh tactic and philosophy of the game.

The people would rally to the New Cricket. Where one man snores in the free seats today a thousand would flock with their savings to the stands. More. So deep-set in the soul of us is the cricket-affair that a fresh start here must have repercussions incalculable throughout the national fabric. Industry, Science, Art – Religion itself – would catch the new breeze and sail off gallantly on the tack of endeavour. Not even statesmanship could avoid the wholesome breath of the fourth stump.

Then the implications international. These are manifest and globe-wide in importance. Let Europe see that Britain has thrust the galvanic needle to the very heart of her national game, and the Continent will know that we intend business in all things. Let virile America have no more excuse to mock at the three-day dawdles of Lord's and Oval and at once we take our rightful place in the family-councils of the world.

(2) End the Weekend

This done, we must reward expectation with performance. It will not be enough to exhibit the promise of vigour. At present we rest upon our laurels before we have gained them; we spend four days of the week in recuperation from the exertions of three. (We speak, particularly, *sans* fear or favour, of the heads of industry, the brains of Britain.) The English weekend must go.

Nothing like it is provided for in the Ten Commandments. 'Six days shalt thou labour' is still, we believe, the authorized text. In current practice we have interpreted it 'Four days shalt thou labour and do all that thou hast to do, and on the sixth, seventh, and most of the first day thou shalt rest from thy labours, thou and thy children, but not thy man-servant and thy maid-servant'. *Quis custodiet ipsos custodes* – the manager who abandons ship at noon on Friday, the director who guides his factory in Manchester from his place in Sussex? The Empire cannot live so long as the heart of the Empire refuses duty on Saturdays and Mondays. These days must come back to the business calendar. On this subject our last word is not yet said.

(3) THE RIGHT – AND RUSSIA

One, two – and still there is a third facet to our practical dream of an England regained. While the civilized nations of the earth drive unanimously on the right side of the road we alone cling obstinately to the left. In no other matter are the voices of the peoples so perfectly in harmony. Britain manifestly cannot much longer shout the one discordant note.

In Politics, in Art, in Literature, a war-tossed world drifts steadily back to the right, and Britain, of all nations, does herself less than justice in paddling a solitary canoe to leftwards, if only on the high-road. The symbolism of a change here is by no means trivial, but pregnant with destiny and not to be neglected if Ministers know their business. Such a gesture by Britain would seal, confirm, and fructify the rightward leanings of the planet. Let the nations see this island stern-set on the right side of the road and even Russia may own that the game is up. Nor from the practical standpoint of trade is it to be forgotten that such a change would require the transformation of every motor we possess, whether in being or on the benches. The left-hand drive will find work for a million.

(4) A Clear Course

Can we put faith in Ministers? The course is clear; but has the pilot the vision to perceive it? Let us briefly recapitulate the three prongs of that dream-trident with which Britannia, if she be but true to herself, shall once more dominate the sphere. Our language, we hope, has been as sharp in meaning as it has been blunt in frankness. But we can never be sure that the whole of our readers will read the whole of our articles. Those who skip the reasoned premises of our beginning may swallow a hasty conclusion. And *vice versa*. Hence without shame, for the general good, we repeat ourselves.

Three things, then: The Fourth Stump – The Six-Day Week – The Right of the Road. Only the small mind will think such matters small. The points of a diamond are infinitesimal, yet without them the jewel is nothing. Our three points are to be the glitter-spots of an England without flaw. Buds only, to vary the metaphor, but they spring from the root of the business and in a small compass conceal the flower of the future. In this affair this journal will permit no paltering by the Government. At the first sign of shifting counsels or feeble grasp we shall not hesitate to write another powerful article.

XLIV

PLEASANT SUNDAY MORNINGS

(2) WITH MR JAMES AGATE

'Cherry Ripe'(at the Golconda)

Let it be posited boldly that two and two do frequently make a total which cannot be described as four. As, peradventure, two elderly persons and two young persons conspiring at matrimony – the sum of which is a crowd; or two shares in oil and two in a coalmine – the answer to which is nothing; or the two eyes of the Duse and the two legs of La Lola – which makes one angel, and two separate blasphemies. Was it not Chateaubriand who said, *'Un, deux – c'est le monde'*? It was not – nor was it anyone else – but no one will know. And here one is enmeshed, *hic, hoc,* and *alorum,* in a difficulty not to be put off without straining a point or two, as *Ardath* said to the traveller. If one is punctilious to avoid the egoistical 'I' beloved of one's pen-fellows, nor will not nightly pepper his pages with 'my readers' and 'my correspondents', after the blushless manner of our Mr Ervine, then how shall one convey that this or that opinion is put forward as a person's and not as the people's, proceeds from a self and not from the shelf, like the wine-songs of Wardour Street? How to be positive without the Papal touch? How to present a pistol in the third person singular? How shall violet cry like peony yet still be violet? Here's fuel indeed for the midnight lamp. But how now! Shall we cry 'Halt!' at the starting-gate? '*Non multum,*' as our old friend Quintus Horatio Flaccus riposted to a certain senator in the Appian Way. 'To feel for the bottom with deprecating foot was ever the best overture to a drowning' – or do we misquote our Emerson? Out, mustard, and to our muttons!

Let it be granted then that for the normal frays of criticism one has forged a sharp and serviceable formula or two wherewith to strike the I out of egoism without doing injury absolute to that breath of personality which is the spark of the weekly scribe. We would not, by our livelihood, ban, bell and book, the first person singular from these our columns; but here at least it must suffer the singular discipline of being singular; so that it shines like a naughty deed in a good world, or, if one may give the trope a twist, like Vega in August and not as the Milky Way. Let others put all their egos into one basket; an I for an I shall never be our motto. Without doubt there were good and sufficient reasons why Henley did not write 'One is the master of one's fate; one is the captain of one's soul'; but he would have earned as many marks for his meaning if he had, and a few extra for his modesty. '*Esto,*' then, or 'Make it so,' as the Admiral whispered.

There is a sort of piece which appears as punctually as the new potato in the early summer and is called musical comedy. That it is no more new than the potato may be postulated boldly; that it hath no more music in it than the vegetable and perchance the same quantum of the comic spirit will here be humbly suggested. But what? Consider the new potato. And then, good coz, consider a world without it. Doth it not fit with an air into the scheme of things necessary? Dost thou think because thou art highbrow there shall be no more ladies of the chorus? Ay, and jazz shall be hot in the mouth! Let it be conceded then that the name of 'Cherry-Ripe' sits ill upon a piece which flits uncertainly between the Lido and a Bond Street milliner's; that the plot is unfathomable, like the appetite of M. Bientôt; that the Brigade of Guards do *not* wear hunting-kit at Venice; that the eldest son of a baronet is not called 'Viscount'; that the Fifth Symphony of Beethoven may not provide the happiest inspiration for a fox-trot; that the words conceivably might have more wit and the chorus more clothes – and still we are left with the naked but agreeable fact of our new potato. What, does one bandy words with a vegetable? Tell me not that a Maupassant could have contrived a better story, and the late Mr Shelley a nobler lyric than:

I love my Baby,
  My Baby loves me.

These gentlemen were not on parade when Mr Sid Froitheim mustered his army of ready writers. And here, faithful as the boomerang, we fly back to our arithmetical beginnings. Two authors and a brace of lyric-manufacturers (to say nothing of three composers) do not make four authors, neither do they make one play; they make Babel, they make Bedlam, they make
– by your leave and the canons of Aristotle – balderdash; natheless in this present affair, an one may hazard a guess, they also make money. '*Et pourquoi pas*?' we sigh with Madame de Sévigné. The haberdasher is worthy of his hire, and shall the balderdasher starve? And if one did not, with one's neighbours, roar like *Falstaff* in the stalls at the easy humours of this noisy trifle let it not be supposed that one slept. We would not of all things be ticketed 'highbrow'; and therefore, *Buzfuz*-fashion, we must swim through a sea benevolent of words to our point, which is that, like the honest Godiva, one cannot conceal from you that I – that is – Oh, Lord, what a play!

XLV

PLEASANT SUNDAY MORNINGS

(3) WITH MR ST JOHN ERVINE

The Contemporary Drama

(1) Pipes

A correspondent writes from Bristol to ask my opinion on a question of some importance to the future of the drama. Since she appears to have a mind (unlike most of our young dramatists) and shows no taint of an Oxford education, I propose to answer her question at length. Most of the people who write to me are nitwits. There is no mind in their remarks. I had a letter from Wolverhampton yesterday which must have been the work of a hippopotamus. I am of course accustomed to abuse, which I enjoy. A dramatic critic who gets no abuse is a critic who has been no use. On Thursday a lady wrote from Hull to complain of what I said last week about short skirts in my article on Ibsen. She said I reminded her of a bull in a china-shop. I will give my readers my answer in full, for it pleases me:

DEAR MADAM,

There are many china-shops in which a bull would do a lot of valuable work; and if there were more bulls in my particular china-shop there would be fewer managers tearing their hair in the box-office, fewer fine actors on the streets, and fewer puling young persons from Oxford and Hampstead on the stage. The cheap and gaudy tea-sets of the Tottenham Court Road cry aloud for an energetic bull. They have no mind. Their makers, having no taste themselves, underestimate the taste of the public. The Shaftesbury Avenue drama is in the same condition, but worse. Not one bull is needed, dear lady, but a drove.

Yours, etc.,

ST JOHN IRVINE

I do not object to personal abuse. It is this absence of *mind* which distresses me in my correspondents, and indeed in nearly everyone else. I often look about me at the spectacle of modern civilization and suddenly realize that nobody else has a brain – with the possible exception of my friend Mr Shaw. Yesterday I saw three young men standing at the edge of a pavement in the West End watching one man working a mechanical drill. Their mouths were wide open. They wore bowler-hats on the backs of their heads. If I were a betting-man I would bet ten pounds to a tiddler that those young men were educated at Oxford and sing folk-songs at Hampstead. They were bat-brains. They were loopy. How can you expect to have a healthy theatre with a population like that?

The problem of the drama in America is a different problem. America is much larger than England and has many more people in it; therefore everything is much worse. When I was in America I was asked, as every distinguished visitor is asked, to state my opinion of American women and American skyscrapers. I said, 'They are very fine, but they have no *mind*'. There are a hundred million people in the United States but I cannot remember meeting anyone who was my intellectual equal. Nevertheless the American theatre is a healthy theatre; the most important people in it are the critics, which is as it should be; the programme-sellers are very attentive and well-dressed, and no smoking is allowed.

That brings me to the subject of my article, which at this rate should run to a column-and-a-half this week. My friend Mr Garvin fills so much space in this paper that it is almost impossible to attract attention with a single column. Nevertheless I know that my readers read me, because so many of them write letters to me from places like Huddersfield and Newcastle. I like my readers to write to me, because it gives me something to write about; and if the letters are long letters I can sometimes fill half a column with quotations, which pleases both me and my correspondents.

I am asked by my friend at Bristol whether as a dramatic critic and lover of the theatre I think that pipes ought to be smoked in the stalls. Now this raises the whole question of the place of the drama in the national life. Before I discuss it I had better say at once that in my opinion it makes no difference whether the pipe is in the stalls or in the pit. The distinction is a purely snobbish one. I have no prejudice against smoking. I don't smoke pipes myself because I don't like the filthy things; and nowadays there are so many theatrical failures and so many first-nights that a dramatic critic would scarcely have time to finish a pipe if he had one. If some of our young men gave less time to lighting their pipes and more to illuminating their minds we should have better playwrights and brighter audiences. I have always said that a nation which cannot create and appreciate great tragedy is a C3 nation. And here is the importance of my correspondent's inquiry. Evidently she has seen some gentleman smoking a pipe in the stalls, whether at Bristol or elsewhere, or she would not have asked the question. Now a man who will smoke a pipe at a musical comedy, whether in the stalls or in the pit, will smoke a pipe at the greatest tragedy that was ever written. He has no mind. He cannot concentrate. Consider the mental equipment of a man who could smoke a pipe at a performance of *Hamlet*. He is batty. He is a sponge. I should like to knock him down. In the days when I tried to smoke a pipe I was constantly striking matches, puffing, blowing, and removing vegetable matter from my mouth. A man who is doing that cannot at the same time give his whole mind to poetry and the growth of character. If anyone can prove to me that the Athenians smoked at the first performance of the *Oedipus Tyrannus* I will give him a new bicycle. And the mere fact that at half of the theatres in London the audience are able to strike matches during a ghost scene and blow smoke at the singers shows how far we are behind the Greeks. When I was in America I did not see anyone smoke in the stalls. If I had I should have hit the man. Tragedy distils the essential greatness of the human spirit, and no one can absorb it who is at the same time engaged in a petty occupation such as the inhaling of nicotine. For the same reason I disapprove of evening-dress at a play by Shakespeare. A man in a stiff shirt and a high collar cannot hope to project himself into the tomb of the *Capulets* or the mind of *Iago*. I should say that the audience at a tragic play ought to wear soft flannel shirts and knickerbockers, except that there is something cranky about knickerbockers, and I detest cranks.

What I have said about smoking in the theatre applies too to the film. A businessman once wrote to me from Leeds to say that he could always judge the character of a strange club by the character of its washing-places. I don't know how far this is true; the arrangements at the United Highbrows are ghastly. But it is true that one can judge the intellectual value of any form of entertainment by looking at the audience. If they cannot enjoy it without enjoying some other distraction at the same time, holding hands or sucking chocolates or nibbling at paper packets of tobacco, then it is bad art. There is no mind in it. At most cinemas most of the audience are doing all these things at the same time, which shows that most films are very bad art, though I detest the word art. When the cinema-audience begins to leave its acid-drops and its fags at home we shall know that mind has come into the film.

And now I must be well into the second column, so that will do for the present. Next week I hope to discuss the place of the programme-girl in contemporary drama, about which three people have written to me, one of them a coal-porter at Runcorn.

XLVI

PINK KNICKERS

(*to be sung by a blonde, with chorus*)

I've formed a lovely Party, but a Shirt we do not wear;
Some other Party's chosen all the colours I can bear;
But some garment is essential if you want to get the mockers,
So I express my policy with my pink knickerbockers:

Pink Knickers! Rally round!
Our policy is sound,
Though I really couldn't tell you where the details may be found.
You mustn't ask me what we mean to do about the poor,
But there really are too many – and there is *a way, I'm sure;*
And if Knicker-boys and Knicker-girls will all together get
In our dinky pinky knickers we'll save the country yet.

I do think all we girls should pull our weight in Britain's boat;
Well, look how everything's improved since woman had the vote.

I'm very much in favour of the miners and the dockers,
And to indicate my programme I wear nice pink knickerbockers:

Pink Knickers! Hail! Hooray!
We're the Party of today,
Though what we'll do tomorrow it is difficult to say.
I do think men are splendid – they've been awfully good to me,
But if they can wear their underclothes in public, why not we?
And if Knicker-boys and Knicker-girls will really get together
We'll make everybody happy and have much more pleasant weather.

We're not Socialists, Conservatives or even Liberal,
But in a kind of way we have the essence of them all;
We won't waste any time upon their prehistoric bickers
And to show our independence we just go about in knickers:

Pink Knickers! Form your fours!
And if oratory bores
You may still impress the people by the vigour of your wars.
When the Pink Knicks are in power all oppression will be dead,
And if anybody says it won't we'll knock him on the head.
So if Knicker-boys and Knicker-girls will all together stand
I think you'll find that everything is absolutely grand.

XLVII

BOMBSHELL IN FLEET STREET

It was very hot. The sub-editor read gloomily. And he had the strange sensation that it had all happened before. He read:

> 'Miss Mavis Bird, a young chorus-girl, took the part of *Marie* in *Love's Lure* at short notice last night, due to the indisposition of Miss Lily Lake. Miss Bird, whose parents reside at Balham, scored a veritable triumph, the audience calling for her again and again. Miss Lake, who will be indisposed for a week or two, has sent Miss Bird a telegram congratulating her on her success.'

The sub-editor groaned. He took his pencil and wrote:

CHORUS GIRL'S TRIUMPH

LONDON SINGER

SNATCHES OPPORTUNITY

Then he groaned again.

'Short notice!' he groaned. 'Don't they have any understudy rehearsals?' It was very hot. The sub-editor pined for beer and beaches. The news of the day repelled him. Also he loved Miss Lily Lake.

He telephoned here and there. And at last he took his pencil again. With a new light in his face he wrote the following surprising words:

UNDERSTUDY FAILS

BALHAM GIRL'S POOR SINGING

'Miss Mavis Bird, a chorus-girl, took the part of *Marie* in *Love's Lure* last night, but not at short notice, as reported in all our contemporaries. *Love's Lure* has been running for ten months, and two days after the opening night the stage-manager summoned the usual understudy-rehearsal. The part of *Marie* was assigned to Miss Bird, and she has been rehearsing it ever since. An ambitious girl, she has not been content with rehearsing, but has made it her practice, whenever possible, to sit in the wings (where she is sometimes joined by Mr Poot, the comic lead) and study the methods of Miss Lake. Moreover, it has been known for some time that Miss Bird and her friends among the Chorus hold a very low opinion of Miss Lake's capacity and charm; and one or two of them have been heard to express surprise at the large salary which Miss Lake receives.

'It was expected therefore, when Miss Bird was at last given her chance, that a performance out of the ordinary would be seen. In such a case the understudy has everything to gain and little to lose; she begins with the sympathy of the audience and of her colleagues, some of whom, after a long run, may be tired of the principal's performance or jealous of her success. The principal, by art or experiment, has made her own creative contribution to the part, has found where the "laughs" lie in the author's lines and added laughs of her own. The understudy has to bring little but a capacity for imitation; the part is ready-made for her and she has only to carry it with an air. And if in addition she can show the smallest signs of individual distinction she is likely to be hailed as a "discovery".

'In the present case, it appears, expectations were cruelly disappointed. Miss Bird was nervous and once or twice forgot her lines. Both her singing and her dialogue were flat. Lines which on the lips of Miss Lake caused hearty laughter were now received in silence. So marked was Miss Bird's incapacity to hit a high note truly that Mr Sopp, the tenor lead, declined to sing two of the love-duets, and the conductor was compelled to cut the numbers out. The audience, perceiving Miss Bird's distress, gave her a generous cheer at the close of the performance; but long before that several well-dressed parties had left their boxes.

'The circumstances of Miss Lake's indisposition are not as stated by our contemporaries. Miss Lake is not in fact indisposed. A quarter of an hour before the curtain rose an old friend of Miss Lake's presented himself at the stage-door but was refused admission to her dressing-room, according to the rule of the theatre that no visitors must enter the dressing-rooms before the fall of the final curtain. Miss Lake sent for the stage-manager and insisted that this childish rule should be suspended to meet the wishes of a leading lady. The stage-manager declined. Miss Lake said that if her friend could not call on her she would not perform that night. The stage-manager was adamant; Miss Lake was as good as her word; and Miss Bird was instructed to play the part.

'Miss Lake will perform as usual this evening; the management have increased her salary, and the company have earnestly expressed the hope that she will never be "indisposed" again. A new understudy has been selected.'

The sub-editor read his work happily and sent it downstairs. He then wrote a letter tendering his resignation, and with a smile on his lips went out into the night.

XLVIII

MR MAFFERTY GOES TO THE TALKIES

'It's a wonder I'm alive,' said Mr Mafferty. 'For I've just been to the talkies itself, an' it's thrown out I was.

'At the end of me own street, Mr Haddock, an' that's a fine little peaceable street was built in the eighteenth century, one house at a time – at the end of me own street, I'm sayin', they've raised up a grand new picture-palace, or talkie-drome, or noise-park, or the divil knows what (for indeed there's no knowin' what name they'd be puttin' to this an' that at the present time, an' they away in their minds with vulgarity an' riches an' a poor education). It stands up over the quiet little houses the way you'd see a hippopotamus rampagin' among the young lambs. The front of it is white tiles, like a public wash-house as large as the Stock Exchange; an' the back an' sides of it is sad dirty bricks like a public prison. Isn't it a wonder now they wouldn't employ a good architect to build an eyesore the like of that one?

'But it's a grand place within, surely. I'm thinkin' if the Queen of Sheba herself set foot in it she'd creep off quietly an' go to her own place with shy thoughts an' a humble heart. There's great fellers standin' without in admirals' uniforms, no less; an' there's marble pillars in the hall, an' the moon an' stars in the ceilin', an' golden stones under your feet; an' there's fountains in the corners of the stairs, an' deep carpets in the corridors a man would sink in the length of his neck, if he should be loiterin' by the way. An' there's girls dressed like colonels in the Austrian cavalry do be waftin' the people to their seats with fairy-lights in the darkness. An' you have a seat for ninepence is like the arm-chairs of emperors a young man could sleep in the rest of his days. An' the hall's as large as St Paul's Cathedral, an' there's lighted grottoes in the walls an' Mexican scenery an' the Italian lakes an' the divil knows what besides. An' it has the world's greatest organ in it, though they do say there's no picture-palace in the world these days hasn't the world's greatest organ. That's what one of the Admirals told me, an' why would he tell me a lie?

'Well, I sank into me rich seat, Mr Haddock, an' I closed me tired eyes, for I'd heard tell it's the great rest the people have in them places, an' they holdin' hands or sleepin' like Peace itself. But I couldn't sleep at all, Mr Haddock, by reason of the quare strange noises. So I opened me eyes an' I looked at the pictures, an' begob, Mr Haddock, it was the strangest noise I ever set eyes on! I see a young girl with no clothes on nearly, an' what she had she was takin' off, for I found in a short while it's a cabaret girl she was, an' she makin' a loud quarrel in the dressin'-room with one of the young gintlemen she did be lovin'. They was both makin' noises the like of no noise meself has heard anny place before, savin' the Zoological Gardens only. There's a quare strange animal in the western end of them Gardens, Mr Haddock, is fed at four in the afternoon. I misremember the name of it, Mr Haddock, but it was the like of that noise the creature makes from three to four each day, an' it howlin' for raw meat. Maybe you know the one is in me mind.

'Well, I turns to the gintleman sits beside me, an' he kissin' a lady at the time, God forgive me, but how would I expect the like of that in a public place? An' I says, "What noise is that?" says I. "What noise at all?" says he, a small piece angry by reason of the interruption. "The noise in me ears," says I. "The noise in this place, though the divil himself could say from what place it comes at all." "That's the American language," says he. "It is not then," says I, "for I'm acquainted with the race. Is it the like of that talk Mr Hoover does be talkin' to Mr Ramsay MacDonald, an' they cementin' the nations with a holy glue?" "It might," says he. "Well, it is not," says I. "An', if it's language, will you tell me now, do you understand a blessed word the young girl is sayin', the one with bare legs changin' her underclothes?" "I do not," says he, "why would I at all?" "It's well for you," says I, "that have an arm round a young lady, an' be huggin' her in the darkness. Maybe the noise is pleasin' to you," says I, "an' it drownin' the sound of your loud caresses an' endearin' words. But it's a poor thing, I'm thinkin', for the like of meself that have come into this place for peace an' quietness. It's a lonesome thing, I'm sayin', to sit in the black night with the sound of she-bears howlin' in the woods or sick cows dyin' on the hills of Kilbay." "Hold your peace," says he, "or I'll call one of them Colonels of Cavalry an' she'll send for an Admiral itself." "The holy angels be about your bed," says I, "an' about your board from this night to the world's end! Let you give the lady a great hug an' not be mindin' me at all." "I will not," says he, an' he kisses the girl again.

' "Well, I wouldn't wonder at your doin' the like of that," says I, "an' you lookin' at pictures the like of this one. I never see so many kisses before. Begob, for two dead poppies I'd kiss the girl meself! Did you see that now?" "I did not," says he. "Well, that's a hard thing," says I, "for there was two couples kissin' at the same time, this gintleman that did the murder an' the lady with the legs, an' the gintleman with the pistol an' the blonde with a bare back an' it shinin' like a side of beef on Saturday night. There's five blondes in this picture, I'm thinkin', an' all as like as two blondes. Bedad, they're kissin' again! Give her another hug, Mister, to relieve me poor feelin's!" "I will so," says he; and every time he sees me blood's on fire with the long kisses in the picture he relieves me feelin's on the lady, an' she smilin' mischief at me under his bowler hat with the fine eyes she had on her, the creature. "Well, it's a quare kind feller you are," says

I at last, "an' you takin' that trouble for a strange man. But why wouldn't the lady sit between us now, the way I could save you the trouble an' not be takin' your mind from the picture?" "She would not," says he. "I would so," says the girl, and, by me uncle's mare, she rises up an' sits her down beside me, the darlin'.

'But it's poor satisfaction I had out of that, Mr Haddock, for at that livin' instant up comes the Manager an' one of the Admirals with a great torch shinin' on us; an' the Manager says will we go out of that place, the three of us, by reason of the scandal an' noise ourselves was makin' among the people. "Scandal, is it?" says I. "Will you tell me now what day it is?" " 'Tis the twenty-seventh of October," says he. " 'Tis the Lord's Day," says I. " 'Tis neither here nor there," says the Admiral, seizin' the back of me throat. "It is so, surely," says I. "Think shame of yourself, Mr Manager," says I, "to be enticin' decent folks on the Sabbath evenin' an' inflamin' their passions with pictures the like of that one. Is there no place in the world but Broadway, America? An' is there nobody in Broadway but bootleggers an' homicides an' girls in the chorus, an' they talkin' the talk of Bedlam? An' have they nothin' to do but kissin' an' revolver-shootin'?" "Let you go out now," says the Manager, givin' me a push. "I'll have the law on you," says I, "for corruptin' me emotions. I wonder now you haven't the whole audience huggin' an' kissin' an' usin' fire-arms after the things they've seen this night. An' I wonder them American kissin's an' shootin's is lawful in London on the Lord's Day but not the plays of Shakespeare himself. Ideals, is it? Disarmament, is it? What harm in the world can ten battleships do to equal one picture the like of that one?" "Hold his arms," says the Manager; an' at that moment up rises the keyboard of the organ out of the floor itself, with a little organist feller in it, like it might be the Fairy Queen in a pantomime, an' he illuminated with the purple limelight. An' he begins to play a little jigglin' kind of a dance-tune on the world's greatest organ. An' I says to the

Manager the time they carried me out, " 'Tis the noblest instrument of music, the organ, Mr Manager; an' even on that you play lascivious tunes."

'So they flung me through the door into the cold street. 'Tis a quare hard world.'

XLIX

'IT MIGHT BE WORSE'

OR, THE PHILOSOPHER

Yes, milord, I'd like to say a word, as you suggest;
The jury find me guilty, and I'm sure that they know best.
And now you'll give me seven years – but what I'd like to say
Is, I hope you won't upset yourself on my account today.

It might be worse, your worship,
It always might be worse;
It never does no good, is what I say, to cry or curse.
It's not a bad old world
If it doesn't get you down;
I'm not so keen on Dartmoor,
But I'm never well in Town.
It's a little disappointing spending summer in a cell;
But it's Providence, my lord, they didn't cop my wife as well.
Things look black, I know,
But they're never quite so low
But they might be a darn sight worse.

Concentrate, my rule is, on the brighter side of things;
You may have to sleep in hedges, but our snakes have got no stings.
There's many a man would whine in a predicament like mine,

But I haven't got the toothache and my appetite is fine.
It might be worse, your worship,
It always might be worse;
I don't like the Black Maria, but it might have been a hearse.
Life, I say, is sweet,
Though now and then disgusting;
If you haven't got a home
You're not bothered with no dusting.
I'm inclined to drink too much, sir, and, though prison makes me shiver,
It's a comfort to be safe, sir, from cirrhosis of the liver.
Things look pretty lousy at the present time of speaking,
But they might be a darn sight worse.

You've troubles of your own, milord – the income-tax, no doubt;
But you might have got no income – and you might have got the gout.
P'r'aps you wish you'd gone into a business when a lad,
But look at me and think what might have happened if you had.
It might be worse, your worship,
It always might be worse;
She might have lost her honour, but I only took her purse.
However black things look
We should all be giving thanks;
It's true I robbed that safe,
But it might have been your bank's.
I can't break myself of burglary, but then I never bet;
Old England lost the cricket, but we've had no earthquake yet…

Blimey! only five, milord? And me expecting seven!
Well, it might be a darn sight worse.

L

SIGHTS

I have twice visited Naples for a few hours but have never seen Pompeii. Is this a record?

I have four times visited Ceylon but never travelled to Nuwara Eliya. This, I know, is a record.

I have had two half-days in Lisbon, but declined to dash out to Estoril, to inspect the old Coaches, or visit Cintra. This was naughty. I have spent many days in Gibraltar but never 'did' the rock-galleries. I have spent a week in Madeira and never left the hotel grounds, except to swim and book my passage home; never climbed the mountains by funicular or car, never descended them in one of the celebrated baskets or sledges. I must have missed hundreds of cathedrals in my time, thousands of picture-galleries, millions of excellent museums. I am disgraceful. In Berlin I 'did' nothing but the Zoo; in Egypt I darned nearly missed Tutankhamen, though I 'did' the Pyramids and desert thoroughly. In Australia I wantonly avoided the Blue Mountains. At Honolulu I was in trouble because I cut the Naval Base and Canning Factories and went surf-riding instead. The other day I was at Coruña for a few hours and they could not get me ashore to see Sir John Moore's tomb; but I sat in the sun and searched for it with magnifying-glasses.

In Jamaica I simply swam and swam and watched the humming-birds; and I never went for a Beautiful Drive if I could possibly avoid it. I don't think I saw many of the pictures at Madrid. I 'did' Niagara Falls, but under duress. High mountains bore me. I am awful about 'sights'. What is the matter with me?

Freud would know, I suppose.

It worries me. I feel that I do not deserve to travel about. Yet I enjoy myself travelling, and I work hard at my holidays. I will walk miles to find a famous café; I never miss an opportunity to plunge into a properly warmed sea. I dance with vigour on the Equator and leap from my deck-chair to look at flying-fish or see the porpoises enjoying themselves. But cathedrals, mountains, museums... Can it be that I have no Sense of the Sublime?

No, they shall not say that I am lazy. In the delicious island of Ceylon I twice did the long tour through the jungle to see the Buried Cities; but even there it was more the monkeys and the fireflies and the elephants that drew me than the noble remnants of the Temples of Buddha and the admirable bits of ancient palaces. I went to see the Temple elephants bathing on a very hot day; I visited the jolly planters and studied the manufacture of tea; but they could not lure me up their lofty mountains to the enchanting Nuwara Eliya of which they all talked so much.

They gave the oddest reasons for wanting me to go to Nuwara Eliya. They said that up there it was blissfully cool, like England, and I should see nasturtiums and sweet peas growing. I said that I had not travelled to the tropics to be cool – I wanted to have a good sweat. Nor had I sailed the seas for three weeks to see nasturtiums growing – we had them at Hammersmith. But I find this everywhere in the world. In Madeira the other day, when I was about to swim, they said that I ought to enter a motor-car and drive up through the clouds to the top of the mountains, where I should find that the air was sparkling – 'like Scotland'. I said, 'Good heavens!' and hurried into the sea.

I sympathize with our gallant exiles, who weary of being warm and, after years of palms, bananas, and bougainvillea, delight to look upon a British pansy. But we swift visitors, who within a few weeks will be thawing our sponges again, are not to be attracted thus.

Especially, in my case, if the inspection of nasturtiums, superb views or waterfalls, involves motor-drives along the edge of circuitous precipices. And I find, outside these shores, that nearly all sights do involve this. It is a most extraordinary thing – no matter where I land, the first thing the residents want to do is to put me in a motor-car and send me up a mountain or along very high cliffs. And I do dislike it so!

I think it was those horrible Canadian Rockies that destroyed my nerve for motor-mountaineering. We used to lurch along in a charabanc with one or two wheels over the edge of Dead Horse Canyon, many miles deep, and at all the hairpin – and unfenced – turns the driver would explain the statistics of timber. In Ceylon, as you whizz along the *cud* (?*kud*) or cliff, your host explains about rubber or tea; but every few miles he says, 'If you look down there you'll see the remains of a bus'. You look down and you do. In Lisbon, forty yards behind a Portuguese driver determined me to ignore Cintra (which I believe to be on a slight eminence); for the capital chap kept taking both hands off the wheel, lighting a cigarette, turning round, grinning radiantly and saying, 'Inglees very good. Italiano no bon.' It is my considered judgement that neither he nor the Jamaican driver (equally genial) has the smallest regard for the sanctity of human life. A man who deliberately goes to see a 'sight' in their company is simply cheating the insurance companies.

I suppose the truth is that residents do not realize how dangerous it is to see their sights, because when the drivers are driving 'locals' they do not think it necessary to discuss timber or politics or make gestures of international friendship.

At all events, I always assume now that to see almost any foreign sight is tantamount to suicide by car; for it is sure to mean motoreering, and the guide will talk politics at Dead Bus Corner.

This, I admit, is seldom a very good excuse for missing cathedrals and museums, Blue Caves, morgues, and botanical gardens.

It worries me. I feel wicked, as we steam away, thinking that I have missed the Sight, though I know very well that next time, unless we stay much longer, I shall miss the Sight again and sit on deck in the sun. It worries me; for I know how it pains good people if you fail to see their favourite Sight. It is hard to say why this should be so; for if they have seen it that, one would say, should content them. But I understand; indeed I have this noble weakness too, and grieve bitterly if my friends fail to enjoy my Sights.

But then, my Sights are the best. Was I not right to surf-ride at Honolulu (the only morning I was there) instead of goggling at a Pineapple Canning Factory? Was I not right to go and view those extraordinary 'apartments' at that hotel in Lisbon, thus missing cathedrals (if any), palaces, and casinos? There are many of these in the world; but I never saw anything like those apartments. That spacious bathroom, with the Portuguese mosaic floor, and the Portuguese marble steps leading up to the sunken bath, crushed-strawberry in colour; concealed lights at the four corners, high up in ornate holders of, I presume, gold! It was more like an altar or a royal tomb. It was my idea of the Queen of Sheba's bath and the film-fan's idea of the bath of Marlene Dietrich. And the rest of the suite was to match. There is a Sight, boys, if ever you visit Lisbon; and, if you are rich, you may actually hire the 'apartment' and wash your ears in the strawberry bath, though I did not feel that anything so vulgar as washing would there be suitable.

But I still worry, I confess, about the cathedrals, the museums, and the mountains. I must, I fear, be singularly lacking in Sense of the Sublime. Or am I just an unusually honest and strong-minded fellow?

LI

TRIAL BY PEERS

I sat in the Royal Gallery and admired the terraces of gorgeous Peers, like two herbaceous borders. It was a grand spectacle; and only the addition of music was required to raise it to the sublime standards of Savoy. And I thought, 'It would be a pity to do away with this altogether, if only because this is almost the only surviving remnant of Magna Carta'.

Let us at least preserve it, this gaudy ceremony, for cases of treason and treason-felony; for in the troublous periods which without doubt lie ahead of us, who knows what noble lords may not be up to? But let us, if we are going to do anything, do something thorough.

For the important absurdity is not that a peer should be tried by his peers, but that he should be tried by his peers upon a charge of manslaughter (which is a felony) and be tried by my peers upon a charge of fraud (which is only a misdemeanour).

If it is decided, then, that the trial of peers by peers for felony has 'outlived its usefulness'(as the Lord Chancellor and Lord Sankey have suggested), this will really mean the abolition of one distinction between felony and misdemeanour in the case of Members of the House of Lords. But what about the other distinctions? What about Members of the House of Commons – and, indeed, Members of the 'Black Horse' Skittles Club?

If, shall we say, the Junior Burgess for Oxford University were to commit a mild burglary or inadvertent bigamy he could neither vote for nor sit in Parliament (for these offences are felonies). But if he were found guilty of perjury, false pretences, or some gigantic fraud (which are only misdemeanours) he could still, I believe, represent the University already mentioned.

As for the common herd who are not Members of P, they may find themselves in a fix any day through the distinction between felony and misdemeanour.

If they do a small bit of housebreaking they will lose their pensions; but not if they commit perjury (which may cost a man his life) or a very big fraud (which may ruin thousands). And even if they commit no crime they may be in trouble about this branch of jurisprudence. Have you ever, citizen-reader, considered for a single instant what are your Powers of Arrest? Never. Well –

But first perhaps we had better give you a bird's-eye view of the

CLASSIFICATION OF INDICTABLE OFFENCES

Now, reader, you are a good citizen, eager to uphold the forces of law and order and to assist in the suppression of crime.

A – *Felonies*	B – *Misdemeanours*
Murder	Conspiracy to Murder
Manslaughter	Libel
Keeping a horse-slaughterer's yard without a licence	Assault
	Riot
Bigamy	Trespass
Burglary and Housebreaking	False pretences
Stealing mineral ores	Perjury
Larceny	Fraud
Forgery (some kinds)	Forgery (other kinds)

You should always therefore carry in your pocket a list (or lists) such as you see above. For if you chance to see another citizen committing one of the crimes in List A it is not only your right but your *duty* to arrest the fellow.

But if the miscreant is committing one of the minor offences in List B you are entitled only

(a) to obtain a warrant from a magistrate for his arrest;
(b) to summon a police-officer; or
(c) to deliver a moral lecture.

And if you exceed your powers the miscreant may have you summoned before the magistrates for assault. Do not suppose that this is idle fancy. There was a case not long ago in which a Noble Citizen tried to collar a Miscreant who was slashing the tyres of a stationary motor-car. Miscreant was punished for what he did, but Noble Citizen was found guilty of assault! Because to slash the tyres of a motor-car is a misdemeanour and not a felony.

Moreover, there is the offence called 'misprision of felony', which means failing to give information about a felony or felon, and may be punished by imprisonment. But there is no 'misprision of misdemeanour'; so that you may keep quiet about any crime in List B without fear of doing time yourself.

By this time, good citizen and reader, you will realize how important it is to carry your lists with you. If you see a man in another man's house he may be either (a) housebreaking or (b) trespassing. In the latter case you may get into trouble if you lay a finger on him; and in the former you will be failing in your duty if you don't. If he has just done a murder you must arrest or tell; but if he is only conspiring to murder you need say nothing about it. And not even your lists will always save you, for forgery is sometimes a felony and sometimes a misdemeanour; and so, I think, is the abduction of a young lady.

Now, all these bits of nonsense and many others like them are operating every day all over the country; but nobody minds. They perplex the public but bring needed bread to the legal profession, which I for one do not begrudge. The aggregate annual cost of them must far exceed the cost of the recent trial in the Royal Chamber. But, as is usual in this vague but beloved land, we excite ourselves (yes, even Lord Chancellors) about the exceptional accident and do nothing about the daily nonsense. And so, I suppose, we shall do always.

EXERCISE

If you see (1) a Duke, (2) an MP, (3) a Chartered Accountant (A) keeping a horse-slaughterer's yard without a licence; (B) puncturing another man's bicycle; (C) forging (i) a passport (ii) a telegram; (D) conspiring to commit embezzlement:

(a)May you arrest him?
(b)Where will he be tried?
(c)Must you tell the police?
(d)Can you tell his mother?
(e)What time is it?

LII

THE TAPIOCA KING

I met at Wapping, by the London Docks,
  In a great warehouse full of scented bales
A little fellow like a hunted fox
  Who sadly told the dismalest of tales:

'You wouldn't think to look at me
  That I'm a Captain of Finance –
Not quite Napoleon, as you see,
  Yet by a most unhappy chance
I am the Man who Cornered Tapioca.

A City man, I earned my feed,
  As others in that busy spot,
By buying things I did not need
  Or selling things I hadn't got,
Until I turned my thoughts to Tapioca.

Far off in Eastern lands they grow
  The beastly tapioca-plant,
And British children, as you know,
  Are made to eat it by their aunt –
That's what attracted me to Tapioca.

For children always will be fed,

I thought, as children always are;
Besides, I met a man who said
That Tapioca cured catarrh –
"Ah, ha!" said I, "I'll corner Tapioca!"

"Go, Broker, go!" I cry, "and buy
From Singapore to Bandikoot,
The world-, the universe-supply
Of leaf or berry, fruit or root,
Or whatsoever causes Tapioca."

At once the farmers of Japan
Gave up the growth of hay and hops;
The sugar-planters to a man
Abandoned their accustomed crops
And took to cultivating Tapioca.

It seemed to flourish like a weed.
Ship after ship the cargoes came –
Far more than all the world could need.
I had to buy it all the same.
For I was out to corner Tapioca.

The price was up, the price was high,
And I who caused the price to soar
Soon found it very hard to buy –
Still, I was sure to sell for more.
My wife had twins; we called one Tapioca.

You know how tiresome doctors are,
And one just now expressed a doubt;
So far from finishing catarrh,
He thought that asthma, croup, and gout
Were due to acids found in Tapioca.[1]

The parents frightened by the price,
  The aunts alarmed about the croup,
Nourished their young on sago, rice,
  On semolina, nuts, and soup –
On anything, in short, but Tapioca.

The market dropped to three or four;
  From Shadwell Basin to the sea
There's nothing else in ship or store,
  And all of it belongs to me –
While every tide brings in more Tapioca.

I am the Tapioca King;
  You may have seen the photographs,
For I was really quite the thing;
  But now the fickle public laughs,
For not a soul will touch my Tapioca.

Still, there is hope. For one fine day,
  Maybe some scientific ass
Will find that tapioca may
  Be used for making poison-gas,
And Governments will buy my Tapioca.

Meanwhile – and this is rather steep –
  I have brought off a little sale;
I sold a ticket in a sweep,
  And they are sending me to jail,
For that upsets them more than Tapioca.'

1. Since this imaginative work was written I have learned that one doctor, the celebrated enemy of acidosis, Dr Hay, has in fact condemned the use of tapioca.

LIII

MILK-O!

Queer stuff, milk.

I like milk. I drink it daily. And I like milkmen. But *must* the milkman wake me up every day 'twixt five and six in the morning?

I know that a peculiar holiness is attached to milk, a kind of moral flavour which is not possessed by the other edible products of the farm. Neither butter nor eggs nor bacon have the power to make us feel small. I do not necessarily regard the man who sells me calf's-liver or sausages as my moral superior; though calf's-liver, I believe, contains almost as many and good vitamins as milk. But milk and those associated with milk do somehow contrive to make us feel small. Milkmaids have always been famous for their purity, though there is no evidence that they have in fact higher standards of behaviour than barmaids, nursemaids, or parlourmaids.

And as the purity of the milkmaid, so is the cheerfulness of the milkman – a famous and inimitable quality which puts us all to shame. Hear him carol the fact of his presence down the area steps. He has a *joie de vivre*, an effervescence, a bubbling sense of contentment which is not approached by any other, though others may bring commodities not less important to our doors. The butcher's man sings no exciting 'Meat-O!' from afar off. He waits till the door is opened and then he says without excitement, 'Butcher'. Yet the butcher's man, I swear, is as good a fellow as the milkman. Perhaps the milkman is inflated by that thrilling passage in the *Memorandum by the Advisory Committee on Nutrition on the Nutritive Value of Milk,* issued by the Ministry of Health and the Secretary of State for Scotland, March 1936:

> 'Milk contains the energy-giving nutrients, protein, fat, and carbohydrate: all the known essential vitamins; calcium, phosphorus, iron, sulphur, iodine, magnesium, potassium, sodium, chlorine, and copper and a number of other elements, present only in minute amounts, such as manganese, zinc, and fluorine…

What a drink! It is not so much a drink as a mining area.

How old is the joke about the reveller who returns to his place of residence 'with the milk'? I know not, but it was one of the first jokes I heard; and all through boyhood and early manhood it lingered with me. That reveller was the type and example of wickedness found out and made ridiculous. Here again the accent is on the *milk*; the essence of the joke is not the dissipation of the dissipated one, but the hideous incongruity of finding a dissipated one in juxtaposition to the impeccable person who delivers milk. If you said, 'He came home with the meat or the vegetables' there would be nothing in it.

Anyhow, that is my theory of the thing; and I shall never forget the first time I actually 'came home with the milk' myself. It was a lovely midsummer morning, the sort of morning on which everybody ought to be up and about. Nobody, however, was 'up' in our little street except the milkman and myself. I was feeling pretty good in every sense. Some of us had been on a rather aesthetic expedition to the City in an open taxi. We had admired St Paul's Cathedral; and St Paul's Cathedral against the early morning sky, with Ludgate Hill deserted and silent, is a rare and wonderful sight, a sight which you poor mutts who never come home with the milk will never see and cannot imagine. I strolled along in my beautiful evening dress, filled with the poetry of living, the soft summer air, the pale blue sky, the song of the lark (or some other bird). And then I saw the milkman. The milkman saw me, and he gave me such a look!

I slunk past that milkman like a frightened dog and scuttled into my home. All the light had gone out of the sky, all the poetry from life. *I had come home with the milk*. I was the ludicrous figure of a thousand comic songs about 'wife and hubby'; I was a big laugh; and, above all, I had been shamed and shown up by that paragon, the milkman. Always afterwards when I came home at that hour (those days are gone now) I used to peep round the corner of the street to make sure that it was free of milkmen, and if one of the tribe were still upon his pious rounds I would hide till he had gone.

But I have never in my heart admitted his right to make me feel small. If it is proper for him to be up and about in the glorious dawn, I argue, so it is for me. Besides, he is paid for it and has been sleeping hoggishly all night; if I stay up all night to admire the glorious dawn and do it for nothing, I am surely the better man. Nevertheless I used to hide till he had gone.

I do *not* accept the very common view that everyone should sleep at the same time, that it is virtuous to do your sleeping at one hour and vicious to do it at another. Dogs, the most sensible of beings, sleep when they feel like sleeping, and no man thinks the worse of them.

The peace and happiness of our tropical possessions are founded on the custom by which the rulers of those possessions go to sleep after lunch. The same custom, it is true, is condemned whenever it rears its head among our rulers in this country. But the point is, there can be no hard-and-fast rule. And when I choose to be active all night and go to bed after breakfast the milkman has absolutely no right to make me feel small.

Nevertheless, when I returned from my first All-Night Sitting in Parliament he saw me, and I still felt small.

And the wretch has it both ways – indeed every way. Even when I am in bed at the right time he gets me down. In the first place, he wakes me up. Between five and six he brings a rattling cart along the street and halts it underneath my window. The cart is full of cans and bottles, and these are so arranged as to make the maximum of noise when the cart is in motion. When the cart is at rest he takes out all the cans and clinks them together out of sheer *joie de vivre*; then he collects all the empty milk-bottles from all the doorsteps and plays bells on them. Empty milk-bottles dashed together have a very effective ring (the 'milking tone'), and when dropped in the gutter make a pleasing crash. And all this time the merry fellow is whistling, humming, and even singing away, refusing to be downcast by the earliness of the hour or the necessity for toil. Presently another milkman approaches (for there are at least two operating in this street) with another cart; there is the little ceremony of Clashing Carts (well, that is what it sounds like), and then the lads exchange gay greetings and jests and sometimes even whistle two tunes instead of one.

Well, you know, it is all very well; but if I were to walk along our street at that hour of the morning singing, whistling, or even humming for no more than three days in the week the nastiest things would be said by the neighbours. And singing just after you get up is logically no less offensive than singing just before you go to bed. Yet I lie awake and listen, and cannot even be cross with the merry fellow. If it were anyone else I should be inclined to jump up and shout from the window, 'Look here, sir, do you realize that other people are trying to *sleep*?' But I cannot. It is the milkman. And therefore I feel small as usual. I say to myself, 'Here I am hogging it in a warm bed while that poor fellow is out in the cold distributing among the people the blessed benefits of milk'. Extraordinary stuff, milk…

All the same, I wish the scientists would stop messing about with the atom and think out some way of distributing milk in silence.

LIV

SAD FATE OF A ROYAL COMMISSION

I saw an old man in the Park;
  I asked the old man why
He watched the couples after dark;
  He made this strange reply:

'I am the Royal Commission on Kissing
  Appointed by Gladstone in '74;
The rest of my colleagues are buried or missing;
  Our Minutes were lost in the last Great War.
But still I'm a Royal Commission.
  My task I intend to see through,
Though I know, as an old politician,
  Not a thing will be done if I do.

I never can remember how exactly we began,
But I seem to recollect a case about a clergyman;
A mountain was delivered, rather strangely, by a mouse;
There were meetings, there were articles and questions in the
  House;
The necessity for action was clear to everyone,
But the view was very general that nothing could be done,
And the Government courageously decided that the Crown
Should appoint a score of gentlemen to track the trouble
  down –

Which always takes a long, long time.

We first explored the history of human osculation,
The views of the Mahommedans, the morals of the nation
The significance (if any) of existing legislation –
And that took a long, long time.

Next a little doubt arose about the limits of our reference,
We accordingly consulted the Government with deference;
Having ascertained that kisses were of every kind and sort –
Some kisses, for example, being long and others short –
Did the Government expect us to investigate the latter?
The Government replied that it didn't really matter –
But that took a long, long time.

Disraeli was a member, but he very soon resigned;
Lord Arrow died in '98, old Rattle lost his mind;
Still, once a month, in winter, we assembled to discuss;
And then the Boer War broke out, which interrupted us –
And that took a long, long time.

We then collected evidence, but carefully dismissed
The opinion of anyone who actually kissed;
We examined social workers from the cities of the North,
Good magistrates from Monmouth, nonconformists from the Forth;
We summoned all the bishops who were over sixty-one
And asked if they were kissed and, if they were, how it was done.
They answered in the negative and said there was abundant
Support for the opinion that the practice was redundant –
And that took a long, long time.

We next examined doctors with extremely high degrees,

Who thought that osculation was the cause of Bright's
Disease,
And one or two Societies existing to suppress
All frivolous activity, including the caress.
Industrial employers said that kissing always tends
To uneconomic conduct and is bad for dividends.
Just then the Great War happened; our proceedings were
adjourned;
Two members joined the constables and seven were
interned.
And I think that it was during that unfortunate campaign
Our Minutes must have vanished – they were never seen
again –
For the War took a long, long time.

There were ten of us surviving at the finish of the War,
And some of us were not so energetic as before;
But the sense of civic duty still invigorated all
And we gathered once a quarter in a cellar in Whitehall.
These things take a long, long time.

One little question puzzled us for many a weary year:
"What is the right procedure when the Minutes disappear?"
The Secretary said he thought the predecents were small,
The Chairman said he didn't know a precedent at all.
The Secretary thought we should remember where we
were
And continue our inquiry, without prejudice, from there.
But a lot of time had passed since the inquiry was begun,
And we none of us remembered what exactly we had done.
And it has to be conceded that you can't go very far
Towards a definite objective if you don't know where you
are.
The Chairman took the view that we should just begin
again,

For the absence of the Minutes would be awkward to explain.
We resolved it was a question we could not at once decide,
And that was the position when the Secretary died –
But it all took a long, long time.

That left the members seven. I should hate to call to mind
The melancholy steps by which our membership declined;
I know that on the suicide of Prebendary Gunn
I suddenly discovered that our membership was one.
And that's the reason why you may observe me in the spring
Investigating park-seats and places where they cling.
That kissing is proceeding there is very little doubt –
I can't imagine why it's done or what it's all about;
But whenever it's discovered that the plebs are having fun
It's generally granted that something should be done.
Civic duty's food and drink to me, and, though it may be short,
I can promise you at least a unanimous Report –
But it does take a long, long time.

I am the Royal Commission on Kissing
Appointed by Gladstone in '74;
The rest of my colleagues are buried or missing;
Our Minutes were lost in the last Great War.
But still I'm a Royal Commission
Which never has made a Report,
And acutely I feel my position,
For it must be a crime (or a tort)
To be such a Royal Commission.
My task I intend to see through,
Though I know, as an old politician,
Not a thing will be done if I do.'

LV

THE JOY OF YOUTH

I remember a time when the Young used to go to pubs – and that was awful.

Then the Young stopped going to pubs and went to cinemas instead – and now that's awful.

If the Young go 'hiking' in the daylight that seems to be awful.

And if the Young go for walks in country lanes after dark, that's worse.

If the Young sit in motor-cars they have the police after them.

If the Young sit on the Common they have the Watch Committee after them.

If the Young sit in the parlour and listen to the wireless they have No Sense of Adventure.

And if the Young sit on pillions and motor-bikes they're Dangers to the Public.

If the Young sit in their studies they have No Spirit.

But if the Young go to political meetings they're Insubordinate and Uppish.

And even if the Young start a religious movement it's pretty scandalous.

If the Young go to the dog-races the old boys talk about it.

But if the Young go into Parliament the old boys still go on talking.

Oh, dear! will anyone tell me where the Young *ought* to go?

LVI

HOUSEWORK

If I had my way I should do nothing but housework. Not house*keeping*, for that is foul, but house*work*. I am amazed (so far as women can still amaze me) by the complaints of women that they have to stay at home and do domestic drudgery while we lucky men go out into the world and do big things.

Drudgery? The real drudges are the poor chaps who have to go to the same office every day and do the same things all day every day, and have nothing to show for their labours at the end of the day. Consider the life of the unhappy wretch who has to keep account of my overdraft (among others). All day, every day, he sits on his high stool entering up cheque after cheque on the debit side of the great ledger; and in the evening what has he to tell his wife? 'Poor old Haddock is down another twenty.' 'Lord Hammersmith is overdrawn again.' The 'shop' talked by bank-clerks in these hard times must be dismal in the extreme. And I doubt if it is much more exciting when they are able to report that poor old Haddock's account is very nearly in funds this week.

But what of the bank-clerk's fortunate wife? She too has laboured, but not in vain. She has scrubbed the garden-seat so that it looks like new; she has polished the dining-room floor so that you can see your face in it (if you wish to); she has weeded the garden; she has painted the conservatory blue – *she has something to show*. Even if she has done no more than cook two secret meals for herself and wash up after them she has something to show; for everything was dirty and is now clean again. The march of life is going on for her; whereas to him who tends my overdraft life must look like one long retreat. But there it is – she thinks she has been 'drudging': and she thinks her spouse has been having fun all day. Queer.

The other queer thing about women is that they are so bad at housework. I know all about this because I keep a sort of mobile houseboat – a houseboat? nay, a noble ship. Not that I have not done my due share of housework on land. Many's the fair pile of washed-up plates that stand to my credit, many the stopped-up sink I have assaulted, many the midnight orgy I've tidied up after for fear the staff should say things in the morning.

But on land the women are always in command of housework. One obeys orders; and, though one may deem their proceedings fantastic and erroneous, one seldom dares to say so. Indeed, as a rule, one generously assumes that they know best.

But at sea, in my noble ship, now riding at anchor at the bottom of the garden (due South of W.6), *I* am in command; the presumption of female omniscience is not present; and I perceive with clear eyes that women really know nothing about housework.

Cooking, you say? Well, yes, perhaps their cooking. Yes, certainly their cooking is comforting and pleasant – and even good; and perhaps – yes, frankly, I cannot do without it. Though even there, if we men had time to give our minds to it…

However, let us take tidying, long regarded as one of the pinnacles of female superiority. The principle of female tidying is, roughly speaking, to put everything away in the wrong place. Or, more softly speaking, the female does not care where she puts everything as long as she puts everything away *somewhere*. Put manuscripts in the coal-cellar and the corkscrew in the work-basket – so long as neither manuscript nor corkscrew is visible when company comes, everything is quite all right. This is the real reason, by the way, why men leave home.

Now, in their own homes the ladies can get away with it. Further, when a house is on land, the safety of the house will rarely depend on the immediate finding of manuscripts, or even the corkscrew. The continued concealment of these and other desirable objects in the sacred cause of tidiness merely causes continual small wastages of time and a small but continual exodus of men from their homes.

But when the house is at sea quite other considerations arise. The principle of tidiness in a ship – the grand male principle – is that everything should be put away in the *right* place. The safety of the ship may depend, indeed in these rushing tidal waters *does* often depend, on the immediate finding and casting of the anchor.[1] And if the anchor has been put away in the engine-room or under one of the beds it is a very small consolation to the captain that the ship looked tidier so.

I do not say that I have ever at a moment of peril found the anchor under one of the beds; but that is only because it is too heavy for most women to move. I have found it festooned with knitting or covered with dishcloths hung out to dry; and I have found the cable hopelessly entangled with the legs of the tea-table. The Mind of Woman may have its special qualities, superb Intuition and all that; but it does not react rationally to such things as anchors. Woman thinks the anchor is one of those queer fads men have, and resents its presence in the prow of the vessel. She would like to deal with it as she deals with

1. No, do not write to me and say that Mr Conrad did not approve the expression 'casting anchor'. Mr Conrad travelled in big ships, where somebody said, 'Let go!' and the anchor was then dropped. If anyone said 'Let go!' in my ship nothing would happen. I have to go forward myself, pick the anchor up, and throw, fling, or cast it over the side. The expression, in this queer vessel, is correct.

manuscripts and corkscrews; and I advise all seamen to keep a very heavy anchor.

I have also to report that even in her own sphere Woman falls short upon the water (always excepting the cooking; and I must say that she does get up nice and early and get the fire going). As soon as the ladies leave my ship I set to and have a thorough tidying. I put everything back in its right place. I sweep (and even scrub); and I am sorry to say that I sometimes find unwashed dishes and pans concealed here and there; and I boil a little of the Thames and, with a smile of Christian resignation, I wash these relics up. Yet these same ladies would say that in the home I am an untidy person. Pshaw!

However, I did not set out upon this discussion in order to belabour Woman, or even to advertise my great domestic virtues. My simple aim is to sing the joy of housework and brighten the lives of all those women (if any) whose place is still the home.

Painting, now. I know no joy so exquisite, no toil so satisfying as the putting of fresh, bright, shiny paint upon some dingy bench, boat, rudder, or cabin-door. Nor do I know anything quite so disappointing as the spectacle the same work presents sometimes in the morning, when the paint was improperly mixed, or dogs, ducks, or cats have gambolled o'er the surface during the night.

But generally there is something to show as the result of the exquisite agony of painting in white along a border of blue, so that the white does not drip or trickle over the blue (as it nearly always does); and there are all sorts of semi-ethical problems – as, for instance, if you are painting a cabin-wall behind a bed, should you paint conscientiously down to the floor or stop at the point where the bed or bedclothes conceal the wall from view? Personally I generally go the whole hog, for there is always a chance that some prowling woman (bent on concealing an anchor or manuscript) may look under the bed and discover that you have scamped your work.

Such are some of the delights of painting. Happy must be the housepainter, I feel, and happier still is he who paints his own house blue. Were I a woman I should seldom cease from painting my house.

But then again the extraordinary thing is that women are not really good at the job. They are impetuous and impatient. They dash along, leaving blurred edges everywhere, flinging white paint over blue and green over both. When the women have stopped painting in my ship I find that I have to go round with a rag and some turpentine and clean up the – But no more of that.

LVII

'MR CHAIRMAN'

Christmas approaches: and now is the time of Annual Dinners. Societies, Clubs, Associations, Movements, Regiments. Night by night, all over the country, men (and even women) are gathering in public places to eat strange foods at unusual expense, to pat the dying year upon the back and wave a cheerful send-off to the next (not forgetting the new President and Secretary).

At all these gatherings agreeable speeches will be suffered by all; and a few words of warning, advice, and entreaty to those who are mixed up with the speeches, actively or passively, may not be unseasonable.

It is, perhaps, too late in the history of this planet to inquire into the origin and justification of after-dinner speeches. Man, I believe, is the only animal who has the habit. At least, no other animals I know consider it necessary for one or more of those present to give tongue at the end of a hearty meal: most of them have the sense to lie down and sleep. Imagine what we should think of our noble friends, the horse and the dog, if it were their custom to howl, bark, whinny or neigh for twenty minutes after an unusually enjoyable repast in good company. I do not know whether the practice obtains among cannibal tribes, but dim recollections of African romances suggest to me that among savage peoples the talk, or 'pow-wow', generally *precedes* the meal; and, subject to correction by the professors, I incline to the view that post-prandial oratory is one of the vices peculiar to what we call the civilized races.

On the other hand, it would be quite wrong to suppose that it is the sign of a physically decadent or over-intellectual society. No one enjoys speeches so much as the vigorous Americans and manly Australians – yes, even way back in the vast open spaces. When I was touring Australia with some colleagues of the Press, I listened, I remember, to twenty-seven speeches in a single day, all taken with or after food: ten after dinner, three (reading backwards) after tea, eight after lunch, three after tea-at-eleven (at an agricultural college), and three – believe it or not – after breakfast! Yes, sir, we had travelled through the night, by railway, and at 6 a.m. we arrived at an enormous open space, almost entirely inhabited by sheep, cattle, and kangaroos. We had a fine breakfast at the railway station, and at 7.45, just as I was plunging a fork into my second fried egg, a man rose up beside me and said, 'Mr Mayor, Lord What-not, Ladies and Gentlemen, this is a proud moment in the history of Woollawoolla. This is without doubt the most important delegation–' etcetera.

And *I* had to reply – the mouth still stained with egg!

No, there it is: this thing has grown up, and I do not see how it is to be stamped out. It is like road accidents: all we can hope for is, by unceasing vigilance, to keep the evil down.

Having suffered extensively in both capacities, I can claim to be beautifully impartial as between speaker and speakee. But the speaker, after all, is the 'producer', the 'worker', so let us discuss his agonies first.

I shall never cease to be surprised by the lack of consideration which is shown by most of the high priests of Dinners towards their victims at the sacrifice. The cause, I think, is not cold brutality or callousness, but simple ignorance, and in particular a complete failure to appreciate the character of after-dinner speaking.

In my view, it is one of those things which, unless they are very well done, should not be done at all. It is an art, a very delicate and difficult art, one of the most difficult of all the arts connected with the use of language, since it combines the functions of composer and entertainer. It is like asking the author to go on the stage and speak his own lines, or the actor to write his own part.

Many can write an amusing speech who could never deliver it audibly or effectively: and many have a confident and breezy manner at the festive board but have nothing much to say. The perfect combination is very rare: and, that being so, the number of after-dinner speeches should be diminished. But my observation tells me that it is increasing. It should be regarded as an exceptional thing for a man to be considered worthy to attempt to do this delicate and difficult thing on any formal occasion; but too many of those responsible seem to think (a) that almost anyone can do it, and (b) that it does not much matter how it is done. Strange error! For from the purely practical point of view, remember, Mr Chairman and Secretary, that at your big formal dinner the speaking occupies much more time than the mere eating and drinking. You start at 7.30 or 7.45; the coffee is on by 9.0; but the speakers may be still at it at 11.0 or 11.30. From which it follows that immense trouble should be taken by all to see that those hours are filled pleasantly – assuming, which I do not, that they must be filled with speeches. In other words, as much care and attention should be devoted to the Toast list as to the Wine list. But is it?

A good illustration of the difference of attitude is the genial but extraordinary notion that anyone who can make a good prepared after-dinner speech can make an equally good after-dinner speech extempore. Of the late Lord Birkenhead this was probably true; and there may be men living who have the same power, though I do not know the names of many of them. There are, without doubt, numbers of public (and even private) men who can at a few minutes' notice string a few pleasant and fluent sentences together, round off with an irrelevant anecdote, and propose the health of the Mayor with a felicitous reference to his work for the Fire Brigade. But this is not what I call an after-dinner speech in the full, fine sense of the term. For that, to me, means a work of art, and works of art do not spring up suddenly, like mushrooms. They have to be worked at.

I do not mean that they should sound like set pieces, sticky with midnight oil and delivered like a recitation. No, *ars est celare artem* is more than usually true in this department. By all means let there be the spontaneous quip, or graceful aside, arising out of something the Chairman has said or the face of an old friend seen at the next table; and by all means let the spontaneous stuff emerge so easily that none can distinguish it from that which has been prepared. But the main framework should be as carefully studied and thought out as the plot of a play; and so, I am sure, by the masters, it is. I have delighted in after-dinner addresses by the Lord Chief Justice, Mr Winston Churchill, Mr Baldwin, Sir John Simon, and many others. All these gentlemen are very well able to make a speech without elaborate preparation, but I will wager that none of them would claim that without it they could do real justice to themselves or their audience on a big occasion.

And what is true of the big shots must be still more true of the smaller fry. But now, Mr Chairman, consider what you do. Just as you insert the first spoonful of soup your Secretary panics up with a message from Sir Roderick Rock. Sir Roderick, the famous raconteur, was to make the second reply for 'The Guests', but has been stricken down by ''flu' or alcohol. You send the Secretary off to some poor fish like me with a request that I will step into the breach. I dissent, hotly. I seem to be among good company, and had promised myself a pleasant evening, without, for once, the trouble and worry of holding forth. I say 'I can't speak extempore, I don't know the Guests, and I've nothing whatever to say'. The Secretary says, 'Don't worry, old boy. Say the first thing that comes into your head. The boys will love it.'

I rage. 'The boys will love it!' A compliment, no doubt; but it is the supreme insult to the art. You wouldn't go to the head waiter and say 'Don't bother about the wine, old man. Just take the first few bottles you see in the cellar. The boys will love 'em.' You don't say to the *chef* 'Don't worry about the soup; throw in the first thing you think of – the boys will love it.' The flowers – even the guests – are not arranged haphazard but after careful thought. In short, all the material side of the entertainment is prepared – yes, *prepared* – upon the principle that nothing but the best will do. But when you come to the intellectual items you are ready to gamble on the chance that a poor fish like me has got something in his head worth saying or can think of something while he is wolfing sole and making conversation to the Mayor's daughter and a female barrister.

Still more, Mr Chairman, do I resent it when you lure me to your orgy on the distinct understanding that there are to be *no* speeches, at any rate by me – and then spring one on me at the sherry stage. It is an affront to the art, unfair to the company and cruel to me. It is like asking an actor to act without rehearsal. One does not want to be boorish, so one tackles the task; but one stumbles, stutters, and gives a bad performance (I do, anyhow), and, if one regards the art and craft with proper seriousness, that is depressing, especially as few people really believe that one is not prepared, or minds if one is. Many a dismal night I have spent trying to remember exactly what were the clumsy things I said in a would-be extempore speech, and shaking the bed with shudders when I did.

Moreover, there is no more certain road to pernicious dyspepsia than the mental effort of making conversation to two strange women with one half of the brain, and trying to think out well-phrased witticisms about The Guests with the other. In all my long experience of public yapping I have only encountered one blessed female neighbour who had the wit to imagine my agonies and the grace to say, 'Don't talk to me – you want to think of something to say'. And the fellow on the other side was in the same trouble, so she had a pretty silent dinner, poor lady. And that's a nice position in which to put one of your lady guests, Mr Chairman! Barbarous!

You ask me what you are to do about it: I have told you already. If you can't get a good speech, don't have a speech at all. And, in the first case posited, if Sir Roderick can't answer for The Guests, as arranged, cut out that item altogether. It is fantastic, anyhow, to expect your guests to get up and formally thank you for your hospitality. (This, I suppose, is a relic from the days of the wandering minstrels, who called at feudal castles in snowy weather and were expected to sing for their supper and board.)

But I am sorry to say, Mr Chairman, that care and consideration are sometimes lacking even when one is officially *warned* for a speech. And in this case there is no excuse. You have placed upon a fellow-citizen a fearful, difficult, and thankless task, and you should use your imagination about it. 'Thankless?' Yes. For one thing, it means much work, and no real reward. Speaking, rather smugly, for myself, when booked to utter at an important meal, I have always taken immense trouble – too much, perhaps, certainly too much for my own interests; the best part, often, of two days' work. A twenty-minute speech contains as many words as two ordinary newspaper articles. And for the speech one is paid nothing. You give the man a good dinner with one hand and ruin it with the other. It is a lunatic way of spending labour and time, and I, for one, have given it up. Not that that is so easy. The more successful one is, the more of a nuisance it is; for people are dining all the year round and kind Chairmen badger one. Still, for charity, or friendship, or even, sometimes, fun, one yields from time to time; and all I want to say, Mr Chairman, is, when you do catch your bird, consider what has gone before, and do the best you can for him.

First of all, *assist* the poor dupe. Probably you have no idea what brutal things you do to him, with your easy-going ways. You persuade him, whether by your own charm or the demands of some charity, to say that he will 'say a few words.' You give him, perhaps, a specific toast – 'Floreat Filchester!' or 'Stet Fortuna', 'Sailors All!' 'Absent Friends', or 'The Ladies'. And the wretched fellow, if he is a conscientious ass like myself, sits down and builds up an elaborate edifice on the brief you have given him. He starts with four or five carefully constructed sentences founded on 'Floreat', 'Stet Fortuna', 'Sailors All', or what-not. Or he combs the Dictionaries of Quotations for kindly references to 'The Ladies'. He has produced, for what it is worth, a complete and logical whole in accordance with your own specification. He comes to the hotel, nervous but fairly confident, because he thinks that he has the goods. You greet him kindly, and tell him how much you appreciate his turning up and making a speech.

Feeling a little better, he proceeds to his table. And there (just as the complete stranger on his right has opened the ball by saying, 'I hope there are not too many speeches'), he picks up the Toast list and finds, with horror and indignation, that you (or somebody) have changed his toast – without telling him! Instead of 'Stet Fortuna' his toast is now 'Salus Populi' or 'Happy Days': instead of proposing 'The Ladies' he is now replying for 'The Guests': instead of answering for 'Literature' he is now proposing 'Trade and Commerce', or 'His Majesty's Forces'. All the subtle phrases, all the sly quotations, with which he was going to play himself in, are now useless, unless he is willing to drag them in with shameless irrelevance: and he must, after all, endure the horror already hinted at, and at the same time compliment his neighbours and compose a speech.

And all this, Mr Chairman, proceeds from your aforesaid erroneous notion that almost anybody can make an after-dinner speech on almost any subject at almost any notice! Well, well; next time I hope that you order grilled salmon three weeks before the dinner, and change the order to fried haddock as you take your seat. And I hope that you will allow me to be present at a conference upon the subject between yourself and the *chef*.

But, short of that enormity, there are many other things you do, or rather, fail to do. Don't you realize, for example, that a good speaker, preparing his speech, is like a producer preparing his play – or a bowler bowling to Bradman: he must, that is, know all the details of the conditions in which he will undertake his formidable task, as, for example, is it desired to get them out or keep the runs down? Can he have two short-legs, and, if so, can they catch? Will the theatre be large, or intimate, or what? And so forth.

The same sort of problems (but there are more of them) confronts the poor fish who is preparing an after-dinner speech. How many will be present? Will there be ladies or not? And, if not, will the company be very respectable, or will the gentlemen be mainly stockbrokers and bookmakers and welcome a touch of the Rabelaisian? At what stage of the evening will he be expected to perform – and then for how long? Will there be many speeches or few? And will they be interlarded with professional 'entertainers' or not? Will the Press be present? And the room – large or small? Intimate or spacious? Oblong or square? Whereabouts will the speaker sit? Will he have to use a microphone – or can he hope to 'fill' the room without that tiresome assistance? What distinguished persons will speak before or after him – and is there anything special which the Chairman would like to be said or avoided?

All these questions are important – particularly those which go to the *physical* conditions of the occasion. If a man has a powerful voice and can be effective in short staccato phrases, that is one thing: he does not care how large the room may be. But if his style inclines to the elegant 'period' or the confidential aside he is happier in a small and intimate company. He must, you say, be prepared to adapt himself to the conditions, like a batsman. Ah, but the parallel is not exact, for you are on his side, presumably: indeed, you are the captain and should have made the conditions clear. But instead, as often as not, you actually deceive him. You tell me, over the telephone, 'So glad you can come, old boy. Just a few friends. You'll like them'. Well, you are, shall we say, an architect. I know about you, and respect you: I spend a day or more preparing an elegant address for the delight of your 'few friends', full of literary allusions and even, perhaps, Latin quotations. I arrive at the scene of the fray, and find that the company numbers seven hundred and fifty, gathered in a room the size of a swimming-bath (but without the acoustics), to defend dog-racing or the British carburettor. There are seventy-five people at the top table and I am at the end, about a quarter of a mile from the fellow in the opposite corner. You were so genial and pressing on the telephone that I vainly supposed that my speech was one of few, perhaps one of the principal items of the entertainment. You mentioned no time and I prepared for fifteen minutes.

I find now that there are fifteen speeches, interspersed with 'entertainers'. I am Number 12 and shall come on about 11.30. What is wanted is four minutes at most, and short, sharp sentences at that, delivered into the horrible microphone. My Latin quotations are useless and I have not thought of any 'broad' jokes suitable to the company. However, I am in for it. I must play the game and do my best for you. I spend the evening, with one-half of the poor old brain, cutting down my remarks to four minutes, discarding the literary allusions and searching for a 'broad' joke. I come on at 11.35, between a juggler and a comic song. Just before I rise the Toast-master approaches and says, 'The Chairman's compliments, and will you make your remarks as brief as possible?' I feel inclined to answer 'Oy! Did *I* ask to come and make a speech? And do you think I want to make a speech *now*? The archangel Gabriel could not persuade the company that he had anything worth saying at this hour of the night!' However, so strong are the traditions of this lunatic business that I know I must do it. I cut my speech down to one minute, and shout it rather crossly into the microphone, which distributes four or five metallic remarks to seven hundred and fifty yawners, and robs even those of any humanity.

Well, if one was paid for this sort of thing one would not complain. But you have given me much unnecessary thought and trouble, and to no good purpose, simply because *you* have not taken trouble and thought; and that is because your ideas about after-dinner speaking are all wrong. I have not the smallest hope that anything I say will cause you to amend your practices: but I must say this – I wish you a very happy Christmas and a riotous Annual Dinner: but don't waste any time on asking *me* to come and make a speech this year. And don't invite me to your delightful proceedings at all, unless the invitation is accompanied by a bond for twenty pounds that in no circumstances shall I have to make one. Hail!

And now, I see, I have not begun to deal with the sufferings of the other side – the *speakees*. However, most of them are attributable to the causes named above. So Hail again!

A P Herbert

The Old Flame

Robin Moon finds Phyllis rather a distraction in the Sunday morning service – after all her golden hair does seem to shine rather more brightly than the Angel Gabriel's heavenly locks. His wife, Angela, on the other hand, is more preoccupied with the cavalier Major Trevor than perhaps she should be during the Litany. Relations between the Moons head towards an unhappy crescendo, and when, after an admirable pot-luck Sunday lunch, Robin descends to the depths of mentioning what happened on their honeymoon, the result is inevitable – they must embark on one of their enforced separations. Finding his independence once more, Robin feels free to link up with Phyllis and her friends, and begins to dabble in some far from innocent matchmaking.

This ingenious work brilliantly addresses that oh so perplexing a problem – that of 'the old flame'.

Honeybubble & Co.

Mr Honeybubble proved to be one of A P Herbert's most popular creations and avid readers followed his progress through life in APH's column in *Punch* where he first appeared. Here his exploits are collected together with a cast of other colourful characters from the riches of their creator's imagination. *Honeybubble & Co.* is a delightful series of sketches revealing some of the more humorous aspects of the human nature.

A P Herbert

Light Articles Only

In this amusing collection of articles and essays, A P Herbert ponders the world around him in his own inimitable style. Witty, droll and a respecter of no man, the admirable APH provides a series of hilarious and unique sketches – and gently points the finger at one or two of our own idiosyncrasies. Such comic dexterity and inspired versatility is beautifully enhanced by a string of ingenious illustrations.

Number Nine

Admiral of the Fleet the Earl of Caraway and Stoke is, as one might expect being an Admiral, a man of the sea. In fact, so much so that for him, all the world's a ship, and all the men and women merely sailors...

The Admiral's dedication to King and country could never be questioned – but surely it was a bit much expecting him to give up his ancestral home for the psychological testing of candidates for the Civil Service. Tired of the constant intrusion, and aided and abetted by his son Anthony and the lovely Peach, he embarks upon a battle of wits against the political hopefuls. The result is a hilarious tale of double-crossing, eavesdropping – and total mayhem.